CONTENTS

Dear Reader,

Have you ever met a man you thought you loved, but not enough to marry? Or so you told yourself?

I mean, you had your reasons for thinking the way you did at the time. Maybe you thought the two of you were too different. Your backgrounds weren't the same or you had different values. Maybe your family didn't like him. It's hard to choose between a man and your own blood. Maybe there were just things about him that irritated you. Chances are it was a combination of all the above.

However, later, when you *couldn't* go back, did dreams of him haunt your sleep? And in those quiet moments of the day did you ever fear that letting him go might have been the biggest mistake of your life?

Trace Cordell was that man for me.

And now I have a second chance.

Provided he isn't hanged from the gallows first!

Yours,

Flanna Kennedy

FLANNA AND THE LAWMAN

Cathy Maxwell

For Helen Voigts

CHAPTER ONE

TRACE CORDELL stared ahead stoically, determined to die better than he'd lived.

The ruddy-faced deputy serving as hangman set the noose around his neck. Trace wove to keep his balance, his hands tied tightly behind his back. His vision blurred as he looked out at the crowd of cattlemen, hired hands and local citizens gathered around the gallows built special in the middle of the street for his hanging. The prickly hemp of the new rope burned his skin and he could smell his own fear.

"Ex-Sheriff Cordell, do you have any *last* words you'd like to say?" Judge Rigby drawled from his front-row seat at the base of the gallows. The boys had brought out a table and chair from the saloon for the monkey-faced jurist to sit in comfort while he witnessed the hanging, a whiskey bottle in his right hand, a fat, half-smoked cigar in his left.

Trace shook his head. He couldn't answer. His throat was dry and there was a buzzing in his head right behind his eyes from a night of hard drinking.

Besides, what could he say he hadn't already in the kangaroo court they'd held minutes ago? He'd told the truth. He'd not remembered killing the man. That sometimes, lately, drink made him forget and lose time? Half the men in the crowd had the same problem, including the judge. The last thing Trace had remembered from the night before was the joy of being dealt a winning poker hand.

He woke to his own trial for murder.

"You've got nothing to say for your last words?" Rigby repeated as if he couldn't fathom such a thing. He pushed his bowler hat back from his forehead and looked over his shoulder at the crowd. "Doesn't seem right a man should pass from this life to the next without last words."

"How 'bout goodbye?" a cowpoke shouted.

"And good riddance?" another chimed in. The others laughed.

Rigby banged his bottle on the table for order. "We'll have some respect here. A man is about to die. And if he don't have anything to say, then as a fellow lawman, I think I will speak for him."

His audience groaned. Judge Rigby was a man who liked to hear himself talk. Well, he could talk until Doomsday as far as Trace was concerned, anything to put off the inevitable.

Carefully, the stubby judge placed the butt end of his cigar on the edge of the table and stepped up on the chair so he could best address the crowd. More than a bit tipsy himself, he had to hold the bottle out for balance. He removed his hat. The few strands of reddish hair on his bald pate stood straight up in the air like tiny flagpoles.

"Trace Cordell was at one time a good lawman. One of the best. Fierce and proud. We've all heard tales of him. But those who live by the sword will die by it and you other fellows out there better look at this man and heed the warning in your own lives." He nodded toward the broken door and glass windows of Birdie's Emporium, a saloon for the hard-bitten. "Justice is the rule of law, even for ex-lawmen and we don't ignore killing…" He then went off into a lecture about what makes a man a man in the West.

Trace stopped listening. Instead, he shifted his focus to the blueness of the sky that seemed to stretch out forever. The dry, ever present Kansas wind swirled around him, carrying with it pieces of dust and grit and the hint of summer heat.

He didn't want to die like this with his feet

dancing on air and everyone watching. He'd seen too many men hanged not to know the indignities of this death.

And yet, he'd killed a man.

It wasn't as if he'd not killed before. As sheriff back in Loveless, he'd sent more than a dozen men to meet their Maker. But he could remember the look in their eyes, the determination in their faces. However, this man—? No face formed in Trace's mind. His head throbbed harder the more he tried to remember. Whatever had happened was lost to him.

He wasn't a praying man, but a prayer formed in his mind. *Dear God, please, not like this.*

There was no answer. No clap of thunder. No giant hand coming down from the sky to save his unworthy soul.

He was going to hang.

Rigby wound up his eulogy by placing his hat on his head with a flourish and jumping down from the chair. He picked up his cigar butt, clamped it between his teeth and said, "Let's get on with it."

The crowd cheered.

Rigby's henchman tightened the noose around Trace's neck. "Won't be long now, Cordell." He gave Trace a friendly pat on the back and went down the steps to yank open the trap door beneath Trace's feet on command. Two other fellows stood ready and armed with shotguns in case Trace attempted to escape.

A preacher man stepped forward, opened his Bible, and began to recite some last words.

Trace saw some men remove their hats out of respect for the Good Book while others stepped forward for a better view of his death. He deliberately kept his mind blank. The pounding in his head increased.

Then, from the far corner of the crowd, he noticed movement. A woman in a straw bonnet worked her way forward, elbowing this man and that out of her way. She appeared anxious to get to the front row for his hanging.

The preacher finished. Rigby stood, his expression solemn. He raised his hand. "Now, with the power inves—"

The bonneted woman shouted, "Wait! Don't hang him! I saw what happened. Trace Cordell is innocent. He didn't shoot anyone." There was a hint of Irish in her voice, a voice Trace instantly recognized, and he groaned aloud.

Flanna Kennedy.

If his life was in her hands, he might as well step off the platform and hang himself.

She and her father had traveled Texas peddling rotgut in medicine bottles with enough charm and false promises to sweet talk a month's wages out of a saint. Trace had been forced to personally escort them out of Loveless. Unfortunately, that had been after they'd bled everyone dry and the reason for his carelessness was Flanna. He'd fallen in love with her. Head over heels. And that was the beginning of the end of his career as sheriff of Loveless.

Stood to reason he'd see her again with a noose around his neck.

Not that she didn't make a credible impression on his behalf. She was dressed for church, her straw bonnet trimmed in yellow ribbons and the blue of her sprigged calico dress the perfect match for her catlike eyes. Her hair was the vibrant strawberry-blond of the Irish and the few artful curls around her face caught and held the sunlight.

She even wore gloves. White leather ones. Obviously the year and a half since Trace had last seen her had been prosperous ones for Flanna.

He scanned the crowd searching for her rogue of a father. The overprotective Rory Kennedy was never far from his daughter. He wondered what game the old scoundrel was playing now.

Like so many others before him, Rigby fawned over Flanna's beauty. He pulled his hat off his head and slicked back his few hairs. A half dozen love-struck cowpokes did the same. "Miss Kennedy, we didn't know you were in town for the day."

Trace almost barked in surprised laughter at the respect in the judge's voice. Obviously he didn't know Flanna very well.

"I know who shot that man and it wasn't Sheriff Cordell," she said to Rigby in a breathless voice.

"*Ex*-sheriff," Rigby corrected with mild distraction, then said, "We've already had the trial."

"But you've had no justice."

The judge frowned. The crowd inched closer to hear better. Trace was listening especially closely, stunned by the revelation that he may not have committed the murder.

"How do you know who shot William Bates?" Rigby asked suspiciously.

"I was there at Birdie's," she confessed.

Now the idea of Flanna Kennedy patronizing a saloon did not surprise Trace at all...but apparently it did the good folks of Harwood. They acted like she was all milk and honey and not the stone-cold thief he knew.

A cowboy named Curly who had testified to the shooting murmured to his companions, "I would 'ave noticed her if she'd been here.

Wouldn't 'ave been able to take my eyes off her.'' The others agreed.

"What *were* you doing there?'' Rigby asked Flanna with interest. He dropped his cigar butt to the ground and pulled a fresh one from his suit coat. "Birdie's isn't the sort of place for a fine young woman like yourself.''

Trace almost choked. Rigby didn't know Flanna at all.

"I came looking for Sheriff Cordell,'' she said. "I'd heard he was in town and we had some, um, business to attend between us. I saw everything that happened. I was standing in the back room trying to manage a way of catching Mr. Cordell's attention without drawing notice to myself when the fight over a hand of cards broke out.''

Rigby clamped the unlit cigar in his mouth, interested. "Go on.''

Miss Kennedy continued. "The gentleman who was killed—''

"Bates,'' the judge supplied.

"Yes, Mr. Bates. He pushed over the card table and accused Mr. Cordell of cheating, but before Mr. Cordell could speak, that gentleman with curly hair—''

"Curly?'' Rigby asked. The cowhand of the same name stood close to the judge's elbow, a scowl on his face.

Flanna nodded. "Curly broke a chair over Mr. Cordell's head and knocked him out cold."

"Me?" Curly protested.

No wonder Trace's head hurt so bad.

"So if Cordell didn't shoot him, who did?" Rigby asked.

"Curly." She pointed a gloved finger right at him. "When Mr. Cordell went down, everyone started fighting save for Bates and Curly. Bates hurriedly grabbed up the money off the floor while Curly picked up Mr. Cordell's famous pearl-handled Colts. I thought it best to hide. No sense advertising my presence what with a group of wild men going at it. They were all acting like barbarians."

Several people nodded agreement.

"Curly and Bates ran for the back door where I was hiding," Flanna continued. "There they stopped and Curly demanded the money. Bates refused. They had angry words and Curly shot him. Bang! Just like that."

The accused cowhand doubled his fist. "I never did no such thing. Bill and I rode the trail together."

"But you never liked each other," a grizzled cowpoke pointed out.

"Yup, there was bad blood between them," said another.

"I liked him well enough," Curly shot back.

"Oh, yes," Flanna agreed. "You liked him enough to take the money. Then you went back into the saloon, and put the gun close to Mr. Cordell to make it look like his doing. I saw it all, you shot poor Mr. Bates right in the back."

During Trace's trial it was the shot in the back that had so many folks riled up. Flanna's comment spurred their sense of injustice.

For a moment Curly appeared ready to argue—and then he bolted for freedom, an action more telling than any admission of guilt. He was stopped by his compatriots before he'd taken three steps.

Rigby shouted for order. Curly shoved his way to toward the judge. "I had to shoot him," he told everyone. "He was stealing *our* money. Just like she said."

"And what were *you* doing?" someone challenged.

"I bet the money is in his saddlebag," another answered. "He told me he was leaving town after he saw Cordell hang."

"Yeah, with our money!"

The call went out for someone to check Curly's horse and a party of men charged off to do exactly that.

Curly fell to his knees, shaking. He turned to the judge. "I didn't mean to shoot him. Just made me so mad he'd start a fight and then would try and steal it all. He was selfish that way.''

Rigby answered by biting off the tip of the cigar and spitting it down at Curly. "You can tell me all about it later when I reconvene my court. Keep an eye on him, boys. I'll deal with him in a moment.'' He looked up at Trace. "Looks like what they say about you having nine lives is true, Cordell. Thanks to Miss Kennedy, you are going to walk. It's too bad. I was looking forward to hanging you."

"Maybe some other day,'' Trace said. And if he had his way, never. He couldn't wait to kick the dust of Harwood from his heels—especially now he knew Flanna was here. She may have saved his life, but he knew her too well. He wanted no part of Rory's schemes. The cost of the last one had been too high. "Someone get up here and cut my hands loose."

Rigby signaled his deputy to take care of the matter. The portly man climbed the stairs with obvious disappointment but did what he was told, slicing the ropes with a knife.

Meanwhile Rigby turned his full flirtatious attention on Flanna. "So, tell me, Miss Kennedy, why were you searching for Cordell last night?''

Yes, why was she? Trace wanted to pretend he wasn't interested in the answer, but he was.

He rubbed his numb wrists. The pain of what felt like a thousand needles shot through them as his blood started circulating again. He couldn't even lift the noose from his neck.

Flanna hedged, apparently at a loss for words. "Why I was looking for him?" she repeated. Trace could see the wheels in her wily brain churning, and knew whatever she was about to say would be a lie. She'd never learn. She and her father were the devil's own playmates.

But even he, who knew her so well, was unprepared for what popped from her mouth.

"Oh, I was looking for him…because he's, um, he's my husband. Yes. He ran out on me almost two years ago and I've come to fetch him back."

Trace surged forward. "What a load of bull—" His words were cut off as the noose still around his neck pressed his windpipe.

CHAPTER TWO

FLANNA RAN TO THE EDGE of the gallows platform and gave Trace's leg a quick squeeze. As lies went, this wasn't a bad one. She gave him a pleading look. He had to go along with her on this. If anyone suspected she'd been searching for him because she needed a gunman, there would be hell to pay.

For a second, he stood stiff, his refusal clear in his distrustful eyes.

Please, she silently begged.

His gaze narrowed. He frowned. Then he stepped back, grabbed at the noose around his neck, and yanked it up over his head.

Flanna turned her attention back to the judge. "He's a little irritated about the hanging," she explained to her stunned audience.

"I didn't know you were married," Judge Rigby continued as if the fact he'd almost hanged an innocent man was of little importance. He put his hat back on his head. "If I'd known, I wouldn't have come courting."

"Well, Trace and I have one of *those* relationships."

The cowhands nodded. More than a handful of them had wives and sweethearts tucked away someplace, easily forgotten.

Trace came down the rickety stairs and to her side. He took her elbow, his grip tight. He was not in a good mood. "We'll be leaving now, *sweetheart*."

Judge Rigby blocked their way. "I just don't know why I wasn't told," he complained. "I mean, I used to sit on your doorstep and drink tea with you."

"I—" Flanna started, not certain what to say. Some men accepted gracefully their attentions were unwanted, while others, the tiresome ones, of whom Judge Rigby was one, always asked for an explanation. She'd never quite figured out how to let them down gently.

Her "husband" had no such pretense of manners. "You know how women are, Rigby. They either can't make up their minds or every other word out of their mouths is a lie."

"Yeah, that's right," Curly quickly seconded.

Trace sent him a look that could have crushed a rattler.

Flanna's temper flared at being publicly

called a liar. "I'd forgotten what an arrogant bull you are—"

"Oh, what a tender reunion," Trace taunted.

With a hard, steely glare of her own, she said succinctly, "A man whose wife just saved him from a noose around his neck had better watch his back."

Laughter broke out from the cowhands, as she'd known it would. She also knew the mighty Trace Cordell hated to be laughed at. She'd learned that little detail about him the hard way.

"You're not my w—"

Flanna cut him off, pleading her case directly to her small audience with a skillful weaving of truth and fiction. "My father never liked him. The two of them got in a terrible fight. You all knew how stubborn Rory could be. I was forced to choose between my father and Trace." She met his hard gaze. That was truth. But then, Trace had been the one to turn his back on her. Trace and his high-minded principles. Her father had warned her he would always be the lawman.

Except something about Trace had changed. She'd noticed it the night before.

Physically, he appeared the same: overlong straight dark hair that begged for a trim, silver eyes that could cut a person to pieces with a look, broad shoulders and slim hips. He seemed taller than she remembered, and harder. The lines around his eyes from the sun appeared deeper and his gaze lacked any of the warm humor he'd once possessed. Perhaps the change was the disreputable-looking two days' growth of beard on his jaw. Or the scent of hard liquor lingering on his skin.

Whatever the difference was, she sensed it went soul deep. This wasn't the Trace Cordell she'd once fallen in love with it. This was the sort of man no wise woman would ever trust.

But she had no choice.

"And you chose your father," Trace reminded her softly. "So that cuts me loose."

"Rory's dead," she said flatly. Grief welled inside her. For a second, she couldn't speak.

"Rory Kennedy dead?" Trace repeated with uncertainty. He glanced around as if expecting folks to contradict her. His grip on her arm softened and his hand came down to clasp hers. "I can't believe it. I thought the old rooster would live forever."

"He would have," Flanna said, unable to screen the bitterness from her voice, "if Burrell Slayton hadn't shot him."

Judge Rigby jumped into the discussion like the lapdog he was. "Here now. It was a hunting accident. We all know it was."

"Yes," she agreed, "except my father was the prey."

"There's no proof to your accusation, Miss Kennedy," Judge Rigby said evenly, then paused. His gaze shifted from her to Trace. "Or should I say, Mrs. Cordell?" he added thoughtfully. "You know, it's convenient of you to turn up married to one of the fastest guns in the West."

Panic rose in her throat, but Trace gave her hand a reassuring squeeze. "Yes, it is," he agreed. "Wonder if Rory would have had his hunting accident if I'd been around."

"Can't say," Rigby replied. "Mr. Slayton had made his wants known. Old Rory didn't listen."

"I don't know if my hearing is any better."

The gauntlet had been thrown down. The cowboys shuffled back while Rigby's nervous henchmen edged closer. Their hands dropped to their guns.

Flanna stepped forward between them all. Her fight was with Burrell Slayton, not the judge. Trace would do her no good if he was shot before they left Harwood. "Come, Trace. Let me take you home. We need to talk." To her relief, he didn't argue, even while a few "wooo's" and catcalls met her words.

"I'll get my horse."

"Oh, your horse has been sold," Judge Rigby said, cockily hooking his thumbs in his suspenders.

"What?" Trace cocked his head as if he hadn't heard correctly.

The judge shrugged. "We had to pay for the damage to Birdie's saloon."

"And you thought it would be me?"

"We thought you'd be hanged," Judge Rigby answered. "A dead man doesn't need a horse."

His gallows humor drew a chuckle or two from the hard-bitten crowd gathered around but Trace obviously wasn't in the mood for jokes. He said quietly, "I want my horse."

"You can have it," the judge replied. "Your *wife* bought it."

Slowly, Trace turned to Flanna. "You bought my horse?"

She was almost afraid to nod yes. "And your guns. And your hat. Everything is at the ranch. Well, except for the hat. I have it in the wagon."

"Good." He took her arm and turned her around. "Let's go get them and while we do that, I'm going to talk to you about taking your sweet time before speaking up. Five minutes later and I'd have been dancing on air."

"Well, I can explain."

"You are going to have a *lot* of explaining to do, *honey*."

"I hadn't expected them to charge you with the murder," she demurred.

"Mmm-hmm."

The cowboys and townsfolk moved out of their way but Judge Rigby's voice called them back. "Wait a minute, Cordell."

Trace turned. "What do you want now?"

"To give you advice. You know, Burrell Slayton isn't going to take well to the news you're married to Miss Kennedy."

"Who the hell is Slayton?"

"A man you don't want to cross. You might be wise to drift on."

Sliding a protective arm around Flanna's shoulders, Trace said, "And leave my wife?"

Rigby pushed back his bowler. "You already did once. 'Course I can't understand why any man would leave a woman like Miss Kennedy."

Trace's lips twisted into a smile. "Have you lived with her yet?" His quick rejoinder was met with a smattering of laughter.

The judge shook his head. "No, something is wrong here." He waved his hands to include both Flanna and Trace. "This doesn't feel right. I don't know if I believe the two of your are married."

Before Flanna could protest, Trace asked, "Why should she lie?"

"She might have her reasons," the judge said, "reasons she'd best not pursue if she's smart." He put his cigar in his mouth. "After all, you two act like the furtherest thing from being loverly."

"'Loverly'?" Trace's voice dropped to a deadly note. "I've had a chair broken over my head, spent the night in jail, almost got myself hanged...and now you are telling me I'm not *loverly* enough."

"The two of you act like strangers."

Flanna opened her mouth. "We know each other well enough—" she started. But her words were cut off as Trace grabbed her arm, swung her around and, without warning, kissed her.

For a second she couldn't think. She couldn't move. Having been caught in midsentence, her mouth was still open and the kiss was awkward.

In spite of the vagrant life she'd led, her father had been overly protective. She'd allowed a few demure pecks on the cheek but nothing like having her mouth swallowed whole like this. And by the one man whose kisses she'd longed for.

Her heart pounded in her ears. Her eyes were open. Everyone was staring. Stiff and unnatural, she waved her arms in the air, not certain what to do with them.

Trace eased up slightly. The anger left him and his bruising lips softened, taking a more intimate turn.

Now, *this* was nice. With a soft sigh, Flanna closed her eyes and relaxed. His kiss became hungry and she couldn't help but taste him back.

Now she understood why everyone liked kissing so much. This was beyond pleasant. It made her vibrate with things she'd never felt with anyone else save him—need, desire, wanting.

She wrapped her arms around him. He responded by gathering her closer. His possessiveness sent a shiver of anticipation through her. But when his tongue stroked hers, she couldn't help a start of surprise…until she discovered she liked this.

He sucked lightly and she felt the tug all the way to the deepest recesses of her woman's body—and she wanted *more*.

Time stood still. She lost all awareness. The dusty street, the watching crowd, even the earth beneath her feet faded from consciousness. Nothing existed save this kiss and the heady feeling of his hard body melding against hers. They fit perfectly like spoons. Her good bonnet fell back, the ribbon around her neck. Her hard, tight nipples pushed against his hard chest. His erection pressing between them gave evidence of his own reaction.

Dear God, she could kiss him all day—

Trace broke off the kiss. He stepped back and Flanna would have fallen to the ground, her legs unable to support her weight. He held her steady with an arm around her waist. "Satisfied?" he asked Judge Rigby.

The judge stared as slack-jawed as everyone else and Flanna realized she and Trace had given them quite a show. Rory must be turning in his grave!

A flood of heat burned her face. Self-consciously she fussed with her bonnet, attempting to set herself back to rights.

Trace smiled at the judge. "We'll be leaving. Flanna and I have some *unfinished* business to attend to."

Low whistles and jostling met his proclamation. Judge Rigby didn't say a word, but Flanna could feel his hard gaze on them as she and Trace headed for the wagon parked in front of the Mercantile.

He helped her into the seat without a word, then climbed up beside her. She reached for the reins but his hand covered hers. His eyes were like slivers of ice. She wondered what he was thinking.

"I'll drive," he said.

She nodded and sat back. With a whack of the reins, he started the horse forward, heading out of town. The judge, his compatriots and the small crowd followed their every movement.

Within moments they were alone. Trace drove in silence until they were a good mile away from Harwood. He stopped the wagon.

"Now what the hell is going on?"

His expression was anything but *loverly*.

CHAPTER THREE

"THEY SHOT HIM," Flanna said, the corners of her mouth tight, her eyes bright. "He was unarmed, Trace. He went to talk to Slayton, to work out a compromise, and they shot him cold. They didn't even bring him back to me but buried him in Harwood quick as a cat can blink."

Surprisingly, grief washed over him. There'd been no love lost between himself and the wily Irishman. As her father, Rory had believed no man was good enough for his daughter in spite of his own two-bit swindles and petty schemes. He'd flat-out told Trace that when Flanna married it would be to a better man than some whore's son who'd made a name for himself with a gun—even if he was a lawman.

Trace had countered he didn't know how Rory thought he was going to meet such a man for his daughter while peddling rotgut disguised as medicinal tonic and getting thrown out of every town they drove through. He had as much right to Flanna as anyone.

Besides, Flanna loved him…or so he had thought.

In the end, Rory had proved him wrong. She'd left with her father without a backward glance.

Still, Trace hadn't wished the rascal dead.

"I warned him," he said tightly. "I told Rory he'd better change his ways or someone would put a bullet through him."

Her gaze hardened. "He did change, Trace. After we left Loveless…" Her voice trailed off. She turned her attention to the line of the far horizon beyond the green prairie of the high plains. "After we left Loveless," she began again, "I told him I didn't want to live that way anymore. I thought about what you'd said, about how out here in the West a person could have a second chance to be whatever he or she wanted to be. No past, no regrets. Just move on and make yourself into someone new, someone meaningful." She swung her gaze to him. "Do you remember?"

He'd always talked that way. It had been his "sheriff" sermon, his friendly advice to those on the wrong path. The words sounded foreign to him now. "Yeah."

She crossed her arms tight against her middle. "After...after what happened between us, when we parted—"

"Oh, you mean you've finally remembered we are *not* married?"

Her hesitation evaporated at his sarcasm. "I had to cobble together a story for why I was searching for you. I couldn't let Judge Rigby be thinking I wanted you to bring Slayton to justice. They're all afraid of him and his friends."

"But to claim we're *married?*" He shook his head. "That was more than a bald-faced lie, Flanna. It was—" It was what? An insult? An injury? A reminder of what he couldn't have?

"I hated choosing between the two of you, but he was my father. You couldn't have expected me to turn my back on him?"

Yes, he had. "You can skip the explanations." He swung his gaze away from her, preferring the ruts in the dirt road to the face of the woman he'd once loved. "Anything between us is in the past. I've managed fine without you." He started to pick up the reins but her tart words stopped him.

"Yes, I can see you have. When did you last shave, Trace? Or bathe? You smell of the bottle."

"I'm sorry, m'lady, but I've spent the night in jail, I was almost hanged, otherwise I would have taken a perfumed bath for you. Eau de lillies.''

"I doubt that. The high-and-mighty Sheriff Cordell doesn't put himself out for anyone. It's his way or no way.''

"I would have married you," Trace charged. "I offered you everything I had, but it wasn't enough.''

"Aye, and you would have reminded me every day of what *grand* favor you did not throwing me out of town," she replied. "Rory warned me. He said you were too self-righteous. A prig.''

"He called me a pig?" Anger felt good. Anger offered protection.

"Not a pig," she corrected, her Irishness coming out. "A *prig*. You ken? A sanctimonious, rigid, know-it-all who must have his own way.''

"If you felt that way, why didn't you let me hang?" He'd almost prefer hanging versus sitting here in the sun taking a tongue-lashing off the one woman he'd ever wanted and couldn't have.

"Because I need you," she told him bleakly. "No one else will help me. They're all afraid of Slayton. And then, just when I was ready to give up, I heard from a passing neighbor that the great Sheriff Cordell was sitting in Harwood playing cards. It was an omen, Trace. God sent you here to help me.''

''God had nothing to do with it.'' He slapped the horse with the reins. ''I was passing through and I'm going to keep moving, Flanna. I'm not looking for any fights. I've had enough.''

''You'll change your mind once you hear my story,'' she insisted stubbornly.

He ignored her.

''Besides, it's all your fault.''

He held his tongue.

She glanced his way and then added, ''If not for you, Rory would still be alive.''

Temper seared through him. Trace pulled the wagon to a halt. He faced her. ''How do you figure that?''

With a haughty lift of her stubborn chin, she said, ''Because we wouldn't even be here if it wasn't for you. I didn't want to wander aimlessly anymore. I wanted a home, honest work, and a place that I could put down roots. Have you ever wanted such a thing?''

Yeah, he had. With her. ''So what did Rory do, swindle this Slayton out of land and earn a bullet for his efforts?''

Anger flashed in her eyes. ''No. We decided to change our lives just like you advised, *Sheriff*. Rory bought this parcel of land from a man who was selling and we decided to change who we were. We're ranchers now and doing well even in such a short time. We have fifty head of cattle."

Trace didn't like hearing she was fine without him. His life hadn't been worth a damn since she walked out. "So what did happen? What did Slayton have against Rory?"

"Nothing against him. He wanted what Rory had—water. Here on the high plains, water is like gold. The parcel we bought has a stream that runs right into the Cimarron and a spring that bubbles with the sweetest water you can ever imagine."

"Sounds like a prime stake."

"It is. And Slayton wants it. He needs the water for his herds. Turns out the man we'd bought it from had been chased out by Slayton's threats, but Rory was not one to run, especially since we were making a good go of it." She placed her hand on Trace's arm. "I have a rage in me for vengeance that could shake the heavens. Rory was no saint, but he didn't deserve to die like that, either. Slayton expects me to sell, but I won't. He'll have to kill me to for my land. And that's why I need you. You are a man of justice. You'll stop Slayton."

That's why I need you. Trace dropped his

gaze to her fingers on his arm…and he wanted to be her hero.

Yup, the time had come to leave.

"Didn't you hear Rigby?" he asked. "I'm an *ex*-lawman. I'm not the sheriff of Loveless anymore."

She drew back as if first hearing the news. "You left Loveless? I can't believe such a thing. You were the pillar of that town. Everyone respected you."

"Respected me enough to give me the boot." He couldn't look at her. Instead, he drove the horse forward. Better to get where they were going so he could leave.

Flanna sat in stunned, gratifying silence. It lasted only a moment. "Why would the people of Loveless do that? You took that town from a wild cattle stop to a thriving village."

He focused on the road ahead. "Well, a good number of folks were upset that you and Rory had separated them from their hard-earned cash."

"We *sold* those bottles to them and we never asked for more than what a person was willing to pay."

"You also made some promises about the elixir."

"It does what we promised," she told him primly, "if a person is in the proper frame of mind. You have to work with it to make the magic happen." She paused. "Turn here and follow this trail over beyond that ridge." She sat back. "So why did they really ask you to leave?"

"Because times are changing," Trace said dully. "A man who has killed as often as I have is not suited for the kind of town Loveless had become. They have churches there now and stores, families."

"You do have a reputation."

"And how did I earn it?" He swore softly. "I gave them everything I had. When there was fighting to do, I did it. I took the town back from the Watkins gang and I kept it. I made something of myself in Loveless. Because of my *reputation* as a gunfighter, the streets were safe. There was law. And then, some medicine man comes through and people start to think I don't fit the town anymore."

They'd also remembered about his being born a bastard. Most of them had known his mother. Hell, years ago, she'd been a cornerstone of the community in spite of her trade. Of course, with civilization, people's opinions changed. "They started thinking they wanted a better man. So they hired some policeman from the east and wished me well. They even asked me to leave."

Bitter humiliation and injustice choked him. And it had all started with her. Before she'd come, everyone had liked him fine. Of course, he'd known his place back then. He'd never have courted a town gal, but Flanna's love had let him believe he was one of them.

God, he wished he had a drink!

Flanna sat quietly. He didn't look at her. He hated himself this way…and he didn't want pity. Especially hers. He'd make his way. One way or the other.

But he was tired. Damn tired…

"I have your guns. And your horse."

He glanced at her. He couldn't tell what she was thinking. But there was no pity. "When we get to your place, I'll pick them up and be off."

She didn't answer but leaned forward, placing her hand right beside his thigh on the hard, wood seat. Another half inch over and she'd touch him.

Every fiber of his being honed in on that one tantalizing possibility…especially after that kiss back in Harwood.

"I need you."

Her throaty words stirred his imagination.

"I did love you," she added. "It was like cutting out my heart to leave you, but I couldn't abandon my father, and the two of you were oil and water."

He tightened his grip on the reins. The trail across the prairie curved, disappearing into the high grass. He could feel her watching him.

"You could start new, too," she offered. "Just as Rory and I did."

Trace didn't answer. That had been his advice for others, not himself.

At last, she sat back. "What shall I do about Slayton?"

"I'd sell. You know how to drive a hard bargain." There, he'd absolved himself of responsibility.

"And what? Move on from the first home I've known?"

He chose his words deliberately. "You're good at moving on, Flanna. You won't have any problems at all."

She crossed her arms. There was a beat of silence and then she said, "Rory was right—you can be a bastard, Trace Cordell."

"That's what they tell me," he replied grimly.

As if sensing the tension, the horse picked up his pace. "We're almost home," Flanna said.

"Ah, yes. Kennedy's paradise," Trace countered.

She didn't reply. At the same moment the trail took them up over a bluff—and there it was.

The horse lifted his head and whinnied, an announcement he was home. An answering call came from Trace's horse, Bill, down in a makeshift corral.

Trace felt a stab of disappointment.

The homestead—a soddy and a barn a little larger than a stable—was like a hundred others he'd seen across the prairie. He hadn't really known what to expect. Something in Flanna's tone when she'd spoken of the place had made him picture grandeur on a scale that common sense told him couldn't be found in Kansas. But he wasn't expecting a soddy. He hated the small houses made out of blocks of tough sod. They smelled of earth and the stories he'd heard of snakes put a shudder through him. Even the barn, really nothing more than a lean-to, had sod walls. A chicken coop with some of the sorriest-looking poultry he'd ever seen had been built against the barn.

A line of huge cottonwoods, locust trees, and hedges marked the path of the stream. There was water in the air. He could smell it. He knew many ranchers would kill for this parcel of land.

"Isn't it wonderful?" Flanna said proudly. She reached for the reins.

"It's something," he agreed truthfully.

"We started with nothing, not even the sod house."

"You made money fast."

She bit back a smile. "Well, we had that bit of a stake we'd earned in Loveless."

"Oh, yes, *that*," he replied dryly, and she wisely let the matter rest.

She drove down the bluff into the yard. Two hound dogs of dubious heritage barked a warning and then jumped up into the wagon to jubilantly greet their mistress. They even had some slobber for Trace.

Flanna laughed at their happy eagerness. "Calm down," she ordered, removing her straw bonnet and holding it high so the dogs wouldn't get it. Immediately, the ever present wind captured her red-gold hair and playfully lifted it in the breeze. She jumped down before Trace could offer a hand. "Let me put this horse up and I'll show you around the place."

Trace thought he could see everything from where he sat. His buckskin, Bill, came to the edge of the corral where Flanna had him penned and nickered.

Flanna's laughing gaze met Trace's. "Your horse is a bit of a stud. He has his eye on my Spice."

"Well, he'd best be thinking about leaving," Trace said, and the smile disappeared from her face.

"Yes. Of course."

He told himself he had no reason to feel like a deserter. There were no promises between them. Flanna shouldn't have assumed. Still…even the dogs seemed to look at him with recriminations.

"Here, you go put your bonnet away before the dogs eat it and I'll see to Spice," he offered as penance. In truth, his conscience was bothering him, but he knew about battles over land. Where money was involved, some men were ruthless. Flanna would be safer selling and starting anew somewhere else.

She nodded and hurried inside. He'd just finished unharnessing the horse when she returned. She held his guns and holster in her hand. "I thought you'd want these."

He stared at the pearl handles of his guns and felt a sudden unease. What good had these guns ever done him? This morning he'd woke thinking he'd killed a man. He took a step back. "Set them up on the wagon," he said, turning away. "I'll get them later."

If Flanna noticed a change in him, she gave no indication. Instead she said, "Let Spice graze. She'll not wander far. I want to show you something." Without waiting for his response, she turned and walked toward the stream.

"It won't do any good," he called after her.

He waited. She kept walking. "Flanna, I'm not staying. I'm not your hero."

She stopped, turned. "Are you coming?"

"You told me no once. I'm not some lapdog to hang around."

She kept walking. "You made yourself perfectly clear. You'll not champion my battle. But I want you to see this, to understand why I won't go without a fight. Wait until you see what I want to show you."

His feet started moving. He didn't know why, but he didn't stop himself.

She led him down by the stream and then turned with a smile. "What do you think?"

On a level bit of land along the banks of the stream stood the foundations of a house. The first floor had been built with supporting beams set in. To his right was a stack of lumber for building, almost as high as his chest.

"It's not much now," she told him. "Rory and I sketched it in a bit on the ground and had been working on it as we got a chance. Wood is expensive, but we want the best. We already have the glass windows. They arrived in Dodge the day after they shot my father."

She stepped up on the boards. "I wanted it by the stream so we'd have its music in the morning. Rory wanted a big porch so he could sit in his chair in the evenings and enjoy the shade. In the summer, this is the only place to catch a breeze.'' She ran her hand over a piece of rough wood, her expression wistful. ''I can't give it up. I've been traveling since I was wee thing. This is my first home. I'll never sell. Can you understand now how I feel?''

Oh, yes, he could. Her eyes were shiny with pride and the wind blew her curls around her face. He felt a need the likes of which he'd never experienced before. For her.

This was Flanna, he reminded himself. She was a tease, a lure used by her father to turn men's minds from his true purpose. And she'd been very good at ensnaring him. She'd cost him everything he'd valued—his position as sheriff, his pride...and in turn had spurned his love.

''I want you to stay.'' Her husky voice cut through his doubts. Her gaze slid from his as if she found the words difficult to say. ''I need you.''

She knew how to twist him in knots.

Trace took a step back, and then another. ''I don't know how you do it, but you have the touch.''

Flanna stiffened. ''What do you mean?''

''You know exactly what you're doing. It's as if you are trying to grab my soul. Well, it won't work, not this time. I thank you for saving my life, but, lady, we're through."

He turned to walk away just as the dogs began barking. Riders were coming over the bluff. "Do you know them?" he asked Flanna.

"Yes." Her mouth flattened. "It's Burrell Slayton and his men. Well, it appears you are going to be making his acquaintance, after all. Shall I invite them for tea?" She didn't wait for an answer but walked forward to greet her "guests."

CHAPTER FOUR

SLAYTON RODE on a white horse at the head of a small party of rough-looking men.

Her heart pounding in her ears, Flanna stopped in the middle of the yard waiting for him to come to her. Trace had followed, and now stood no more than five feet away, his expression wary.

Her pride refused to drag him into a fight he did not want. But his refusal to help her cause hit her full-force. She'd counted on his help. From the moment she'd heard he was in town, she'd known he'd been sent to help her...and she'd thought she'd have a second chance at his love. Leaving him had been a mistake.

Now, she knew she was alone. The Trace who stood behind her wasn't the man she remembered. That man had an inborn sense of justice. He'd have fought for what was right regardless of the circumstances.

This man thought only of himself.

She directed her resentment toward her unwanted guests.

Dust swirled around the hooves of the horses as Slayton called his band to a halt ten feet from where she stood. "Miss Kennedy," he greeted with jovial humor. He was a lean man, fastidious in dress and manner—especially when compared to the coarse men riding with him. His boots were polished to a shine the trail could never dull, his shirt, a crisp white against the black of his jacket, and his ribbon tie made him appear as if he'd just come from church.

Rory had always liked the vain. He claimed they were the easiest marks. For that reason, he'd assumed he could handle Slayton. He hadn't expected to be shot.

"Or should I say, *Mrs. Cordell?*" Slayton queried in soft, polite tones, leaning one lazy arm over his saddle horn. His gaze moved past her to where Trace stood, a silent witness. "How convenient for you to turn out to be married to one of the fastest guns in the West. I'm surprised Rory didn't brag about it."

"What do you want?" she demanded.

Slayton grinned. "I want what I've always wanted, Mrs. Cordell. I want to buy your property. I was hoping I could have a word with your *husband* about the matter."

Too late, Flanna realized the shortcoming of

her marriage scheme. By law, a wife's property belonged to her husband. Trace's advice for her to sell rang in her ears. She blocked his path. "It's not for sale. It'll *never* be for sale. Not to you."

"That's all well and good, Mrs. Cordell," Slayton replied, "but I'd like to hear from your husband. This is men's business now."

"How much are you offering?" Trace's rough voice cut right to her soul.

Slayton's teeth flashed in triumphant. "Three hundred dollars. Gold."

"Only three hundred?" Trace repeated.

The smile on Slayton's face flattened. "My price is more than generous."

"I have another price in mind." Trace came up to stand by Flanna. "How about admitting to the murder of Rory Kennedy?"

Flanna's heart gave a glad leap. Burrell Slayton sat up on his horse, his lazy good humor gone. The riders behind him tensed.

"I didn't have anything to do with Rory's accident. I wasn't even close to where it happened."

"You were the last person to see him," Trace replied evenly. "If you didn't shoot him, you know who did."

Slayton's eyes turned cold. "I had nothing to do with Kennedy's death, Cordell."

"Well, naming the killer is my price for this land."

Flanna linked her arm in Trace's. She saw the trap he'd laid. Slayton could never admit to the murder. And if he turned in one of his own men, well, there was no doubt in her mind the killer would squeal like a cowardly dog to save his own neck.

"You are making a mistake, Cordell," Slayton said. "A fatal one if you continue to accuse me of something I didn't do." The three men behind him shifted their hands to their guns.

Trace didn't waver. "Threats won't get you what you want."

"I don't make threats. I make promises."

Flanna clenched her fists, but Trace smiled easily. "Any time you want to carry out a *promise,* you go right ahead. I'm not Rory Kennedy. I know how to watch my back."

"We'll see." Slayton nodded to his men and, with a sharp jerk of the reins, turned his horse around. But as he passed one of his men, Flanna caught a signal pass between them.

"Watch out," she warned Trace even as the man pulled his gun and fired.

The bullet whizzed into the dirt right at the toe of Trace's boot. Flanna gave a small yelp of surprise and jumped back, but Trace didn't flinch.

Instead, a change seemed to come over him. His eyes took on a blazing light. He actually seemed to grow in stature. He looked up at the man who had shot at him, a trail-beaten cowboy with a toothless grin, still proudly holding the gun on him.

In two giant, quick steps, Trace was in front of him. He grabbed the cowhand by the front of his shirt and yanked him off his horse as if he weighed no more than a rag doll. His movements had been so unexpected, the man hadn't had the presence of mind to shoot.

Trace knocked the gun from his hand. It flew through the air to land close to Flanna who promptly snatched it up.

Wrapping both hands around the cowboy's neck, Trace held him high. The man's face started to turn red, his mouth gaped for breath. His comrades pulled their guns. Her knees shaking, Flanna trained the gun on them.

Trace ignored them all. He acted possessed, his focus was on the cowboy who struggled for breath. "If you ever take another shot at me, you'd better not miss," he said in a low, dangerous voice Flanna had never heard from him before. "Because if you do, the next time, I'll kill you."

The cowboy's feet were kicking out now, trying to swing free of Trace's dangerous grip.

Then Trace let him go. The cowpoke fell to the ground, his legs unable to support his weight. On all fours, he started hacking, trying to catch his breath.

Trace pinned Slayton with his hard gaze. "Leave Flanna alone. I'll not let harm come to her."

Slayton's lips formed a firm line as if he bit back a retort. Instead, he looked at the two remaining men. "Pick Tom up. Let's get out of here." He rode off while his men scurried to obey under Trace's watchful eye.

One caught Tom's horse while the other rode over and held down a hand. Tom took a minute before he could gather enough strength to reach up for help. His burly friend swung him up behind his saddle and the trio followed their boss.

Flanna watched until they had gone over the bluff and out of sight. Any triumph she felt was tempered by the swift, controlled violence of Trace's actions. Tom could have shot him. And yet Trace's reaction had unsettled her. The way he had walked into the line of the cowboy's gun had been suicidal and yet Trace had not hesitated. Something dangerous and unrestrained had overtaken him. Something she didn't understand.

But she could appreciate why the people of Loveless had asked him to move on. And her own father's doubts. Slowly, she turned to face him and what she saw almost broke her heart.

He studied some point on the ground, a statue of a man made of muscle and flesh. His shoulders were hunched in thought and deep lines etched his face. She wondered what he was thinking...and knew the answer.

He hated what he had become. She understood as if she could read his mind.

Immediately she stepped forward. "You were wonderful," she whispered. "You were like the archangel Michael with his avenging sword. The way you walked right into the gun sight and grabbed that cowboy by the neck." She hooked her arm in his. "The man was quivering with fright and his friends were, too."

Trace watched her, silent.

His quietness made her uneasy. "You did it," she assured him. "Slayton will think twice before crossing you."

"He'll be back. And when he comes, he'll bring more men. I've challenged him. It's personal now."

His words sobered her. "Why do you say that?"

"Because I know his kind. Hell, I *am* his kind."

"No, you're not." She gave his arm a

squeeze, feeling the hard muscle there. "You're a good man, a brave one. You're no more like him than a Thoroughbred is like a burro."

"Yeah." He turned from her, but she drew her hand down his arm to capture his hand.

He looked at her, expectant. When they stood this close, she was so aware of him, of his size, of those hard silver eyes, of the long, tapered fingers rough with calluses.

Merciful God, she was still in love with him.

She thought she'd been over him but then there'd been the kiss…and all the arguing…and then the confrontation with Slayton—

She dropped his hand as if it had turned into a burning ember.

He noticed and he didn't like it. "What's the matter?" he said carefully.

Her stomach did a nervous twist. She wasn't about to admit her feelings. He wouldn't believe her even if she did. He was not the kind of man who gave second chances. "Nothing. I'm, uh—" Words failed her, especially under his scrutiny. She attempted to recover. "What are you going to do now?"

"Stay and fight." He walked toward Spice, grazing by the wagon. He took the horse by the mane and guided it toward the barn.

Flanna took after him, skipping to catch up. Placing a hand on his arm, she made him stop.

"Listen, Trace, this isn't your fight. Maybe I was wrong to draw you in."

His brows lifted in surprise. "You should have thought about that before you claimed to be married to me. Everyone thinks I own the land, Mrs. Cordell."

"Well…yes. But you were going to leave."

"I changed my mind."

She glanced at the creek where the water merrily rushed over stones. The precious, precious water. "I just don't want anything to happen to you." And it would. A sense of impending gloom seemed to hover over her. Perhaps she *should* sell.

"Besides, maybe I like being married."

"Like it?" She looked up, startled. The expression on his face was indiscernible…until his gaze lowered…down to her breasts with raw, hungry desire.

The air crackled with tension.

Flanna didn't dare move. She could barely breathe. Her breasts seemed to fill and tightened. An edgy tingling danced across her skin to settle deep inside her.

And yet the sun was still shining, birds whistling, and the ground was still beneath her feet. The horse nudged Trace as if to tell him to get moving. He let go of the animal and took a step closer, raising his gaze to linger on her lips.

She cleared her throat and then edged back. "But we aren't married."

He smiled.

"I told you earlier I'm willing to pay you for your help," she said stiffly.

"Like a *hired* hand?" he asked softly, his inflection giving the offer a meaning she hadn't intended.

Again she cleared her throat, surprised at how nervous she was. "Yes. Fair's fair."

He nodded as if in agreement. "Well now, what is a 'fair' price?"

Flanna forced herself to pretend she wasn't aware of how tall he was, how intimidating…or how easy it would be to step into his arms. "I did save your life."

He laughed. His chest so close, she could feel the heat from his body. "Yes, you did. Shame you didn't make it for the trial."

"But I was there in time to stop the hanging." Her voice sounded as if she'd run a great distance and she was starting to feel light-headed. Maybe now was a good time to put a little distance between them. But as she started to back away, his hand caught her arm—just as it had in town before he'd kissed her.

"My services don't come cheap, *Mrs.* Cordell."

Her toes curled at his use of her fake married

name. His voice was laden with unspoken promises. "I didn't think they did." She struggled for sanity. This was a bargain they were driving. She must keep her wits. "I'll offer you ten dollars a day."

He laughed.

Annoyed, she retorted, "It's a fair price. More than you earned as sheriff."

"And how did you come by that sort of cash? From the people of Loveless?"

A guilty heat stole across her cheeks. "By the look of you, you shouldn't be turning up your nose at the offer of a little cash."

"No, I shouldn't, should I? Especially covered in trail dust." He pulled her closer, the light of a hundred devils gleaming in his eyes. "And it has been a while since I've had a good meal or other—" he gave her arm a gentle squeeze "—comfort."

Comfort. Oh dear. "What are you thinking?" she asked, cautious and yet so very aware of his legs now pressed against hers.

"That perhaps I might take you up on the offer you made in town."

"Which offer?" she squeaked.

Again, his gaze flicked over her breasts. "About being a wife."

Flanna's mouth went dry. "I was...saving you...when I made that claim," she explained faintly. Good Lord, she could barely think. Or move her gaze from his mouth. She'd always known Trace was a fine-looking man but she'd never noticed how sensual his lips were. Manly lips. The kind of lips that had proved they knew how to kiss.

He grinned, his white teeth in his whiskered face giving him a roguish look. "Well, that's the price, Flanna. You wanted to pretend to be my wife in Harwood. The way I see it, we don't have any other choice but to continue the game."

For a second, the need, the desire, the wanting of him made it difficult for her to reason. Rory would never have approved. But Rory wasn't here.

"This is a Philistine's bargain," she whispered.

"You've struck that kind of a bargain before." He smiled. "It all depends on what you want." His lips mere inches from hers, he said, "It's what *I* want."

Merciful heavens, this was the devil's own pact. Her traitorous body yearned for his body heat. She loved the feeling of his arms around her. He made her feel protected and safe.

"I have needs, Flanna," he said, his voice close to her ear going straight through to her heart. "Needs only a wife can provide."

She made a small sound of distress that sounded embarrassingly like a whimper of desire. "A pretend wife?"

His lips brushed the top of her forehead. "Oh, yes. But a wife in *every* way."

Flanna feared she'd swoon. Rory must be rolling in his grave. Almost as if in a trance, she nodded. "Done."

"Good."

Then to her surprise, he started to remove his shirt.

She looked around wildly. It was broad daylight, no later than midafternoon. He couldn't be thinking of ravishing her now? "Wait. Trace, what are you doing?" His bare chest was rock-hard with muscle. His shoulders made others appear puny. "Oh, my," she murmured, part in distress and part in admiration. She fluttered a hand up to her collar, the heat of the day suddenly overwhelming. "I mean, you can't—I can't— We should at least go inside—"

He cut her off by tossing his dirty, sweat-stained shirt in her face. "Here."

Gagging, she removed the shirt. "What is this for?"

"It needs washing. I've got another in my saddlebags. Best get busy—" He paused and added with smug emphasis, *"Wife."*

Laughing, he drove Spice into the barn.

CHAPTER FIVE

TRACE CONGRATULATED himself as he walked the mare into the barn. *Finally,* he'd gotten a bit of his own back over Flanna. She'd thought he was after something else. The expression on her face when he'd taken off his shirt had been comical. And then, when he'd thrown the shirt at her—*ha!* He'd made her feel like a fool. Just as she'd made him feel back in Loveless.

No sir, she hadn't liked that. Even now she stood holding his shirt away from her as if she'd rather burn than wash it.

But she wouldn't because for once in her life, she needed him.

Trace put Spice in a roped-off stall. Outside, Bill ran around the corral, wanting attention. Or, more likely, company.

The barn itself was a small, low-roofed soddy. Rory had put every inch of space to use. Hanging from the rafters were tools. A plow rested in the corner. A row of bulging sacks were stacked against the wall. Trace wandered over and knelt to investigate. Wheat seed. He'd heard it grew well in these parts. Of course, the seed should have been planted weeks ago…round about the time Rory had been shot.

The lucky Irish bastard. He'd had it all. Land, a future, and a daughter who loved him.

"Perhaps I deserved that."

He turned at the sound of Flanna's crisp voice. She stood a few steps from him, his shirt in her clenched hands, her face pinched. The air in the stable grew close. Too close. He shrugged.

She interpreted his gesture accurately. "You don't want to talk about it, do you? Every time I bring up what happened between us you grow angry and push me away."

He stood, unexpectedly ill-at-ease at being half naked in front of her. What was it about Flanna that made him feel more like an awkward boy instead of a man? It was as if she could see to the heart of his black soul. His saddle and saddlebags were stacked on top of several others draped over a makeshift sawhorse close to the grain bags. He reached into his bag and pulled out his other shirt, giving her his back. It wasn't much cleaner than the one she held. "Forget it. Loveless was a long time ago."

"I feel like it all happened yesterday." When

he didn't speak, she said, "I didn't mean for things to get as tangled up the way they did."

He didn't want this conversation. He pulled his shirt over his head.

"Trace—" she started, and suddenly he'd had enough.

"I'm here, dammit," he swore. "You wanted my help. You have it. Leave the past where it is."

"I can't. I *loved* you."

For a heartbeat he couldn't breathe. He couldn't think.

And then he remembered.

"Damn, you are good." He tucked his shirt into his pants, his movements jerky...and he hated himself because he wanted to believe. She was so lovely, so tempting, and yet—

"You've said those words before, Flanna. They come easy to your lips, especially when you want something. Well, the blinders are off. I'm not the moony-eyed—" He caught himself in time. He'd been about to say "lonely." He wasn't the moony-eyed, lonely man he'd been in Loveless.

But that wasn't true, was it?

He turned and his gaze dropped again to the sacks of seed.

He sensed her take a step toward him. "You feel I betrayed you," she said.

He remained silent…and so very aware of her.

"If I'd thought things could have been different, I'd never have left. But Rory and I milked your town dry, Trace. I wanted to stop, but it was too late and you wouldn't have forgiven me. You still won't." She paused, cleared her throat. "Rory said a man like you didn't forgive easy."

She moved closer until she stood right at his arm. He could feel the heat of her body. When he'd first met her, he remembered thinking she'd smelled like fresh grass on a spring day. New and green, vital, inviting. Now the scent of her filled him. It would be so easy to put his arms around her. To kiss her as he had in town but with deeper intent.

Ah, yes, that kiss had been a mistake.

"You said a person can make herself into whatever she wants to be out here. No matter what her past was. Were you lying to me, Trace? Because I've tried. I am different. Wiser."

The light lilt of her voice wrapped itself around him. He struggled to protect himself. "Maybe I was wrong. Maybe a person can't change."

"Or maybe you are fooling yourself," she

countered. "Especially if you think answers can be found in a whiskey bottle."

He hated the way she shot right to the heart of a matter. She'd never been one to sugar the truth...and if the truth be known, he was starting to feel embarrassed. Perhaps he had overreacted when they'd thrown him out of Loveless. He'd never been one to feel sorry for himself and yet, here he was.

Damn Flanna. She had a talent for making him see the truth in himself. He walked over to where a coil of rope hung from the ceiling. "I've got work to do if I'm going to be ready for Slayton when he comes."

FLANNA RECOGNIZED that she had been dismissed. Trace didn't want to talk...but then he'd always been a man of few words. However, she sensed he wasn't as indifferent to her as he wished her to believe.

And she wasn't about to leave him be. She'd made the mistake of leaving him once. She'd not do it again.

"What do you have planned?" she asked.

He stiffened, a frown coming to his lips.

"After all, we're partners," she explained, her woman's intuition telling her she must keep herself in front of him. No matter how angry he got, she didn't dare let him turn his back on

her. Because she knew now what she wanted—
she wanted him.

"I should know what you are planning so I
can help."

His irritation plain, he replied, "I have it handled."

"Of course you do," she agreed diplomati-
cally, "but I need know what you expect me to
do."

"You don't have to do anything," he said
pointedly.

Flanna sensed she'd best not push him. "Ah,
then, I'll be fixing the supper. And washing
your shirt."

He glanced at her as if he thought she teased
him with her abrupt capitulation. She kept her
expression carefully neutral.

"What is going through your scheming Irish
mind, Flanna?"

"You give me too much credit, Trace. All
I'm trying to do is protect what is mine against
Slayton." She moved now, deliberately walking close as she passed him. "I'll be in the
house, being a good *wife*."

He shifted at her emphasis of the title, wary
as if expecting her to pounce on him. Giving
Spice's nose a rub as she passed, she asked with
studied nonchalance, "So what are you planning to do with the rope? Build a fence?"

She was teasing but he said seriously, "Yes. They may come back tonight. I'll run this rope through the trees by the creek to create a barricade."

"That won't stop a band of armed men," she replied.

"No, but the horses will be confused when they hit the rope. They'll balk, maybe even bolt. Slayton's men are cowards at heart. They get the courage from their numbers. And they are lazy. If the horses act up, if this job looks like the least bit of work, they'll run." He yanked the end of the rope taut. "Then it will just be Slayton and me."

"What about the bluff?"

He smiled, more relaxed now they were discussing something other than their disturbing history. "I'll build a quick fence from the wood Rory has stored for the house. Again, something that will startle the horses. And I'd best get started. We have less than four good hours left to get ready." He escaped out the door.

Thoughtfully, Flanna followed. Trace headed for the stream but she went on inside the soddy. The dogs, having returned from their field chase, eyed the two of them going off in different directions. Samson, the male, loped after Trace. Delilah stayed with her.

Her one-room home was a cozy place, but as

she stepped through the door, the thought struck her it must not appear like much to Trace.

Over time, and because she and her father had built the house themselves, she'd grown accustomed to the single, windowless room. They saved their window money for the new house and when the weather was good did most of their living outdoors. The furnishings were simple but well made—a table, a few chairs, a rocker, and a bed. Her pride and joy was the cast-iron stove that Rory had planned to move to the new house when the time was right.

Taking a pail, she fetched water for washing and then set it on the stove to boil. While waiting for the water to warm, she started a stew for their dinner. As she worked, she decided she was not displeased with matters between herself and Trace. He was doing his best to push her away…and yet she didn't think he was succeeding.

God had brought him back into her life for a reason and this time, she'd not let him go. Her gaze fell on the double bed pushed into one corner of the room. A nervous energy stemming from anticipation fluttered in her stomach.

Trace thought her a tease. Yes, she'd admit part of her father's sales had been her ability to lead men on a wee bit—but not with Trace. Never him. From the first moment she'd laid eyes on him, she'd loved him. Brave, bold, strong—he'd been the epitome of everything she'd dreamed a man could be.

Time had proved her devotion. She'd made a terrible mistake in not staying with him. And yet, in truth, she would have made a miserable sheriff's wife, especially in Loveless. Rory had claimed that the townspeople had been the easiest marks of his career because of their puffed sense of importance. She was not surprised they hadn't treated Trace right.

Still, she had not expected to find him like this. The man she'd known had been full of confidence. For eighteen long months she'd pictured Trace as going on and forgetting about her. After all, there'd been many a lass eyeing him.

But he hadn't turned to solace in the arms of another. Instead, if her woman's soul read the signs right, he'd been as bereft without her as she was without him.

Flanna placed a lid on the stew pot, ready to move the warmed water off for washing, when she was struck by a revelation. Her eyes strayed again to the bed.

Loveless was not for them. But here, on this blessed parcel of land, she and Trace could make a life for themselves. They could build something of substance. Together.

All she had to do was convince him. She knew he'd forgive her, but would he give her another chance?

Her first step, she decided, was to show him she had changed...and that she'd make a man a fine *wife*.

CHAPTER SIX

TRACE DROVE HIMSELF HARD to get as much as possible done before dark—and to erase Flanna's disturbing presence from the edges of his mind.

He was too damn aware of her for his own good. She made his blood hot in a way no woman had before or after her. But he would leave her, as soon as he'd taken care of Slayton.

Burned once, he wasn't fool enough to let her close a second time.

He wove the rope through the trees along the other side of the stream. The dog, a mottled-brown male hound with soulful eyes and a wagging tail, followed his every step. Inside the stable, Trace found two bottles from Rory's medicine-show days and hung them in the tree branches close enough together for them clink quietly when the wind blew. If Slayton sent riders this way, the horses would hear the soft sound and grow skittish...or so Trace hoped.

He loaded the lumber for the house into the

wagon and then pulled it himself to a point half-way up the bluff. The dog tagged along, his tongue hanging loose.

Trace's plan was to make a makeshift barrier by stacking the lumber much like a split-rail fence below the bluff's crest. Slayton's riders would charge over the bluff and then be surprised. With a spade, he started digging into the hard earth to make a posthole to bury a footing.

"I brought you water," Flanna's voice said from behind him. He turned and his breath caught in his throat. She'd braided her hair in a single plait that hung over one shoulder. The simple style made her look younger, vulnerable, except for where the tip of the braid brushed the crest of her breast.

His imagination leaped to a picture of her without the calico dress, with them alone, to-gether. At one time his body had burned for her to the point his nights had been restless.

Now, as she dipped a ladle into the pail of fresh water, he wondered what she would do if he gave in to temptation and ran his hand along her clean, shining hair to the wayward tip of that braid.

"This is from the spring," she said, unaware of the lust drumming in his veins. "It's the sweetest water you can imagine."

He grunted an answer, not trusting his voice,

and tried to focus on anything but the curl resting on her breast. He was all too conscious of his own disheveled state. Lifting the ladle, he drank his fill. The water seemed to spread through his body, renewing him…and slowly, he let down his guard…just a little.

After all, this was Flanna. At one time he'd shared his dreams with her.

If she noticed a change in his stance toward her, she gave no indication. "I washed your shirt and hung it to dry."

He was conscious the shirt he was now wearing was filthy. "Thank you."

Almost shyly, she said, "I found a rip in the sleeve. I sewed it."

He nodded. This conversation about mundane things seemed intimate—like the sort of inconsequential conversation between a husband and a wife.

Abruptly he backed away from the direction of his thoughts and picked up the shovel. "Thanks for the water."

She didn't leave. He dug into the earth, giving her his back.

"Do you think that running a rope through the trees will be enough?" she asked.

"It's the best we can do with what we have."

"I'll help you dig," she offered.

"I'm fine, Flanna. Go back to your house."

"It's no trouble. The stew is on and there is an hour or two before dark. We can get more done if we work together. I'll fetch another shovel." Before he could protest, she'd set down her pail and run down to the stable. The dogs loped along beside her.

Trace swore under his breath. Stubborn. She was the most irritating woman—

He dug his shovel into the earth, pushing it deep. If she thought he'd coddle her, she was wrong. He set a plank of wood in the shallow hole he'd dug and measured the distance for the next hole.

"Here we are," Flanna said, coming up the bluff carrying a short-handled spade. "What do you want me to do? Dig a shallow hole like you did this one?"

He didn't want her to do anything, and he would have told her so—except when he looked up, the words died in his throat. She stood, ready and willing with those two mixed-breed dogs flopped at her feet and happily panting. He tempered his words. "Yes. Like I am."

She nodded and set to work. As he stacked a set of "rails" on top of the other, she said, "Now I see. There's no trick here. Together, we'll have this done in no time."

Her attitude in the face of Slayton's attack

was cheerful. Trace didn't know what to make of her, so he tried to ignore her.

But no such luck.

"Did I tell you the dogs' names?"

He wasn't interested.

"Samson and Delilah," she said as if he'd asked. "They're brother and sister, of course, but we thought the names fitting."

Delilah. Figures. He kept his opinion to himself but as she started sharing with him more details of her and Rory's dreams for the ranch, he couldn't help listening.

Finally she asked a question he had to answer. "This barricade we're building won't be hurting the horses, will it? I wouldn't want that on my conscience even if the animals are being ridden by the worst sort of pigs imaginable."

He smiled at her summation of Slayton's men. Flanna never held back her opinion. "I've thought of the horses, too. They'll be surprised but they should manage fine. Besides, the rails aren't nailed. They will topple off each other."

"Spook the horses and break the necks of their riders!" she finished in triumph. In spite of himself, a rusty chuckle escaped. It had been so long since he'd laughed, the sound almost startled him.

Flanna seemed to sense it, too. A quick, satisfied grin crossed her face before she changed the subject.

"We're almost done here since we're about out of wood. What shall you do with the ground we can't cover?"

"I'm not worried. Slayton's men will take the easy way, depending on speed for their attack. This should catch them. If they try the way of the barn, the animals will tip us off. I'll roll the wagon over by the house and stand watch there. We should be ready for them tonight."

"I can stand watch, too."

He wasn't about to let that happen. Women were to be protected, not to be protectors, but he'd not voice his opinion because he knew Flanna would argue. Instead he said, "Maybe."

She wiped her hands on her skirt. "There's not much daylight left. I'd best check on my stew. You come down as soon as you're finished and I'll have a hot meal for you."

A hot meal. The smell of cooking meat wafted from the stove stack to where Trace stood. It had been a long time since he'd had a home-cooked meal. "Do you have any soap?"

She lifted her shovel handle up to rest on her shoulder. "I do," she said with cocky humor.

"I could use a bit."

Her smile lit her face. "It's scented with Attar of Roses, not eau de lillies."

He caught her joke, and managed a crooked smile. "I don't suppose it would do me any harm."

She laughed, the sound as light as the wind skittering across water. "No, no harm at all. I'll fetch it." She headed toward the barn to deposit her shovel.

Trace watched her come out and then walk toward the soddy. The dogs trailed her heels, probably hoping for their dinner.

The sun was setting and everything was bathed in a mellow, golden light. Even the humble soddy appeared grander than it was and in spite of Slayton, of the danger...for the first time in a long while, Trace felt a sense of peace.

FLANNA WATCHED TRACE sit quietly across the table from her, sipping his coffee, and realized how homey this scene was. The dogs rested on a rug before the stove.

When he walked in for dinner, clean, shaved, his hair slicked back, his lean, muscular body smelling of roses, well, she'd felt a bit giddy, like a girl meeting her first beau. Every time she glanced at him, she was struck anew at what a fine and brawny man he was. A woman could do far worse.

Through dinner, they'd wisely set aside the past and talked about the weather, the livestock and the search Flanna had made for her fifty head. She was certain Slayton had the animals. The hired hand Rory had brought on to watch the beasts had disappeared right after the shooting. Trace knew more about ranching and farming than she'd imagined.

However, now, with their stomachs full, a companionable silence stretched between them. She picked up her darning basket, needing something to do with her fingers and to distract her mind.

This was the way it was between married couples. This space of time in the evening when chores were done and dinner finished. If they really were married, they would blow out the lanterns and go to bed together.

For a second Flanna couldn't move. She could barely breathe at the image her mind conjured. Back in Harwood, during their kiss, she'd felt him, bold and hard.

He wanted her.

And, God save her, she wanted him, too.

In spite of their vagabond existence, Rory had been an overprotective father. He'd not let anyone dally with his daughter and she'd not wanted to—until she'd met Trace.

Now the fact that the two of them were alone

fueled her imagination. Her inattention cost. Accidentally she stabbed herself with the needle. Raising her finger to her lips, she sucked the prick, lifting her gaze to see if he noticed—and then froze.

Trace was sound asleep. He sat upright in his chair, his hand resting loosely curved around the tin coffee mug on the table.

She set her darning aside and rose quietly. Moving around to the back of his chair, she gave in to temptation a moment and curled one strand of his hair around her fingers. "You need a haircut," she whispered and then placed a hand on his shoulder. He didn't move. The man was exhausted and who could blame him after the drinking, the fight, the trial and almost hanging? He'd not be happy he'd fallen asleep. He'd interpret his need for sleep as a sign of weakness…and yet to her it made him endearingly human. This was the side of him she liked best.

"Come along, Trace," she said in his ear. "It's time for bed."

He mumbled something about needing to stand watch.

"Yes," she agreed. "You must stand watch. Here now, come over here."

In his sleep he was as compliant as a child. She easily directed him the few steps to the bed.

"Rest here a moment while I check the horses."

He was so exhausted, he did as she asked.

Flanna looked down at him and her heart filled with her love of him. Rory's rifle rested in a corner, loaded and ready. She picked it up and with a soft command to the dogs to follow, went outside to take a post in the wagon to watch for Slayton.

TRACE WOKE with a start. He'd been dreaming that he had to stand watch and when he woke, he was disoriented.

Slowly he took in his surroundings: the earth walls, the thin wood floor and the smells of coffee and the meal he'd shared with Flanna. The soddy he'd disdained when he'd first seen it had turned out to be a warm, hospitable *home*. He was in bed, comfortable and cozy.

But Flanna. Where was she?

He said her name aloud. No answer. The dogs weren't there, either.

Instantly alert, he sat up. His holster and gun hung from the bedpost. He pulled out his gun and cocked it. His boots were still on his feet but the fire was dying in the stove. He'd been asleep a few hours.

Swiftly, he made his way across the soddy and opened the door. The light of a half moon bathed the landscape in shadow and silver. All seemed quiet. Samson slept on across the threshold. He wagged his tail in greeting and rose to all fours.

His gun still poised, Trace searched for some sign of Flanna. He didn't see her. He thought about calling out and decided against it. She shouldn't have let him fall asleep. What if Slayton had come and taken her?

He bit back panic.

"Where is she?" he said in a low voice. To his surprise, Samson answered by taking off toward the wagon. At his approach, Delilah raised her head and Trace knew Flanna was there.

He lowered his gun and hurried toward the wagon, determined to give her a piece of his mind for not waking him. Samson and Delilah both took off in another direction. "You're right," he whispered. "You don't want to hear this." He raised his voice. "Flanna!"

No answer.

His heartbeat kicked up a notch. What if she *wasn't* there? He leaned over the edge of the wagon and found her sound asleep on the hardboard bed.

Relief washed through him.

She must have been as bone-tired as he'd been. Cradling the rifle to her, she slept with the weariness brought on by a day's hard work.

They were damn lucky Slayton hadn't attacked.

Trace glanced around. He saw no movement on the rise of the bluff or in the shadows of the trees around the stream. There was nothing but the call of a night bird and the music of insects. They could be the only two people in the world.

He returned to the house, grabbed the quilt off the bed and then walked back to the wagon. Flanna didn't even wake when he hopped up beside her on the wagon bed. He spread the quilt over her sleeping form and then settled himself beside her, his back against the wagon seat.

For a second he sat quiet. Then, gingerly, he lifted her shoulders and placed her head on his thigh so she might sleep more comfortably. With a soft sigh, she eased deeper into sleep.

He could have carried her inside...but he liked being with her this way.

Carefully, reverently, he reached out and stroked the silken length of her braid. Her cheek appeared downy-smooth in the moonlight.

And he faced the truth: he'd never gotten over her. Not really. He'd pretended but she was the only woman he'd ever loved.

Love. Such a small word and, yet, he hadn't been the same since she'd introduced him to its full meaning.

He looked out into the night. Dawn was a few hours away. If Slayton hadn't struck by now, he probably wouldn't until later, but still Trace would be prepared for him. He had to protect Flanna.

In the morning, he'd give her a tongue-lashing for not waking him. But for now, it felt good being this close to her. The terrible emptiness he'd felt when she'd left him back in Loveless eased.

And as he stood guard the rest of the night, he wondered if maybe, just maybe, he should take another chance on Flanna.

That is, if she'd have him.

CHAPTER SEVEN

FLANNA WOKE the next morning with the most wonderful sense of well-being. She'd not slept so hard since before her father's death and Slayton's threats.

With a start, she remembered she was in the wagon and her purpose. She should not have fallen asleep.

She scrambled up and was surprised by the quilt around her shoulders. And she was in bed.

She looked around. Where was Trace? Had Slayton come?

Spring sunshine formed a rectangular pattern on the floor. All was quiet. Her panic was eased by the gut feeling that all would not seem so peaceful if Slayton had attacked.

To punctuate her thoughts, her rooster crowed and there was a meadowlark's trill as if in answer. Lambert, the rooster, always strutted and crowed midmorning. The day was well advanced. She'd slept late.

Flipping her sleep-ragged braid back, she put

her feet over the edge of the bed. Trace must have removed her shoes. She had a hole in the sock right over her big toe and her dress was hopelessly wrinkled. Trace couldn't be more furious with her than she was with herself. How could she fall asleep during her watch?

At that moment, as if she had conjured him, Trace appeared in the doorway. His tall, broad-shouldered frame blocked the welcoming sunlight.

She came to her feet, covering one foot self-consciously with the other to hide the hole. "I know what you are thinking and I was wrong, wrong, *wrong* not to have woken you. And then to have fallen asleep myself! I'm so blessed sorry and I won't let anything like that happen again—" She would have continued verbally flogging herself but he held up a hand for quiet.

"Slayton didn't come and no harm done. You didn't do anything wrong. Besides, you must have needed the sleep." He paused, his gaze studying her face, then followed the line of her neck, lingering over her breasts and down all the way to her toes. Her heart beat a funny little trip.

"You look more rested," he said. There was a warmth in his voice that made her toes curl.

"I am," she answered, her voice suddenly a husky squeak. She turned, needing to give herself respite from those silver eyes of his that seemed to see everything. He walked into the soddy, his bold, masculine presence filling the room…and she found it hard to breathe.

Uncertain, she touched her braid. What had she seen in the depths of his eyes? Want? Hunger?

No, something more. Something she'd thought never to see again. So filled with astonishment was she, she dared not put a word to it—yet.

He moved toward the stove. "You were so tired, I made biscuits and you didn't even move. Not even when they were baking."

She could single out the scent of biscuits now that he mentioned them. "You made them?"

"And gravy." He opened the lid of her iron skillet. "It's not fancy but it's pretty tasty."

Her stomach growled in response.

For a moment she was paralyzed with embarrassment. Their gazes met…and then they both laughed, relaxed again.

"Here, I'll dish you up some grub," he said, and reached for a heavy china plate from the pinewood cupboard beside the stove.

Flanna took the moments of his inattention to unplait her hair. She ran her brush through it and decided to leave it be for the moment. Then she pulled on her sturdy shoes.

When she walked over to the table, she was glad she hadn't rebraided her hair. Trace lifted his hand as if to reach out and touch her—but he stopped. "You have the loveliest hair. I used to dream about it."

She held her breath. "I was in your dreams."

His gaze met hers. He gave the smallest of nods and then abruptly stepped back. "I'd best get outside and stand watch. Wouldn't be good for Slayton to come riding in and me standing here moony-eyed."

Moony-eyed. She loved the sound of those words. Before she could speak, he ducked out the door. Both dogs went with him, easily accepting his leadership in the household.

Flanna sat down at the table, her hunger forgotten. Something had happened overnight. He'd decided to let the past be. There was trust again and on trust, one could build love.

Trace loved her.

She knew it all the way down to her woman's soul. He hadn't said the words, but he was *moony-eyed* and mooney-eyed wasn't far from love.

Rory would have told her himself that when a buyer was interested, you kept the product in front of them. She picked up her plate, grabbed a fork, and headed outside to be with Trace.

Trace sat on the wagon seat, the rifle across his lap, alert and watchful for signs of Slayton. But he was also aware of the woman inside the soddy. He knew the moment she stepped out the door.

She walked toward him, her plate in one hand, a fork in the other, and her red-gold hair shining in the morning sun like a bright lure. She'd changed, too, into a practical dress of brown calico. She appeared like the kind of woman a man fought to protect.

The dogs wagged their tails in greeting as Flanna climbed up into the seat and plopped down right beside him. "I was lonely," she explained to his unasked question. "Couldn't see any sense eating inside on a glorious day like today." She dug into a gravy-covered biscuit. Savoring the first bite, she hummed her satisfaction.

Trace watched with a befuddled sense of awe.

"I think the people of Loveless were foolish to let you go," she said, taking a piece of biscuit and sopping up the rest of the gravy.

"Because I can cook?" he asked, using humor to guard against what he feared she might not say.

"Because you are the type of man who will take a stand." She added, "And you know what you're doing. Trust me, Burrell Slayton is quaking in his boots.'' She said the last with relish and he had to smile.

Then he turned serious. "The truth is, I never did fit in Loveless."

"But you were born there."

He shrugged. He'd assumed someone had told her.

"Why is that?" she asked softly. "You were always standoffish but I thought it was because you were sheriff. Was there another reason?"

He studied the line of the bluff, watchful for the appearance of movement, but his mind was on her question. Then, with feigned nonchalance, he said, "My mother was the local whore. Loveless used to know wild days. Some folks have long memories."

He waited, anticipating her reaction with a touch of dread. During his last days in Loveless, his long-dead mother's line of work had been the buzz of gossips.

"Rory had to run from Ireland because he stole a pig from the magistrate," she said. "My mother was the youngest of ten daughters of a Catholic farmer who didn't have an acre of land to his name. She thought her chances for a good life were better with a pig thief than her family."

"Did Rory ever try and not take anything

that wasn't nailed down?'' Trace asked, relieved that she hadn't withdrawn after his small confession.

''No,'' Flanna said simply, and then laughed. ''I never knew my mother. She caught a chill in Missouri and died while I was still a babe. I'm lucky Rory didn't leave me with some farmer's family. He was a rascal, but I loved him. Did you get along with your mother?''

Trace considered the question. No one had ever asked him about her before in a normal, everyday sort of way. ''Yes. She was a good woman and she did what she had to do to survive. She raised me right.''

''But you never knew your father?''

''She never talked about him.'' He leaned forward, warming to the subject. ''When I was a kid I used to ask questions. I know she got pregnant and her family threw her out, but that's about all...and eventually, that got to be enough.''

Flanna set the plate aside and slid a few inches closer to him. Her thigh brushed his... and she hooked her hand in the crook of his arm.

He sat still. The wind ruffled her hair as she looked over to the stream. She smelled of sunshine and woman—a woman he loved. What had been between them once had never died.

"All of this, even down to the scrawniest chicken, is because of you," she said.

"I drove you out of Loveless."

She leaned closer. "Ah, yes, but you also made me want *more*." She paused. "Don't you want more, Trace? Or were you thinking of drifting the rest of your life?"

Was she asking him to stay? To help build the house over by the stream with the big porch to enjoy during the evenings?

He could see himself there, raising the walls...creating a home.

"You know, Flanna, Rory was right about me. I really am not good enough for you."

She smiled, not looking at him, and said quietly, "You're all I ever wanted."

For a second Trace feared his ears played tricks but then she swung toward him and, there, in the depths of her eyes was the truth. She loved him!

And in her love was power. Loneliness, anger, regret, doubts—all fell away from him. Flanna Kennedy, this wondrous, mercurial woman, loved *him*. He wrapped his arm around her—

Samson sat up and barked. Delilah quickly joined him. They jumped off the wagon and ran toward the barricade blocking the path over the bluff. Trace lifted the rifle, ready to fire.

"Get down," he ordered, "as close under the seat as you can."

Of course she didn't obey him. "Hand me your gun."

"And let you shoot off your toe? Get down." He pushed her off the seat and, with a hand on her head, forced her to follow his orders.

A wagon drove over the bluff. "Hello!" the driver yelled, and then reined in when he saw the barricade. "Flanna? It's Jacob Gustaf."

Flanna's head popped up. "It's my neighbor." She climbed backward out of the wagon. Waving, she started up the hill toward Mr. Gustaf.

With a soft oath, Trace followed, keeping his rifle at the ready.

Mr. Gustaf was a tall, long-nosed man dressed in somber clothes. He nodded at Trace but turned his attention to Flanna. "I've come to warn you, Miss Kennedy, Slayton is planning to come out here and burn you to the ground, but I can see by the fence you already know."

"We're surprised he hasn't shown up yet," she said bitterly.

Gustaf sent a nervous glance in Trace's direction. "There are some who don't want to battle Mr. Cordell. He has a reputation. Slayton's having trouble rounding up a party of men. But he plans on coming out here tonight."

"How many men has he gathered?" Trace asked Gustaf.

"Not many. Even Judge Rigby isn't falling into line." Gustaf's gaze drifted down to the rifle in Trace's arms. He shifted nervously. "I came to take Miss Kennedy to my place. She'd be better off there."

"You're right," Trace agreed, and would have put her up in the wagon next to Gustaf but Flanna stepped back.

"I'm not going to run. I'll stay here and fight."

"Flanna—"

"I won't go, Trace. You could tie me up and put me in Mr. Gustaf's wagon and I'd escape and run back."

"Miss Kennedy, this land isn't worth your life," Gustaf said.

"This land is my home," Flanna countered. "I won't leave."

Trace couldn't blame her. He looked up at Gustaf. "Can you fetch the U.S. marshal? He's in Dodge. Then we can stop a man like Slayton for good."

Gustaf shook his head. "I don't know. I've got two sons, a wife. Slayton would destroy my farm. Look what he did to Rory Kennedy."

Flanna placed her hand on Gustaf's wagon. "I understand. It's not your fight."

But Trace didn't understand. This was the way it had been back in Loveless. They'd wanted him to fight the dirty battles, but once the town was clean, they'd expected him to leave.

"Then, get on your way," he told Gustaf coldly. "Tomorrow evening come around. We'll either be here or we'll not. If we're here, you won't ever have to worry about claim jumpers like Slayton again."

"I wish…" Gustaf started but then hung his head. "I wanted you to be warned."

Trace answered, "I'll be waiting for him."

"*We'll* be waiting for him," Flanna corrected. "Goodbye, Mr. Gustaf."

The man didn't like leaving. Trace could understand. He'd not like admitting he was a coward, either.

They watched the wagon turn and drive out of sight.

Trace broke the silence. "You should have gone. I could have handled this by myself."

"You've always been by yourself." She linked her fingers in his. "I left you once. I'll not leave you again."

He felt humbled in the face of her love. "Flanna Kennedy, will you marry me?"

"Yes, Trace. Yes, yes, yesyesyes!"

For a second he could barely believe his

good fortune. With a whoop of joy, he lifted her in his arms and twirled her around. The dogs barked, wanting to join in the play.

Then Trace lost his footing. They both tumbled to the ground, laughing, he protecting her fall with his body, the rifle on the ground beside them.

Flanna looked down at him, her body stretched along his.

The laughter stopped as they both became aware of how intimately they fit together.

He reached up and ran his hand along her bright, shining hair. He wanted her so much. He wanted to brand her with his body, with his love.

"We'll marry tomorrow," he promised, then added with a smile, "We'll have Rigby say the words since he likes to talk so much."

"Tomorrow," she agreed softly.

Again he ran his hand over her gleaming hair, burying his fingers in the curling mass. Dear God, he wanted her, wanted her as he'd never wanted another woman before.

"Tomorrow, we may not be alive," she said soberly.

"I'll not let anything happen to you," he swore fiercely. He'd fight with a superhuman strength to protect her.

She placed a finger over his lips. Her legs

were entwined with his. He could feel the beat of her heart against his chest, its rhythm mingling with his own. "Whatever happens, we'll be together. But I'm not going to wait for some pompous fool like Rigby to say vows before I make mine."

She smiled, her eyes shiny but serious. "Will you, Trace Cordell, take me to be your lawful wife?"

CHAPTER EIGHT

TRACE SAT UP, causing Flanna to straddle him, her skirts hiked up, her knees on either side of his hips. "Flanna, are you sure?"

She knew what he was asking. She trained her gaze on his and continued, "To love and cherish. To hold fast in your heart through sickness and in health."

The dogs, stretched out on the grass, watched with lazy curiosity. A bird flitted to the wagon seat and cocked its head. Even Bill, Trace's gelding, and her Spice had wandered over to the fence to witness.

He took her hands in his. "I do. Do you, Flanna Kennedy, promise to love, honor—" a smile came to his lips "—and *obey* me?"

She laughed. "I shall love, honor, and listen to you the best I can," she vowed.

His teeth flashed white in his smile. Then he added soberly, "Till death do us part?"

"Yes." She pulled her hands from his and

cupped the sides of his square jaw. His skin was warm beneath her touch. "Forever."

"Forever," he echoed.

For the space of several heartbeats, in which she could have sworn neither one of them breathed, they stared at each other, caught up in the miracle of their love. "Yes," she confirmed aloud, "this is a miracle. I thought you were lost to me and here we are."

"Husband and wife," he said. In one smooth movement he rose to his feet, carrying her with him. His arms supported her as he walked down the bluff toward the soddy.

Flanna clung to him, her arms around his neck. This was right. This was the way it should be. But Trace walked right by her small house. Instead he carried her to the wood house. He stepped onto the first floor, the frame of the walls all around them.

"Wait for me," he said, and headed off to the soddy. A moment later he came out carrying the cotton mattress and quilts. He spread the mattress out on the floor and threw the blankets over it.

"I don't want us to be together in that dank soddy," he explained. "I'd rather have the fresh air and cottonwood trees for a roof. After we beat Slayton, we'll build this house and this ranch into the finest in all Kansas."

She stepped into his arms. "I love you."

Pride lit his silvery eyes. "I love you." Then he kissed her. This kiss was different than the one yesterday. This kiss held promises, commitments.

Flanna opened herself to him, her heart pounding in her chest. When his tongue first touched hers, she started but then relaxed. This was Trace. This was her husband. She knew any vows she took on the morrow would pale in comparison to these vows of her heart.

Trace started undressing her.

Samson and Delilah, sensing they were not wanted, jogged off to chase rabbits. Above in the trees and around the prairie, the birds sang but it was as if they'd created a wondrous choir just for Flanna and Trace.

Without modesty, she held her arms up and he pulled her calico over her head. He tossed the dress aside.

Flanna held her breath. Her nipples pressed against the thin material of her chemise. He began untying the tapes of her petticoats. His lips brushed her breasts, wetting the thin cotton material. She buried her hands in his thick curls, bringing him to her.

For a second she allowed the sensations to overwhelm her and then her petticoats fell to the ground. He bent, his arms around her knees and gently lowered her to the mattress.

Swiftly, intently, he undressed her until she was gloriously naked in front of him—and completely unashamed.

"You're beautiful," he whispered.

"Come to me." She held out her arms.

Trace undressed. He was hard and ready. She discovered her first glimpse at a boldly naked man did not alarm her. Instead she was ready for this. She'd waited for him.

He lay down beside her and pulled the quilts up over them. "If Slayton comes now, he'll be in for a surprise." His arms hugged her close to the heat of his body. "But I could not stop myself for any reason in the world."

"I know," she agreed, and then gasped as he kissed the hollow of her shoulder. He nibbled the line of her neck and circled her ear with his tongue.

"I want this to be good for you," he whispered in her ear.

"It will be." Beneath the covers, she ran her hand up the velvety length of his shaft, pleased with the low growl of desire she drew from him.

His teeth teased her skin, followed by the smooth caress of his tongue. Soft intakes of breath, small sighs, and loving laughter revealed their progress. Each moment seemed to drive the need Flanna felt for him.

At last, he gave her breast one lingering kiss and then settled himself between her legs. He rested his weight on his arms.

"I want this to be good for you," he said, his expression intent.

Instinctively she cradled his body, her legs around his hips. "It will be."

He smiled. Then, in one smooth movement, he entered her.

Flanna tensed. He stopped, letting her grow accustomed to him. He pressed forward.

There was small pain as he broke through the barrier of her virginity but it was not unpleasant. He was watching her, a line of worry between his eyes.

She soothed that small line with the tips of her fingers, and arched herself up to him. Her movement buried him deeper. Her muscles clenched and then embraced...and she was in heaven.

"Dear God, Flanna. You are so tight, so sweet." Trace began moving.

She had thought them done. Now she discovered there was more, much, much more.

He took his time, paying attention to her pleasure. And, proudly, she met him every step of the way. His thrusts grew more demanding.

She didn't know what to expect. A part of her centered on him and another part was spiraling out of control.

Then she discovered where they were going. One moment she was grounded to him and in the next, she was no longer a creature of this earth. She was like the water that bubbled over the rocks in the stream near where they lay. She was music and art and beauty.

Trace knew where she was. He'd been the one to bring her here. Now he thrust once, twice, and then with a glad cry, he filled her. He completed her.

They lay in each other's arms lost in the aftermath of their lovemaking for what seemed like hours. Flanna stroked his arm, admiring the muscle beneath. "Is it always like this?"

"It's never been like this." He looked down at her. He was still inside, connected with her. "We are one." There was reverence in his voice.

For the first time Flanna understood the meaning of the phrase. She threw her arms around his neck and laughed with joy.

THEY MADE LOVE several times, right there outside beneath the sky. To Flanna, it was as if they'd created their own Garden of Eden. For the space of a few hours, the world was held at bay.

She lost herself in the heady sensation of desire. Her lips tasted his skin. She loved the warmth and scent of his body…and in his arms she felt loved and protected.

No matter what the night would bring, she would not regret giving herself to him.

Ever.

She slid her hand down to her belly. They were snuggled under the quilts, the sky and the cottonwoods their canopy. "I could be with child, even now." The thought gave her a powerful sense of satisfaction.

His hand covered hers, his expression darkening. "Flanna, if something happens to me—"

She silenced him with her lips. "Nothing will happen," she said. "They can't get away with killing my father and you, too. A merciful God would never let such a tragedy come to pass."

"Sometimes, God isn't always watching."

"He is now." She rubbed her cheek along his. "He sees us and is pleased. He will be with us tonight."

Trace's answer was to make love to her, again.

However this time, they moved leisurely, savoring their precious moments together. Afterward, they dressed.

The sun was beginning to set and they prepared to wait for Slayton.

AS THE MOON HIT the highest point in the sky the bottles tied to the line clinked softly together.

"Shh," Trace cautioned. "Wait."

Flanna nodded, her hands trembling around the Colt's smooth handle. Trace stood, easing the rifle to his shoulder.

They'd placed the dogs in the soddy. Trace hadn't wanted them to warn their attackers.

There was a splash in the stream. Flanna could hear horses breathing—and then object with a snort at finding the rope.

Trace fired and she started firing with him. He'd told her to let off no more than three shots.

She discovered why. She doubted she hit anything but chaos broke out among their attackers. They hadn't been expecting the rope. A least one of Trace's bullets hit and she suspected by the cursing and hollering, others did, as well.

"I'm hit. I'm hit," one man moaned while others shouted for a retreat.

"Get down," Trace warned, and pulled her

off the porch of the house, pushing her under the foundation. "Stay here until I call you."

He disappeared into the night as riders charged over the bluff. She could make out their silhouettes and feel the thundering of hooves.

Then the horses hit the barricade. The riders had not noticed it. Horses squealed warnings and skidded to a halt. Riders were unseated. Flanna could hear them holler as they fell.

Then Trace started shooting. This time, there was no free firing, but the systematic crack of a sharp shooter choosing his quarry.

Guns were being fired from the bluff now. Slayton's men were fighting back. What if they saw Trace, standing alone in the moonlight?

Flanna gripped the Colt and climbed out from her haven. She had to get to Trace, to help him.

A second later a pair of strong arms grabbed her from behind.

TRACE WATCHED the last man of the attacking party run retreat.

His plan had worked. The cowards had run.

Several men were dead. He hoped Slayton was one of their number.

He jumped down from the wagon. Bill and Spice raced around the corral, still worked up over the battle. The dogs barked madly inside the soddy. Even the chickens seemed upset.

"Flanna!" He started toward the soddy to release Samson and Delilah.

There was no answer.

His hand on the door, he called again.

This time he was answered but not in the way he expected. "She's here," said Slayton. He stepped out of the shadows of the barn. He held Flanna by the hair, a gag around her mouth, and his pistol pressing against the tender skin of her neck.

Trace felt fear. The dogs seemed to sense what was happening. On the other side of the door, they started growling and acting crazy, wanting to be released.

If Slayton noticed, he gave no sign. "I'm sorry you got involved, Cordell," he said. "Hell, I'm sorry matters got so messy tonight. Maybe if you'd both been a bit more quiet, we could have parted company as friends."

"I doubt that," Trace said carefully.

Slayton's mouth crooked into a smile. "Yeah. You're probably right." He sighed. "Well now, I've got to do what I must do."

"Let her go," Trace said.

"Maybe," Slayton answered. "But first, you toss that rifle off to the side."

Flanna moaned her protest, twisting as she

did so. Slayton viciously pulled her hair. "Settle down," he warned.

Trace threw the rifle aside. He had no choice.

"Good," Slayton said, and pointed the barrel of his gun toward Trace. "It was nice meeting you, Cordell."

In answer, Trace opened the soddy door. Samson and Delilah shot out of the house like Chinese rockets. Delilah moved toward Flanna but Samson went for Slayton.

Trace dove for his rifle. Slayton released Flanna and fired off a shot at the charging dog, but he missed. Trace's shot didn't. He caught Slayton right in the chest.

The man jerked back. Samson jumped on him, pushing him to the ground. Shaking, Flanna reached for her dog. Trace ran forward. "Samson," he said, lifting Flanna into his arms. The animal obeyed immediately, falling back to his side.

Flanna buried her face in his chest. "You told me to stay. I wanted to help."

He kissed the top of her head and then kissed her precious nose, her beautiful eyes and her stubborn chin.

She was crying and he could taste her tears. He hugged her close.

"Is he dead?" she asked.

"Yes."

A shudder went through her and then she relaxed in his arms. At the same moment a party of riders came up over the bluff.

Trace pushed Flanna behind him and raised his rifle. Both Samson and Delilah tensed, ready to attack.

A man called out, "Mr. Cordell, Miss Kennedy, it's me—Gustaf! I brought the marshal from Dodge."

Flanna reached down to soothe the dogs. Traced lowered his rifle but still held it ready. The riders made their way around the barricade, their horses stepping over some of the boards that had been knocked down.

A minute later Gustaf, the marshal, and two men rode into the yard. The marshal was a stocky man with a no-nonsense expression.

Flanna lit a lamp and put water on to boil for coffee.

"It looks like a battlefield around here," the marshal said. "Some of Slayton's men ran right into us. I have a group of men a mile or so down the road holding them in custody." He walked over to Slayton's body and then faced Trace. "Guess you better tell me what happened, Sheriff Cordell."

THE NEXT DAY, an overcast one, Flanna and Trace rode to Dodge to give a formal statement at the marshal's office. Trace brought up the belief that Slayton had rustled Kennedy cattle. The marshal promised Slayton's herds would be searched.

Then Trace walked Flanna down to the wooden church in the field at the edge of town. There, the minister heard their vows.

But in Flanna's heart, no promises carried more weight than the ones she and Trace had made to each other the night before. She told him as much as they walked out the church door.

"And what do you think Rory would have said if I hadn't given you a proper ceremony?" he asked, holding the door open for her.

"I think he would have agreed you are the finest, bravest man I know," she answered.

As if in benediction, rays of sunlight burst through the clouds. She slipped her hand into his. "There, see?" she whispered. "Rory is smiling. Come, Mr. Cordell, and take your wife home. We have a house to build."

Trace set his hat on his head at an angle. "Not just a house, love, but the finest spread in all Kansas."

Flanna laughed, filled with the joy of living. Life held endless promise. "Yes, my love, the finest."

Together, they walked back to their wagon and headed home.

Dear Reader,

My name is Kate McCrea. All I wanted was to protect my nephew, Danny. Who'd have thought that seeking shelter in a little cabin in the wilderness would cause such a chain of events? Events that would forever change our lives.

Ethan Storm looked like some kind of wild mountain man; his dog, Blue, a vicious wolf. And yet, within days, both man and beast had worked their gentle charm, proving to be delightful companions. In Ethan's arms I found my safe haven. But nobody warned me that when love enters the picture, everything changes.

Will Ethan's love survive when my lies are exposed, bringing danger, and even death, to his very doorstep?

Kate McCrea

THIS SIDE OF HEAVEN

Ruth Langan

To all who believe in love.
And to Tom—who made me believe.

CHAPTER ONE

Montana Territory—1880

"COME ON, BLUE." Ethan Storm rolled out of bed and hitched up his suspenders as he walked to the door of his cabin. "You've been skittish the whole night. Go chase those coyotes while I see about our breakfast." He unlatched the cabin door and watched as his dog took off at a run.

Chuckling, he closed the door and rummaged around for the rest of his clothes, idly noting that his shirt had another rip at the shoulder, and both knees of his pants were in desperate need of patches. As he finished dressing he glanced in the chipped mirror hanging over the washbasin and decided he'd shave tomorrow. Of course, he'd been telling himself that for a month or more, so he figured one more day wouldn't matter. He was a man completely comfortable with himself and his life in the Montana wilderness.

After pulling on his scarred boots he ate the last of the dried beef, saving a few bites for his dog. It looked as though he'd have to spend part of the day hunting up a herd of deer, or there'd be nothing left to fortify himself and Blue but a couple of hard biscuits left over from his last attempt at baking.

He banked the fire and searched the entire cabin until he found the little pouch of tobacco that had fallen under a chair. Then he picked up his rifle before letting himself out of the snug cabin he'd called home for the past couple of years. After wandering around the West working as a cowboy and range hand for other ranchers, he'd found himself drawn to this place in the hills. There was just something about it. Its pristine forests. Its spectacular mountains and icy rivers. The vast open ranges below, abloom with grama and bunch grasses, providing ideal food for cattle.

Best of all, in Ethan's mind, was the fact that it was so sparsely settled, he could spend months without seeing another human being. It wasn't that he didn't like people, but he'd spent his twenty-eight years in crowded bunkhouses, first with his father, and later, after Enoch Storm had lost his battle with a grizzly, Ethan had gone on alone. Maybe that was when the dream of having his own spread had been born.

Or maybe it had its beginnings even earlier, when Ethan's mother had still been alive, cooking over campfires, sleeping in the tiny wagon she and her husband and young son had called home, until the cholera had claimed her.

This place was all his. Ethan had cut every tree, hewn every log and sealed every crack with pitch by himself. Every stick of furniture inside had been made by his hand, over the long Montana winters. He'd started his herd with a couple of young stock, and now he had a fine herd.

His, he thought with a sense of pride as he started toward the barn, where Blue stood sniffing and scratching at the door.

"What's got into you, old boy?" Ethan leaned his weight against the barn door. "Don't tell me one of those coyotes slipped in here while we were sleeping."

The dog raced past him and began digging frantically in the straw. Seconds later the straw shifted and two bedraggled figures huddled together while Blue stood, fangs bared, a warning growl issuing from deep in his throat.

"Well, I'll be." Ethan took aim with his rifle, wondering if he looked as startled as the two intruders.

The larger of the two struggled to stand, pushing the smaller figure protectively behind them. "There's no need to shoot. We didn't mean any harm. We just needed shelter for the night. If you'll call off your wolf, we'll be on our way."

The foreign-sounding voice was definitely feminine, though it was hard to tell under all that dirt.

Ethan took a step closer, hoping for a better look. What he saw was straw sticking out of matted hair the color of mud and a torn, filthy gown that had seen better days. The child behind her looked no better, hair sticking out in all directions, face and arms so covered with dirt it was hard to tell where the shirtsleeves ended and the arms began.

"Where'd you come from?"

The female backed up, eyes wide at the look of this wild mountain man towering over her, rifle aimed at her heart. "Ireland."

That would explain the lyrical notes in her voice.

Ethan shook his head. "I didn't mean where you were born. I mean now. There isn't a ranch for miles in any direction."

"We..." She swallowed and glanced at the threatening animal. "Could you be calling off your wolf?"

"Blue. Easy." At his soft tone the growling stopped as the dog dropped down on its haunches and continued watching the strangers with avid interest.

"We're...heading to town. But we got turned 'round."

Ethan noticed that she'd evaded his question. Not that it was any of his business where she'd come from. Still, it was obvious that these two were on the run. What they were running from piqued his interest. "That'll be quite a walk, ma'am. The nearest town's over that mountain. It takes me all day by horseback, if I push. You'll be a week or more on foot in weather like we've been having."

The female looked crestfallen. Then she brightened. "Maybe you'd be willing to take us. I could pay you for your trouble."

He shook his head. "Sorry. I can't leave my herd. Spring is birthing time. Nothing wolves like better than tasty new calves." He saw the way the light went out of her eyes. "I'll tell you what. I have a signal arranged with the stage driver who comes through these parts. I'll run it up the tree, and when he passes through, he'll stop and pick you up."

"Oh." Her spirits lifted. "That would be grand. Danny and I would be grateful."

Danny. At least now Ethan knew that the little one was a boy. He appeared to be no more than six or seven years old.

The girl looked up expectantly. "How soon will the stage come through?"

He shrugged. "Hard to say. Sometime in the next month or so."

"Month?" Her eyes widened in disbelief.

"Yes'm. In this part of the country, we're lucky to have a stage come through at all. But since my spread is in the general direction of town, the driver doesn't mind stopping by when he sees my signal, before heading on to Heaven."

"Heaven?"

He nodded. "That's the name of the town." He looked puzzled. "You sure you know where you're headed?"

"Yes. Of course. Heav…Heaven, Wyoming."

"This is Montana, ma'am."

"It is, yes. Did I say Wyoming? I meant to say Montana." She glanced at the little boy, who hadn't spoken a word. "Danny and I are…in a bit of a hurry."

"Well, I wish I could see my way to taking you." Ethan moved to the stall and sent several chickens squawking while he saddled his horse. "I've got to get down to my herd on the lower range. If you and the boy would like to rest inside, you're welcome to use my cabin while I'm gone."

She was already shaking her head. "That wouldn't be right. Not while you're away."

He shrugged. "Suit yourself, ma'am. There's not much to eat. But there's a sack of sugar and flour and a tin of lard if you've a mind to bake. I banked the fire, but the coals are still hot enough to get a fire started." He led his horse out the door and pulled himself into the saddle. "Oh, and there's a rain barrel on the porch, if you'd like to wash up." He whistled to the dog. "Come on, Blue. We've got work to do."

He rode away, leaving the two intruders staring after him with matching looks of amazement. They hadn't even so much as exchanged names, and he'd invited them to use his cabin.

"HERE, DANNY." Kate McCrea handed the boy a rock-hard biscuit and a cup of steaming coffee. "Dip this in the coffee to soften it."

While the boy ate, she broke open a second biscuit and slathered it with lard, and then with sugar to make it more palatable. As soon as Danny finished the first she urged a second one on him.

She hadn't intended to take the stranger up on his offer. But after so many nights on the run, and days spent hiding out in the woods, the thought of food and warmth were simply too tempting. Though the bearded giant and his vicious wolf frightened her, she figured she and Danny would spend a few hours in the cabin restoring their strength before moving on. They would be gone long before the man returned.

When the boy had eaten what little food she could find, Kate led him toward the bucket of water heating over the fire. "Take off your clothes and wash yourself. Then while you're sleeping, I'll wash our clothes and hang them on tree branches. By the time we're ready to go, they should be dry."

The boy did as she asked. When he was finished washing, she bent him over the bucket and scrubbed his hair. Then she bundled him into a blanket and lay him on a rug in front of the fire. He was asleep within minutes.

Using the sugar and flour and lard she mixed up a batch of biscuit dough. While it was baking over the coals, she stripped off her clothes and washed herself thoroughly, scrubbing her matted hair until it gleamed. Then she used the water to wash their clothes.

Though she disliked intruding on the stranger's privacy, she let herself into his bedroom and rummaged through his clothes in search of something to preserve her modesty. From his meager supply she helped herself to a coarse shirt and a pair of shabby pants. Then, because his clothes were as dirty as hers, she carried the rest of them to the bucket and scrubbed until they were clean.

Outside she hung the clothes on the branches of trees and low-hanging bushes before returning to the cabin.

She resisted the temptation to curl up beside Danny. Instead she picked up a broom and began to sweep, hoping to repay the kindness of the stranger in the only way she could. Judging by the amount of dirt in the cabin, it hadn't been cleaned in years.

When the cloud of dust cleared she made her way to the barn. She'd seen the chickens. Maybe, if her luck held, she would find a few eggs nestled in the straw. Weak with hunger, she returned to the cabin with a handful of eggs.

A short time later she sat back with a smile. It was amazing what a single egg and a biscuit warm from the fire could do to satisfy the soul.

With her strength renewed, she walked outside and checked the clothes. Finding them still damp she returned to the cabin and stretched out on the floor beside Danny. She couldn't afford to fall asleep. But at least she could rest for a few minutes, just until their clothes were dry. They would be wise to be gone before the wild man and his beast returned.

It was the last coherent thought she had before sleep claimed her.

IT WAS NEARLY DUSK when Ethan rode up to his cabin, the carcass of a deer slung over the back of his horse. He lifted his head, sensing a storm rolling in across the hills.

Suddenly he was distracted by the sight of a wispy bit of cloth dangling from the branch of a tree. He reined in his mount to run the fabric between his thumb and finger. It was as soft as a spider's web, with fancy embroidery at the neckline, and a narrow ribbon dangling from either side. It wasn't often that a man living alone had a chance to see such a thing. But he was worldly enough to know that it was a lady's chemise. He found himself sweating at the thought of how it would look on one of Lester Minor's soiled doves at the saloon in Heaven. Not that Lester's women ever owned anything as fine as this.

He slid from the saddle and for the first time noticed that some of his own clothes were hanging from branches, as well.

Puzzled, he stepped into the cabin. The sight that greeted him had his throat going dry. The woman and boy were sound asleep. Even when Blue sniffed them, they didn't stir.

It gave him the strangest feeling to see the female wearing his clothes. He studied the slow, even way she breathed, her breasts rising and falling with each measured breath. That brought an image of her wearing the fancy chemise. He had to swallow hard.

She'd tied his pants with a length of rope that emphasized a waist so tiny his hands could easily span it. Now that she'd taken the time to wash, the change in her was amazing. Her skin was as pale as milk. The hair he'd thought brown was actually a rich red-gold, spilling in soft waves to below her hips.

The boy appeared to be no older than six or seven, with the same pale skin and hair as yellow as a field of wheat.

Outside the horse stomped and blew. Ethan turned away and let himself out of the cabin, leading his mount toward the barn, with Blue following. After forking hay into the stall, and filling the trough with water, he rolled up his sleeves and bent to the task of skinning and gutting the deer.

By the time he returned to the cabin, darkness was falling. Taking a stick from the fireplace he held it to the wick of a lantern. That done, he tossed several hunks of deer meat into a skillet and set them over the coals. Then he filled a bucket from the rain barrel and began to wash away the blood and dirt of the day.

Hearing Blue's warning growl he looked over to see the woman stirring. When she sat up he found himself looking into the most amazing eyes. Eyes the color of the green spring grasses that rippled across the prairie.

"I see you decided to stay."

"I..." She swallowed, stunned by the realization that it was already dark outside. She and Danny should have been on their way hours ago. Now, she thought, they would have to spend the night in the company of this primitive man and his wolf. "We will. Yes. As long as you're sure you don't mind."

CHAPTER TWO

HEARING THEIR VOICES, the boy sat up and instinctively moved closer to Kate. Seeing the way he was eyeing Blue, Ethan walked over to lay a hand on the dog's head. The minute the boy caught sight of his raised hand, he flinched. Seeing it, Ethan kept one hand on the dog, and carefully lowered the other to his side.

"Old Blue here isn't used to seeing strangers. But he won't hurt you, son. As near as I can tell his only enemies are wolves and coyotes. He just can't abide them."

When the boy said nothing Ethan turned to the woman. "My name's Ethan Storm."

"I'm Kate McCrea. And this is my nephew, Danny."

"Nephew?"

She nodded. "My sister Fiona's boy. I'm taking him home with me to Boston."

Ethan gave her a measured look. "Boston's a mighty long way from Montana. You have family there?"

"Danny is all the family I have left." She got to her feet and suddenly glanced down at herself. A flush came to her cheeks. "I'm sorry. I needed something to wear until my clothes dried. I hope you don't mind. I'll see that these are washed before we leave tomorrow."

"No harm done, ma'am." He stared after her as she rushed out the door, noting the way his old britches hugged her backside. He'd never before seen a woman wearing men's clothes, and the effect was unsettling. She seemed to be all lush curves that had him thinking about things better left alone.

Minutes later she returned and handed Danny his clothes. Ethan saw the way she'd folded her more intimate garments inside her gown while she avoided looking at him. Her extreme modesty had him all the more fascinated.

Her voice sounded breathy, though from the work she'd done or nerves, he couldn't tell. "Would you mind if I used your bedroom to dress?"

Ethan shrugged. "Suit yourself."

She disappeared, then returned minutes later smoothing down the skirt of her gown. Now that all the soil had been washed away, it proved to be the color of the pale pink bitterroot that grew in profusion across these Montana hills.

She had tied her hair back with a pink ribbon that seemed lost in all those fiery curls. With a toss of her head she hurried across the room to help Danny into his clothes.

The smell of meat burning snagged Ethan's attention. Hurrying across the room he pulled the skillet from the fire and carried it to the table. While rummaging around the kitchen for plates and cups he spotted the biscuits.

He turned to Kate with a look of surprise. "You baked."

She nodded. "I hope you don't mind."

"They'll go fine with the venison." He lifted the blackened pot of coffee and, seeing that there was some left, set it on the coals to heat.

Because the woman and boy hadn't moved, he paused beside the table. "Supper, or what there is of it, is ready."

Kate shook her head. "You go ahead. Danny and I have already eaten our fill."

He glanced at the food. "If Blue and I eat all this, we won't be able to move for days. I think you'd better help us."

The boy shot a pleading glance at Kate.

Seeing it, she relented. "If you're sure there's too much, I suppose we could eat something."

"I'm sure, ma'am."

Kate caught the boy's hand and led him to

the table. Relieved, Ethan passed her the plate
of venison. She took a small piece, then placed
a piece on Danny's plate before handing it back
to Ethan. When he passed her the biscuits she
did the same, taking only one and placing half
on her own plate and the other half on the boy's
plate, before giving the rest to Ethan.

Just as he was lifting the fork to his mouth
he saw that Kate and the boy had joined hands.
He lowered his fork.

The two bowed their heads and Kate murmured, "Bless this food and the kind stranger
who has offered us shelter."

Ethan waited to see if she intended to say
more. When the woman and boy began to eat,
he did the same.

The venison was tough, but it filled the hole
in his stomach. After several bites he broke one
of the biscuits, and was surprised at how easily
it came apart. His own biscuits often had to be
banged against the edge of the table to break
them apart.

His first bite was a revelation. It almost
melted in his mouth.

He shot her a look. "What did you do to
these?"

"Do?" Kate was caught off guard. "You
don't like them?"

"They're fine. In fact, I don't believe I've ever tasted anything so fine."

He saw the pleasure that lit her eyes. "They're just simple biscuits, like the ones my da used to like with his tea."

When the coffee began boiling he wrapped a length of cloth around the handle and filled three cups. As he set them on the table he frowned. "Sorry. I forgot about the boy. I never thought to bring some milk from the herd."

Kate placed a cup of coffee in front of Danny. "You'll not be apologizing. We're just grateful for food and a warm shelter, Mr. Storm."

His frown deepened. "Mr. Storm was my pa. I prefer Ethan."

She looked down. "As you wish. And I prefer Kate to ma'am."

He nodded, then passed the biscuits around again. "I think, considering how fine these taste, it'd be wrong not to finish all of them."

Kate and Danny needed no coaxing. By the time they pushed away from the table, there wasn't a crumb left.

When Ethan started to clear away the dishes Kate stopped him with a shake of her head. "It's enough that you've given us food and shelter. Danny and I will clean up here. I'm sure you have other chores to see to."

"Too many to count." He nodded toward the deer meat, carefully wrapped in the hide. "I'm thinking I'd better get this roasting over the fire. By morning I can cut it into strips and hang them to dry."

"I'll tend to the meat after I clean up here." She opened the hide. "What did you do with the innards?"

"Left them in the barn."

"If you bring them in I'll cook them in a pot for your dog."

He couldn't hide his surprise, or his pleasure. "I'm thinking old Blue would like that." He pulled open the door to the cabin. "Come on, Blue. Let's go fetch your supper."

When he and the dog were gone, Kate rolled up her sleeves and set to work washing the dishes and scrubbing the wooden table. By the time Ethan returned, she had pots and pans, and even his blackened kettle positioned over the fire. The little cabin was soon filled with the most amazing fragrances. Even the innards, simmering in a pot of water over the coals, smelled good enough to eat.

Kate set aside a small portion to cool. As soon as she set the bowl on the floor the dog attacked it.

Ethan chuckled as he ran a hand down Blue's back. "After a feast like this I doubt you'll be satisfied with my hard biscuits and a hunk of dried meat.''

He picked up a length of harness in need of repair, and settled himself on a bench in front of the fire. As he bent to his work it occurred to Ethan that the same might be said for him. After all these years of seeing to his own needs, it had been pleasant to taste someone else's biscuits. Not to mention the pleasure of sharing his table with these two. Though they were strangers, they weren't the least bit intrusive. In fact, they were easy to be around. He found himself enjoying the sound of the woman's soft brogue. It was so musical, it made him want to smile. She was easy to look at, as well, with the face of an angel. As for the boy, he seemed afraid of his own shadow. And Ethan had yet to hear his voice. But at least he wasn't setting up a howl as some children did.

Ethan paused in his work. Could it be that the boy couldn't talk? Maybe he couldn't hear, either. He glanced across the room, where Kate was busy washing Blue's dish. The boy stood right beside her, keeping one eye on the dog.

When Blue ambled across the room and settled down in front of the fire, the boy remained beside Kate. But now, instead of watching the dog, his gaze focused on Ethan.

Sensing the boy's fear, Ethan kept his voice

low while he continued working. "Why don't you and the boy sit awhile, Kate. You've done enough."

She pushed a strand of damp hair from her face. "I thought I'd start another batch of biscuit dough. That way you'll have some for the morning, and enough left over to take with you for the day."

He kept his gaze fixed on the length of harness. "That'd be much appreciated."

While she mixed and stirred and kneaded he kept glancing over, watching the way she looked working at his little table. He had a quick flash of memory. Of his mother kneading dough in the back of their little wagon. Of the love he'd felt when she would hand him a slice of bread warm from the fire, before he left with his father for the day.

There'd been no time to grieve her death, or, years later, that of his father. He'd simply continued on with his life, doing what was necessary for survival. And until this moment, it had never occurred to him to wish for more than he had.

He pushed the thought aside with a flicker of annoyance. He had all he needed. A place to call his own. A thriving herd. That ought to be enough for any man.

Restless, he got up. While Kate and the boy

watched, he began searching the room, tossing aside his shirt, a wide-brimmed hat.

"What is it you're looking for? Maybe we could help," Kate offered.

"My tobacco pouch." With the toe of his boot he moved aside the rug and found it lying underneath. After rolling a cigarette, he settled back down.

Kate lay a clean square of linen over the dough, then caught Danny's hand and led him toward the fire. When she sat down on the other end of the bench, she pressed a hand to the small of her back. Ethan could hear the little sigh that escaped her lips.

"This is nice."

He glanced over. "What is?"

"This." She spread her hands. "Having your own home. And all of it so snug and sturdy."

He was surprised at the little jolt of pleasure he felt at her words. "What's your place like in Boston?"

She looked down. "It isn't mine. I work as a maid."

"What does a maid do?"

She took a moment to gather her thoughts. "Whatever needs doing. Sometimes I scrub floors by day and pots and pans by night. Other days I'm sent to the market for food, then find myself standing on my feet ironing by the light of the fire throughout the night.''

Ethan paused in his work. ''Is that why you left Ireland? To become a maid?''

She gathered the little boy close, keeping an arm protectively around his shoulders. ''I left Ireland hoping for a better life.''

''What was it like there?''

He could hear the smile in her voice. ''When I was Danny's age, it was a grand time. We lived in my grandfather's fine old house. I remember my da and mum always smiling, and always making music. My da played the fiddle and my mum played the harp. But when my grandfather died his land was claimed by a wealthy landlord from across the Channel.'' She fell silent for a long time. Finally she said softly, ''Life wasn't grand after that.''

Seeing that Danny had fallen asleep, Ethan said, ''Why don't you and the boy sleep in my bed tonight?''

She shook her head. ''It wouldn't be right. We'll be fine here on the floor.''

Before he could protest she lay the boy down on the rug and wrapped him in a blanket.

Ethan set aside the harness and went into his bedroom, returning a few minutes later with a faded quilt over his arm. ''You'll need this later tonight when the fire dies down.''

"Thank you." She studied the bits and pieces of fabric that had been stitched together with a fine, even hand. "Someone put a lot of love into this."

There it was again. That odd little rush of pleasure at her words. "It was my mother's. She made it when I was born. It's been with me ever since."

"What a treasure." She looked up at him.

He was close enough to smell her. Her hair was perfumed with rainwater. Her clothes smelled of cedar and sagebrush. His eyes narrowed and he was forced to absorb a quick, sudden jolt to the heart.

Kate shivered at the intensity of his look. Though he hadn't lifted a hand, she felt as if he'd somehow touched her. She drew the quilt around her shoulders. "Before I leave tomorrow I'll see that it's washed and hung to dry."

"There's no need..."

She shook her head, sending curls dancing. "It's the least I can do for the hospitality you've shown us."

Her lips parted in a sweet smile, which only had his frown deepening. He had the most overpowering urge. An urge to take her in his arms and kiss her until they were both breathless.

He turned away, knowing he needed to put some distance between himself and this woman.

If she had any idea what he was thinking she would be shocked to the core. In truth, he was feeling a bit stunned himself.

He fisted his hands at his sides and looked down at the sleeping boy. "Can he speak?"

She nodded. "He can, yes. But he's fearful."

"Of me?"

"Of many things."

There it was again. That way she had of evading, and letting him know she had no intention of giving away any more than was absolutely necessary.

At the doorway of his bedroom he turned back, his eyes dark and shuttered. "If Blue scratches to get out, ignore him. It usually means there's a coyote or wolf close enough to smell."

"I'll remember."

He paused, keeping his back to her. "I put up the signal for the stage. You and the boy might want to consider staying on awhile, just until the weather gentles a bit. Who knows? Maybe by then the stage will come through, and you'll be able to save yourselves that long trek to town."

She couldn't stop the shiver that raced along her spine. "I'm afraid we don't have time. But I do thank you."

She waited until his door closed. Then she

time I had my hair cut, before someone takes me for a shaggy buffalo.''

That had Danny giggling.

It was, Kate realized, the first time she'd ever heard the little boy laugh. It was the most wonderful sound. For a moment she had to blink back tears of happiness. Her heart was so light she felt as if she could float.

''Well, now.'' She glanced at her nephew and realized that his joy was contagious. ''We can't allow that, can we? Maybe if we cut off enough, you'll just be taken for old Blue's father.''

She took the scissors from Ethan's hand and stepped behind him. The sight of that wide, muscled back had her throat going dry. She breathed deeply before taking hold of a length of hair. It was thick and dark as a raven's wing, and still damp from his bath. Her fingers tingled from the touch of it. As she began cutting, it spilled into the grass at her feet.

Danny stood to one side watching with such fascination he didn't even seem to notice when Blue walked up beside him. Minutes later when the big dog pressed his nose into the boy's hand, it seemed the most natural thing in the world for Danny to begin scratching behind the dog's ears.

Ethan pretended not to notice. No sense letting the boy see what the clever old dog was up to. Leave it to old Blue to find a willing slave to pet him.

He turned his head. "You done yet?"

"Not yet. Hold still." Kate snipped some more, then seemed to measure before cutting even more.

He reached a hand to his head. "Hold on there. I'd like you to leave me a little bit of hair."

"I am. Very little." She couldn't resist winking at Danny, who was convulsed with laughter.

Ethan caught her wrist, stilling her movements. The moment he did, he felt the rush of heat. But this time, instead of being shocked by it, he allowed himself to enjoy the pleasant tingle. "You sure you haven't cut it all off?"

"Maybe you'd better go see for yourself."

She was relieved when he released her and stepped away. It took several moments for her nerves to settle. There was such a wild fluttering inside, she wondered that her heart didn't jump clear out of her chest.

She watched him hurry to the cabin. Through the open door she could see him studying his reflection in the mirror. When he stepped outside he was tucking his shirt into the waist of his pants.

Kate couldn't take her eyes off him. Without

the shaggy beard and long hair he was so handsome he took her breath away. For the first time she could see the strong chin, the perfectly sculpted lips. Lips that were split in a dangerous grin that had her heart hitching.

"This is better than the haircut I got from Jason Skinner in town last summer. And he charged me a whole dollar. Of course, he threw in a shave and a bath. But the water wasn't nearly as warm or as clean as the bath I just enjoyed." He stepped closer, fixing Kate with a look. "Are all your countrymen mind readers?"

She shrugged. "There are those who think so."

He loved the color that flooded her cheeks. "That explains how you knew what I was craving."

Kate's brogue thickened. "When my da came home after days with the sheep, the first thing he wanted was to sleep in his bed from sundown to sunup. And the next day, his greatest pleasure was the bath my mum would prepare for him by the fire."

"Then I'm grateful you had such a fine teacher." He was standing so close he could see himself reflected in her eyes. It occurred to him that he was drowning in those green depths.

He lowered his voice. "I can't remember the last time I've felt this rested."

"That would be from a good night's sleep in your own bed." She turned away, eager to escape. He was too close. Too...potently male. There was something about him that made her heartbeat unsteady. "I'll toss the bathwater."

He put a hand on her arm. Just a touch, but he saw the way she pulled back as though burned. It gave him considerable pleasure to realize he wasn't the only one affected by all this.

"I'll do it, Kate. That tub's too heavy for you to lift."

She stayed where she was, watching him hurry inside. Minutes later he stepped from the cabin and tossed the bathwater into the grass.

Kate couldn't tear her gaze from him. From the muscles that rippled along his arms as he emptied the tub. He seemed...different today. More confident. More in control. Which had her feeling just the opposite. Confused. Uneasy.

To cover the silence she asked, "Will you be going to the herd soon?"

"Not today." He lowered the empty tub and turned to her with a look that had her heart tripping over itself. "Today I'm just going to stay around the cabin and see to the chores I've been neglecting. Tomorrow is soon enough to return to my herd."

He stowed the tub, then nodded toward the barn. "Danny, how's that calf doing with its new mama?"

For a moment it looked as though the boy would revert to his silence. But after glancing at Kate for reassurance, he managed to mumble, "He's eating. Want to see?"

"I believe I do." Ethan started toward the barn, then turned. "Maybe you and Blue would like to come along."

He noticed that the boy kept the dog between them as they walked. Whatever had happened to make him so fearful, it wouldn't be erased with a few kind words or deeds. It would take a heap of patience to persuade this wounded little boy to trust again.

Ethan had never been one to bother about things that weren't his business. But he found himself wondering again what these two were doing in the middle of Montana. And just who or what they were running from.

"OH, ETHAN. MILK." Kate looked up from the lantern she was polishing and gave a delighted laugh when Ethan set the bucket on the table.

"For Danny." Ethan wiped an arm across his forehead. He'd worked up quite a sweat from his chores in the barn.

Kate tried not to notice the way his shirt was

plastered to his back, revealing rippling muscles. "We'll have to use it up before it sours. If I had a churn, I'd make you some butter."

"That'd be nice." He could smell biscuits baking. The cabin looked all shiny and new. Even the hearth had been swept clean of soot.

"I know." She turned away and lifted the sack of sugar. "I'll make you bread pudding for supper."

"Kate." He cleared his throat.

"It's not much work. I'll just scald the milk and add the sugar and an egg and..."

"Kate." He lay a hand on her arm.

Startled, she looked up.

"You don't have to earn your keep."

"But I'm not..."

He struggled to keep the emotion out of his tone. It wasn't easy, when she was standing so close and her pretty face was covered with sheen. "I'm not that rich man in Boston. I'm just a simple rancher, and you and the boy are more than welcome to share what I have."

Her cheeks flamed. "Thank you. But we're eating your food. We're an intrusion in your life. And..."

Before she could say more he dragged her into his arms and kissed her full on the mouth.

Kate was so startled, all she could do was stand perfectly still, absorbing the most amazing sensations that seemed to be exploding all through her body.

Stunned by his bold actions, Ethan lifted his head and stared down at her as if unable to believe what he'd just done. And more, what he'd just felt.

"Sorry."

"Yes. I..." Kate swallowed.

They stepped apart and stared into each other's eyes, wearing matching expressions of guilt. For the space of a heartbeat the two of them remained frozen.

Then Ethan swore savagely and dragged her back into his arms. This time as he lowered his mouth to hers she wrapped her arms around his neck and gave herself up to the pleasure.

In her whole life Kate had never been kissed like this. As though she were some special treasure to be savored. His mouth moved over hers and she felt her heartbeat racing like a runaway carriage. Needs she'd never even known she possessed began pulsing deep inside.

These were the most amazing feelings. Feelings that left her dazed and breathless.

Ethan couldn't get enough of her. There was such sweetness in her. But laced with the sweetness was a simmering heat that matched his. That discovery had the blood roaring in his temples. Now that he'd tasted her, he wanted more. He wanted all.

He gathered her firmly against him, needing to feel her in every part of himself. He ran a hand lightly down her back and felt her trembling response. It only made him bolder.

"I want you, Kate."

It seemed like a dream. No one had ever spoken those words to her before. "And I..." She dragged in a ragged breath and struggled to think. But her mind had begun clouding the moment he'd touched her. Now, with his kisses stirring her blood, she couldn't seem to get her bearings.

His big hands set her flesh on fire, and had the blood in her veins turning to molten lead. She would gladly go on like this forever, being kissed by him, touched by him. He'd taken her higher than she'd ever been.

"Lie with me tonight, Kate."

The words, murmured against her lips sent tremors racing through her. The temptation was so great. What he offered was all that she wanted. All that she would ever need.

"Please, Kate. Come to me after Danny falls asleep."

Danny.

She went very still. How could she have been so foolish? Nothing must be allowed to come between her and the boy entrusted to her care. Not even this man, who so touched her heart.

"I can't." She pushed free of his arms and stood, chest heaving, the threat of tears burning her throat. "I have to think of Danny."

"What does the boy have to do with us?"

"He has everything to do with us. With me." She took in several long deep breaths. "I have to take him away."

"Why? Who's chasing you, Kate?"

"No one." With her hands clenched into fists she turned away, avoiding those dark, knowing eyes.

He touched a hand to her shoulder and felt her flinch. Still, he kept it there as he said softly, "You're not a good liar, Kate. Even while you say one thing, your kiss said something quite different."

"'Twas a kiss. Nothing more."

"Maybe. And maybe you really don't want me. But at least spare me the lies about Danny. If someone's after you, you don't have to run. You can stay here and we'll stand together against whatever it is you're running from."

When she refused to answer, he lowered his hand.

She shivered, feeling suddenly cold. She squeezed her eyes tightly shut and listened as he crossed the room and pulled open the door.

When it slammed shut behind him she crossed her arms over her chest and breathed deeply until the threat of tears had passed.

Then she threw herself into her chores with such fury it was impossible to think. Once or twice she may have trembled at the thought of strong arms holding her, and warm, firm lips moving over hers. But she was able to brush aside such distractions as she drove herself with even more energy than usual.

CHAPTER FIVE

THE DAYS PASSED in a blur of work. Each morning Ethan left to tend his herd, always wondering if this would be the day that he would return to find Kate and Danny gone. The last of the snow had melted, and the days were growing longer. Though the mornings were still frosty, there was a gentleness in the breeze that spoke of spring.

Lately there was a restlessness in Ethan that seemed completely out of character. An impatience with anything that kept him from spending more time with Kate and Danny.

Being a practical man, he figured he understood his feelings toward Kate. He'd been without a woman for a long time. A trip to town would probably solve his problem. Still, the thought of being with one of Lester Minor's women filled him with revulsion. There wasn't one of them that could measure up to Kate. He had to admit that it wasn't just any woman he wanted. It was the one sleeping just a few feet

away in his cabin each night. She played softly
through his mind, even in dreams. That lovely
angel face. That musical brogue that did such
strange things to his heart.

Then there was Danny. Though the boy still
didn't trust him, he was at least beginning to
leave his aunt long enough to sit with Ethan
after supper. At first he'd merely sat on one end
of the big bench and watched as Ethan used the
light of the fire to mend harness or to whittle
wood into practical things for the cabin. Danny
had watched in amazement as Ethan had whit-
tled on a block of wood until he'd made Kate
a butter churn.

"You think I could do that?" the boy asked
timidly.

"I don't see why not." Ethan gave Danny a
smile. "But you'd best start with something
smaller. I'll bring you home some wood tomorrow, and see if you can figure out what to
make of it."

He touched the wood in his saddlebag and
urged his horse into a gallop. Daylight was fad-
ing and time was wasting. Time he'd rather
spend with Kate and Danny than here on the
trail.

The minute he came riding up the cabin door
was thrown open and Danny and Kate stood

framed in the doorway. It was a sight that had Ethan grinning like a boy at Christmas.

"Did you bring the wood?" Danny called.

"I did." Ethan slid from the saddle and drank in the sight of Kate, her hair damp from cooking, her eyes looking soft and dreamy. "I'll be inside in a while."

Kate turned away to get supper on the table, but Danny surprised him by falling into step beside him. As the boy walked he kept a hand on Blue's head. The dog rewarded him with a quick lick of his tongue.

Inside the barn Ethan unsaddled his horse, noting the fresh water and hay already in place in the stall.

"You been taking good care of the cow and calf, boy?"

"Yes, sir. She's a good mama, don't you think?"

Ethan paused to study the nursing calf. "I'd say they're a good match. We're lucky. Some don't work out as well as others."

"Why?"

Ethan shook his head. "Don't know for sure. Some critters just aren't cut out to be good at it."

The boy dropped to his knees to pet Blue. "You think folks are like that, too?"

Ethan nodded. "I expect so. There are some

who just don't know how to take care of their own.''

He started toward the door and noticed that Danny was still kneeling quietly, petting the dog while watching the cow and calf. "You coming, son?"

"Yes, sir." Danny got to his feet and followed Ethan to the cabin.

Inside the air was perfumed with something wonderful. Ethan hung his hat by the door and rolled his sleeves to wash in the basin of fresh water. When he turned, Kate was just setting a batch of biscuits on the table.

"What's that I smell?"

"Apples and cinnamon." Kate seemed delighted with her discovery. "You never mentioned the root cellar under the floor."

Ethan shrugged. "Not worth mentioning. Near as I can recall, there's nothing left down there until I replenish it with summer stock."

"Nothing left? When I started cleaning it, I found a treasure. Two dried apples, buried in the dirt. And on a shelf was an old cinnamon stick. So I added them to my biscuits."

Ethan grinned at Danny. "If they taste half as good as they smell, we'll be mighty grateful."

Kate set dinner out while the man and boy took their places. As always, Kate took Danny's hand and the two bowed their heads. Before she could say a blessing she felt the warmth of Ethan's hand on hers. She looked up in surprise as he reached his other hand to Danny's. For a moment she felt her heart catch in her throat. Then she bowed her head.

"Bless this food and those of us gathered here to enjoy it."

They passed the food and filled their plates.

"I have another surprise." Kate showed off the butter she'd made with her new butter churn. "I think my biscuits will taste even better now."

Both Ethan and Danny eagerly broke open their biscuits and slathered on butter before tasting.

Kate waited while they chewed and swallowed.

Ethan's eyes widened. "Well I'll be..." He turned to Kate with a look of astonishment. "You've made my mother's son-of-a-gun biscuits."

"I don't understand." She was looking puzzled. "Why did you call them that?"

He chuckled. "At the time, I didn't understand why every time I'd ask for those son-of-a-gun biscuits, it'd make my folks roar with laughter. But now I realize I was too young to say cinnamon, and so I called it son-of-a-gun.

And they got such a kick out of it, they never bothered to correct me.''

Danny was listening with interest. ''You mean you were little like me once?''

Ethan winked. ''Even smaller. I can remember thinking my dad was the biggest, strongest man in the whole world.''

''Did you...like your pa?'' The boy was watching Ethan closely.

''I couldn't wait to grow up and be like him. He was my hero.'' Ethan dug into his meal, and helped himself to another biscuit.

''Did he live on a big ranch like this?''

Ethan shook his head. ''He never had a place of his own. My pa and I traveled all around the West, working for other ranchers. But I saw how much they respected him. He always did the job they paid him to do. And when he left, they'd always ask him to come back the next year, to help with the roundup in late summer, or to help with the calving in the spring.''

Danny drained his milk and wiped his mouth on his sleeve. ''What about your ma?''

''She died when I was seven. After that I went everywhere with my pa.''

The boy's eyes widened. ''You worked alongside him?''

Ethan nodded. ''There were a lot of ranch chores for a boy. Milking. Mucking stalls. By the time I was nine or ten I was working along-side grown men, riding range, mending fence.''

He looked down at his plate and realized he'd eaten everything. He glanced at Kate. ''That was a fine meal. I don't believe I've ever tasted one better.''

She laughed. ''You say that every night.''

''Do I?'' He looked genuinely surprised. ''You're spoiling me, Kate. I don't know how I'll ever be able to eat my own cooking again.''

While he tore around the cabin searching for his tobacco pouch, she ducked her head and sipped her coffee. And wondered why his words should make her feel sad.

''YOU HOLD THE KNIFE away from you like this.'' By the light of the fire Ethan patiently showed Danny how to begin whittling. ''You start by studying the piece of wood and seeing if it reminds you of something. Maybe it's the shape of the wood, or the grain. Then you whit-tle away until you have the shape. The finer details will come later.''

While the man and boy sat together on the bench, Kate prepared a fresh batch of biscuit dough. Afterward she positioned a chair by the fireplace and picked up a basket of clothes that needed mending.

Ethan glanced at Blue, lying at Danny's feet,

and then at Kate, head bent, hair gleaming in the light of the fire. If someone asked him to describe heaven, it would be this. Just this.

He cleared his throat. "I worked with a cowboy once from Ireland. Everyone called him Irish. His voice sounded like yours, Kate."

She smiled. "I've tried to sound American. But the tongue doesn't want to oblige."

He shook his head. "Don't ever change it. It's pleasant to the ear."

Kate felt her cheeks burning and blamed it on the fire.

Ethan was determined to keep her talking. The sound of her voice did such soothing things to his heart. "How old were you when you left Ireland?"

"Ten and two."

"So young."

She laughed. "This from the one who did a man's work at the age of nine or ten?" She fell silent for a moment, then looked at Danny, absorbed in his work. "When my mum was dying, she asked my sister and me to seek a better life. So after we put her in the ground, Fiona and I boarded a ship to America."

"You must have been worried about how you'd survive."

"Aye. But when you've nothing, you're willing to risk everything."

He marveled at her spunk. "How old was Fiona?"

"She was ten and five. And so beautiful. Fiona was always the pretty one."

Ethan couldn't imagine that anyone could be more beautiful than Kate, but he kept his thoughts to himself.

Kate sighed, lost in her memories. "She had hair the color of coal, and eyes as blue as a summer sky." Her voice lowered. "Danny has his mother's eyes."

"Did she work with you as a maid?"

Kate nodded. "Aye. But Fiona was a dreamer. She always wanted more." She seemed to catch herself and let her words trail off as she bent to her sewing.

"Where is Fiona now?"

"She's dead." Kate bit the thread and picked up another of Ethan's shirts.

"And her husband?"

Kate took her time examining the rip in the fabric. "He's dead, too."

Not long after, Kate set aside the basket of sewing and got to her feet. "I believe I'll just walk to the barn and see how our wee calf is getting along."

Ethan watched as she quietly closed the cabin door. He listened to her footsteps fade as she walked away. Then he turned his attention to Danny, who was stifling a yawn.

"WELL." Kate stepped close to the calf and ran a hand along the soft hide, while the cow hovered protectively. "Look at you. Warm and safe and well-fed."

In answer the calf swished its tail.

"Lucky little thing. Soon you'll be out on the range, running with the herd. That's as it should be." Her voice took on a dreamy edge. "Every creature should be free to grow and run with its own kind. To live in freedom and achieve all that the heart desires. And no one—" her voice quivered with emotion "—no one should be allowed to stand in the way of one's freedom. Especially not one who is precious and sweet and innocent…"

Without warning the tears came. She dropped to her knees in the hay and found herself weeping uncontrollably. Hard, wrenching sobs that burned the throat and rolled down her cheeks like a river.

She didn't try to stem the flow. Instead she allowed herself to wallow in the grief that until this moment she'd been denying. There'd been no time to grieve. Not seven years ago when she'd buried her mother and turned her back on her homeland forever. Certainly not now, as she'd struggled against overwhelming odds to fulfill a dying sister's request. It seemed to her that her life had been one long road of uncertainty and hard work. There had been times when she'd feared she wouldn't live to see another day.

But here she was in this peaceful haven, so like the place she'd once called home. What she wouldn't give to be able to remain here. But she knew in her heart it wasn't to be. Sooner or later the danger would catch up with her. And she dare not linger, lest she bring it here to Ethan's doorstep.

"What this?"

At the sound of Ethan's voice she lifted her head.

He dropped to the hay beside her. "Tears?"

"They're nothing." Embarrassed, she scrubbed her hands over her face to erase the evidence. "Just a foolish woman's moment of weakness. I'd best see to Danny."

Before she could scramble to her feet Ethan put a hand on her arm. "Danny's asleep. Wrapped in a blanket in front of the fire, with Blue keeping watch over him."

"They've begun—" she looked into his eyes "—to care about each other."

He nodded. "It's happened to us, too, Kate. I don't know how much longer I can go on fighting these feelings. Every day I want you. While I'm tending the herd. While I'm doing my chores. And the nights." He touched a finger to her cheek. Just a touch, but she felt a ripple through her entire body. "Every night has become a test of my strength."

She longed to throw herself into his arms. To beg him to lie with her and love her. Instead she scrambled to her feet, her eyes wide with absolute terror. "Ethan, we musn't. I can't do this to you. It wouldn't be right."

His voice was a hoarse cry as he stood over her and caught her arm. "Have mercy on me, Kate. How much can a man take?"

The tears were still too close to the surface. She knew if she didn't run now, she would embarrass herself again.

"I can't, Ethan. I know you don't understand, but I...can't."

His puzzlement turned to anger as she fled.

CHAPTER SIX

THOUGH THE BARN was already clean, Ethan had a need to vent his anger. He grabbed up a pitchfork and began mucking the stall, muttering as he worked.

What kind of fool was he, that he'd allowed himself to think a woman like Kate McCrea could ever want him? She'd seen how the rich men in the east lived. Big houses and fine carriages, and people to do their dirty work. She'd made it plain that she couldn't wait to get back to that life. But he'd foolishly thought he could persuade her to stay with him. He'd even begun thinking of Danny as the son he'd never had.

Family. It's what he had once been part of. It was what he yearned for in his heart of hearts. And until Kate and Danny came along, he'd thought it was beyond his reach. He'd been happy. Content with his life as it had been. But here they were, three lonely people who fit together perfectly, and he'd begun tempting himself with the thought of some kind of permanence.

"Nothing but a damned fool." He tossed a forkful of dung into the cart and scattered fresh straw.

As he turned to retrieve the pitchfork he saw her, standing directly behind him.

His scowl deepened. "I thought you'd gone back to the cabin."

"I...tried. I was halfway there when I turned back."

"Is there some insult you forgot to fling in my face?"

"Don't, Ethan." She reached a hand to his face but he drew back.

"It's late. Go to bed, Kate."

"Not until I tell you what's in my heart."

"You've already made very clear that you don't want what I'm offering."

"If you think that you're a fool. And the man I've been watching these past weeks is anything but that. Will you hear me out, Ethan?"

He sighed. Without a word he crossed his arms over his chest, determined not to touch her again.

"This isn't easy for me, Ethan. I'm not... accustomed to baring my soul. But this needs saying." She avoided his eyes. "I think you're the finest man I've ever met."

"And so you refuse my love."

"I refuse it because I don't deserve it. You deserve better than the likes of me."

"It's you I want, Kate."

A long, deep sigh welled up from deep inside her chest. "And it's you I want, Ethan."

"Then why...?"

She reached up to press a finger to his lips. That simple touch had sweat beading his forehead. "If I stay here, I could bring trouble to your doorstep."

"Then we'll face it together."

"It isn't that simple, Ethan."

"Just tell me what it is that's dogging your trail, Kate. And we'll deal with it. Together."

She was shaking her head as she started to back away. He brought his hands to her shoulders to stop her. That was his undoing. The mere touch of her had the need building like a sudden, violent summer storm.

His voice was a husky plea. "Stay with me, Kate. Lie with me. Let me love you."

"Oh, Ethan." The words were torn from her lips. "Do you have any idea how desperately I want to do just that?"

His head snapped back as though he'd been struck. For long minutes he simply stared at her, unable to believe what he'd just heard. Then, without a word, he drew her into the circle of his arms and lowered his mouth to hers.

She thought about resisting. But it was too late. His mouth was on hers, weaving its magic. That warm, clever mouth that could cloud her mind, steal her heart, her very soul with but a touch.

"Oh, Ethan." She sighed and wrapped her arms around his waist, needing to cling to his strength. "Promise me you won't hate me later."

"Oh, my sweet, foolish, darling Kate. How could I possibly hate you when my heart is overflowing with so much love?"

Love. That single word was the final straw.

And then there were no more words as he crushed her mouth with his.

He'd never known such heat. Or such need. He took the kiss deeper and knew that he'd crossed the line from reason into insanity. If he could, he would take her here and now, and end this terrible, consuming need. But he'd waited so long. Had wanted her so desperately. If this was all he could give her, he would make it as special as she was to him.

"Kate. My beautiful Kate." He forced himself to slow the pace, raining kisses over her forehead, her eyelids, the tip of her nose.

Kate took in a long, deep breath and wondered if her poor heart would ever slow its crazed pace. She felt as she'd been running for a lifetime. And now, in this man's arms, she'd found all that she'd been seeking.

She brought her arms around his neck and lifted her mouth to his. He kissed her with such reverence, as though unable to believe she was really here with him. But as he lingered over her lips she could feel the way he struggled to bank his passion.

A thrill raced up her spine. It was deeply arousing to know that she was the cause of his desire.

He lowered his mouth to the column of her throat. With a sigh she arched her neck, giving him easier access. But as he pressed soft kisses to her throat, then lower to the swell of her breast, she was forced to suck in a breath at the feelings that jolted through her. Despite the barrier of her gown, his mouth closed around one erect nipple, causing her to groan and clutch his waist, afraid that her legs would fail her.

As if sensing her need, he lowered her to the straw and lay beside her, nibbling at her earlobe. "I'll understand if you change your mind, Kate."

His words, whispered against her ear, sent a rush of heat that staggered her. "I'll not be changing my mind, Ethan. It's you I want. And this." She touched a hand to his heart and felt it thundering. "Just this."

He knew he'd been holding his breath, afraid that she might have a change of heart. He wasn't sure his own heart would ever recover if that should happen now.

"Kiss me, Ethan. I need your mouth on mine."

He kissed her with such urgency, they were both stunned and reeling. As he reached a hand to the buttons of her gown, he was forced to wage a terrible battle within himself. On the one hand he wanted to tear the gown from her and ravish her. On the other, he knew that what she needed was tenderness. And so he forced himself to move slowly, to touch, to taste, to savor.

As he slipped the gown from her shoulders he caught sight of the fine, embroidered chemise that he'd seen hanging on a branch of a tree. He'd dreamed of seeing her in this. And now that she was here in the flesh, it was so much more satisfying than any fantasy.

His throat went dry as he untied the ribbons and the fabric parted.

"Oh, Kate." His gaze swept her, drinking in the pale, porcelain flesh, the high, firm breasts, the tiny waist. "You're so beautiful you take my breath away."

She touched a hand to his cheek. "I'm glad you think me beautiful, Ethan. I want to be beautiful in your eyes, for no man but you has ever seen me like this."

Her admission left him speechless. With soft kisses and whispered sighs he showed her, in the only way he could, just how grateful he was for the gift she was giving him.

She lay in his arms, steeped in pleasure. As his kisses deepened, so did her pleasure, until, desperate to touch him as he was touching her, she reached a hand to the buttons of his shirt. When she fumbled, he helped her, until his clothes joined hers in a heap beside them in the hay.

"You're so strong, Ethan. So beautiful." She brushed her lips across his hair-roughened chest and heard a low, gutteral moan that seemed more animal than human.

At her touch, he could feel his control snap.

The change in him was frightening. His kisses were no longer gentle. The fierce look in his eyes had her heart pounding as he dragged her close and savaged her mouth with his. Yet even while she marveled at this darker side of him, she felt a thrill knowing it was her touch, her kiss that aroused him.

Growing bolder, she pressed kisses across his shoulder, down his chest, then lower still, until he gave a hiss of frustration and covered her mouth with his.

He kissed her like a man starving. She returned his kisses with a hunger of her own, feasting on his mouth until the dark, mysterious taste of him filled her.

With their passion unleashed, they rolled

around in the straw, lungs straining, bodies alive with need.

Though he'd intended to take her slowly, all his good intentions were gone in a moment. One touch of her and he'd been lost. Now all he could do was drink his fill of the sweet, clean taste of her. Pleasure was so exquisite, it bordered on pain. Need was a beast inside him, struggling to be free.

Despite the cold in the barn, their bodies were slick with sheen. The heat rose up between them, clogging their lungs, making their breathing ragged.

Kate trembled as Ethan moved over her, bringing his mouth down her body until he brought her to the first peak. He felt her stiffen, then gasp with unbelievable pleasure. Stunned, she fisted her hands in the straw, struggling for breath. But he gave her no time to recover as he took her again.

The world beyond this place no longer existed. Though the horse stomped and whinnied, she didn't hear. The wind sighing in the trees outside seemed nothing more than a distant chorus. Now there was only Ethan. His voice, low, urgent, as he took her to a place she'd never been.

He studied her, eyes glazed with passion, body tense with need. This was how he'd wanted her. Unafraid. Open to all he had to give.

His woman. Only his.

He kept his eyes steady on hers as he entered her. At her hiss of breath he hesitated, afraid to hurt her. But when her lips parted in a smile, and she wrapped herself around him, he was lost.

He buried his face in her hair and felt her move with him, climb with him. With the blood roaring in his temples he breathed her name, or thought he did. Then there was only the sound of their two hearts pounding as they stepped off the very edge of a mountain into space. And soared.

It was the journey of a lifetime.

"KATE." At the sound of Ethan's voice, she stirred, then opened her eyes.

Seeing the first rays of morning light streaming in through the cracks in the barn door, she sat up with a cry. "Danny. He's alone."

"Shh." He dropped to his knees and kissed her into silence. "I just left the cabin. He's sound asleep, with Blue beside him."

"The fire..."

"Is stoked. Relax, love. The world hasn't come to an end."

She laughed, a light musical sound that never failed to wrap itself around his heart. "Are you sure? I thought it ended several times during the night.''

''That was the earth moving.'' He gathered her into his arms and held her, just as he'd held her all through the night.

There'd been little time to sleep. They had rolled around the hay like two eager children, loving with an abandon that left them dazed and delighted.

Several times while she slept Ethan had left her side to go to the cabin. The first time he'd returned with quilts, which he'd wrapped around her. The second time he'd brought her biscuits and the last of the coffee. Whenever she dozed, he slipped away, seeing that Danny was safe and warm.

''I'd better get washed and start breakfast. You'll want to get to the herd.''

He shook his head. ''Not today.''

She paused and looked into his eyes. ''Why? What will you do today?''

''What I'd like to do is strut around like a proud, contented old rooster. But what I'll most likely do is a few ranch chores. I just want to stay close so I can look at you.''

She blushed. ''Whatever for?''

''Because it makes me happy to look at you, Kate. Do you know how beautiful you are?''

Her blush deepened. ''I told you. Fiona was the pretty one.''

"To you, maybe. To me, there couldn't be a prettier woman in the whole world than you."

She got to her feet and began rummaging around for her clothes. As she pulled on her chemise, Ethan stood and caught her hands.

"Let me do that."

She watched his eyes as he tied the ribbons. She'd never felt like this before. So loved. So cherished.

She picked up her gown and slipped it over her head. As the skirt drifted down around her ankles, Ethan began buttoning. With each touch of his hands she felt the heat grow. She could tell, by the narrowing of his eyes, that he felt it, too.

When they were both dressed he caught her hand. "Come on. I can't wait for the day to be over."

"You can't?" She pulled back. "Why?"

He gave her a smoldering look. "Because tonight, after Danny falls asleep, I can lie with you and love you again."

They raced toward the cabin, their laughter ringing in the warm spring air.

CHAPTER SEVEN

KATE MOVED AROUND the little cabin, baking biscuits, setting strips of venison in a skillet to heat over the fire. Her heart was so light, she felt as if she were flying. She marveled that her feet even touched the floor.

When she paused to poke at the fire she felt strong arms encircle her waist. She was drawn back against a wall of muscle, while warm, firm lips pressed soft kisses to the back of her neck.

In her thickest brogue she asked, "Now who might this be?"

"Little witch. I thought after the night we spent, you'd recognize your man."

"Oh. It's Ethan Storm, is it?" She gave a delighted laugh. "I was expecting a wild, hairy buffalo, and instead I find this handsome young lad who has probably set all the Montana lasses' hearts aflutter with his charm."

"There's only one lass I care to charm." He boldly touched a hand to her heart. "Hmm. I believe I feel a little flutter."

She turned in his arms and pressed her mouth to his throat. "More than a little, if truth be told. You fill my heart to overflowing, Ethan Storm."

Just then Danny sat up from the spot on the floor where he'd been sleeping and rubbed his eyes. Beside him, Blue lay with his head on his paws, eyes open and watchful.

The boy seemed fascinated at the sight of his aunt being embraced by Ethan.

He looked at the man with an eagerness that tugged at Kate's heart. "Can we work on my whittling tonight after supper?"

Ethan gave Kate a last lingering look before releasing her and walking across the room. "No need to wait until tonight, Danny. I've decided to stay here today and see to some chores. Maybe after our work is done we can take the knife and wood outside and work on it in the shade of a tree."

"You're staying here all day?" The boy seemed delighted. "Can I help with the chores?"

Ethan grinned as Kate called them to the table. "I think that can be arranged."

As they took their seats Ethan reached out and caught both Kate's and Danny's hands in his and bowed his head, waiting for Kate to say the blessing.

She had to swallow the little lump in her throat before she could speak. Afterward she passed the eggs and biscuits and meat and watched as man and boy devoured their food.

Every so often she saw Danny pass a bite of meat or biscuit to Blue, who hovered behind him, watching his every move. When she looked up she realized that Ethan had seen it, as well. The two shared a smile and continued on with their meal.

Later, as she began to clear the table, Ethan lay a hand on her arm and brushed a kiss over her cheek. It was such a simple gesture. But it occurred to Kate that just a day ago, it would have seemed too bold, too intimate. Now it seemed as natural as breathing.

"Danny and I are going to take a look at the barn. I'm thinking that I'll add a coop to one end, so the chickens won't have to share space with the horse, cow and calf."

She set the dishes in the basin of steaming water. "Oh, now that's a grand idea, Ethan. With warmer weather coming, you'll want to be letting some of the hens nest. Perhaps we can soon double their number."

"I was thinking the same thing." He strolled out the door, then stopped dead in his tracks.

Did she have any idea what she'd just said?

As he started toward the barn his smile came

slow and easy, until his eyes were dancing with laughter. Unless he missed his guess, Kate's little slip of the tongue meant she was making plans for the future. A future that included being here on his ranch with him.

"THAT'S IT, DANNY." Ethan fastened a heavy timber to a length of chain and waited while the boy took hold of the horse's reins and led him slowly forward. When the timber had rolled into position Ethan shouted, "Good work. Stop right there."

In no time he'd shouldered the log into place and secured it, before stepping back to admire his handiwork.

He put a sweaty arm around the boy, whose own clothes were soiled and damp from the work he'd done. "While I unhitch the horse, you run up to the cabin and fetch your aunt."

"Yes, sir."

The minute Danny turned away, Blue was beside him, tongue lolling, tail wagging furiously.

Danny was beaming with pride. It was the first time he could ever recall being praised by a man. Coming from this man, it was all the more special.

He could still recall his first glimpse of Ethan Storm. He'd been absolutely terrified. And he'd been prepared to hate the man and his dog. He paused to run a hand down Blue's back. Now he couldn't imagine a better friend in all the world than this big gentle dog.

"Aunt Kate." He slammed into the cabin with Blue just managing to dodge the door as it nearly closed on his tail.

Kate looked up from the dough she was kneading, and wiped a strand of damp hair with the back of her hand. "What is it, Danny?"

"Ethan wants you to come see what we made."

"All right." She gave the dough one last punch, then covered it with a clean linen cloth and washed her flour-dusted hands in the basin before following the boy out the door.

Danny had a hand on Blue's head as he walked beside her. "Ethan says I'm a good worker."

"That you are, luv. You take after the McCreas. Not an idle one in the bunch. We've always known how to do a day's work."

The boy's pride went up another notch.

Ethan was waiting for them. When they walked up, he pointed. "What do you think of your new coop?"

"Oh." She pressed her hands together. "It's lovely. I didn't expect it to be so big."

"You said the chickens would be doubling

their number by summer's end. I figured we'd better be prepared.'' Ethan held the door open and waited for her to lead the way inside.

She stood between the man and boy and slowly turned to take it all in. There were waist-high perches for the chickens to roost, and fresh hay scattered along three walls for the hens to nest.

''Oh, my.'' Her voice was hushed. ''They'll think they've moved into a palace. It's even finer and bigger than my room in Boston. Both of my men did grand work, indeed.'' She paused to brush a kiss on Danny's cheek, then stood on tiptoe to kiss Ethan's cheek, as well, before stepping outside.

Danny could hardly control his excitement. ''Can we move the chickens in now, Ethan?''

''I don't see why not. Why don't you do that while I muck the stall.'' Ethan followed the boy out the door, then turned to watch as Kate lifted her skirts and hurried back to the cabin to tend to her baking.

If he'd had any doubt about Kate staying, it had just been erased. What woman would trade all this for a room smaller than a chicken coop? His heart was feeling light as air while he finished his chores.

"Now you've got the hang of it." Ethan sat beside Danny in the shade of a big tree and showed him how to hollow out the inside of the wood. "Take nice slow, even strokes. You're not running a race here. If it takes you the rest of the week to do the job, what do you care?"

The boy smiled up at him and returned his attention to the task at hand.

Because the air had turned unseasonably warm and the sun had climbed high in the sky, Ethan rolled up his sleeves and mopped at his forehead. Danny did the same.

Kate stepped out of the cabin and handed each of them a glass of milk before placing a plate of biscuits between them. In no time the plate was empty, as were the glasses.

Kate settled herself in the grass and leaned against the trunk of the tree, watching the progress of the little boy. "What are you making?"

"It's a secret." Danny wiped the milky mustache from his upper lip with the back of his hand.

"Oh." She glanced at Ethan, who winked. "Sorry. I shouldn't have asked."

"That's all right." The boy held the wood a little away, studying it with a critical eye before turning it and resuming his work.

Kate sat watching him awhile longer before

getting to her feet. "Guess I'd better start supper."

"Let it go, Kate." Ethan caught her hand. "The day's too pretty to spend indoors. Sit and visit with us instead."

"But what about supper?"

"We'll eat cold meat and biscuits tonight." He squeezed her hand, urging her down beside him. When she was seated in the grass he put an arm around her shoulders. "And after supper we'll come back outside and watch the sun go down and the moon and stars come out to play."

Kate touched a hand to her heart. "I had no idea you were such a grand poet, Ethan."

He chuckled. "Neither did I. Maybe it's having you and Danny here that put such thoughts in my head. All I know is, I've never felt such peace."

"It's the same for me." She rested her head on his shoulder.

Just then Blue, dozing in the sun, sniffed the air and came to attention before issuing a low, menacing growl.

They looked up to see a cloud of dust as a horse and rider came thundering over the ridge.

Ethan swore. "I can't believe I was so careless. I left my rifle in the cabin. You and Danny get inside while I see who this is."

Kate scrambled to her feet and caught Danny's hand with such force the knife and block of wood went sailing. When he paused to retrieve them she yanked him roughly away, sprinting the distance to the cabin without a backward glance.

Once inside she shoved him into Ethan's bedroom. "No matter what you hear, you must stay here." She stared into the boy's frightened eyes. "Do you understand me?"

"Yes." Though his lip trembled, Danny remained there when she closed the door.

Kate hurried across the room and snatched up Ethan's rifle.

As she stepped out the cabin door she could see the horseman struggling to control his mount while Blue kept up a fierce yammering.

When the horseman spotted her he took aim with his rifle.

In a voice that sent chills racing down her spine he shouted, "Kate McCrea. I warned you not to cross me. Now fetch my son out here before I blow you to kingdom come."

CHAPTER EIGHT

AT THE MAN'S WORDS Ethan looked thunder-struck.

His eyes narrowed on Kate. "I thought you said the boy's father and mother were dead. Is this man Danny's father?"

"He is, yes." Her cheeks were suffused with color. "Though God knows he doesn't deserve to be."

The horseman waved his rifle. "That's not for you to say. Fetch the boy and be quick about it."

Kate's head came up. "I'll die before I see him leave with you."

The man's hand tightened on the trigger. "That can be arranged, woman."

Her brogue thickened. "I'm sure you'd have no regret about putting another woman in the grave."

"That's right." He turned to Ethan. "You seem a reasonable man. If you know what's good for you, you'd better fetch my boy now.

I'll remind you that the law is on my side. I'd be within my rights to kill you both for stealing my son.''

Ethan moved to stand beside Kate. ''Tell me what's going on here.''

In a pained voice she said, ''I told you that my sister Fiona wanted more than the life she'd found in Boston. She had some foolish romantic notion and answered an ad for a mail-order bride. This man—'' Kate's chin came up as she glanced at the horseman ''—Ezra Boomer sent Fiona enough money for train fare. I begged her not to go, but she wouldn't be talked out of it. The year after she left there was a letter, telling me she'd had a son.'' Kate's tone softened. ''She'd named him Daniel, after our father.'' She swallowed. ''Fiona's next letter said she'd made a mistake. Ezra Boomer, she said, was a cruel drunk who often beat her. There were no more letters until the one that arrived this year. Fiona wrote begging me to come and get her and Danny. She feared for their lives. I used my life's savings to head West, only to find I was too late. Fiona was already in the ground, and Danny was so afraid, he could barely speak. His poor little back was scarred from beatings. When I offered to look after the boy Ezra flew into a rage and told me I'd have to leave the next morning.''

"Instead the little thief waited until I'd fallen asleep and went sneaking off in the night with my boy. I figured she'd head for the nearest town. I wasted a lot of time going the wrong way. Then I heard from a rancher about a woman and kid crossing his pasture. That's when I knew she was headed this way." Ezra Boomer waved his rifle. "I warned you, woman. Now go fetch him. I'm losing my patience."

Ethan held up a hand. "You don't deny beating Fiona and the boy?"

"Deny it?" Boomer gave a chilling laugh. "Why should I? The woman was my property. Just like the brat. If they don't do like I tell them, they deserve what they get." His voice went up a notch as his temper grew. He took careful aim with his rifle. "Now get him. If I have to do it myself, it'll be over both your bodies."

"No!" The cabin door slammed as Danny came rushing out to stand protectively in front of Kate and Ethan. "Don't hurt them. I'll..." He was shaking so badly his voice could barely be heard. "I'll go back with you."

Boomer spat a stream of tobacco juice. "About time. Get over here you sniveling little coward. When I'm through with you you'll never try running away again."

Before Danny had taken two steps Ethan snatched the rifle from Kate's hand and lifted it to his shoulder. "I may not have the right, but I can't let you take the boy. Not when I know you're going to hurt him."

"Why you damned fool." Boomer fired off a shot that seemed to echo like thunder across the hills.

Kate let out a scream as Ethan fell to the ground. She dropped down beside him, trying vainly to stem the river of blood that was staining the front of his shirt, but it was impossible. The blood spilled through her fingers and soaked the ground beneath him.

She looked up, tears streaming down her cheeks. "You've killed Ethan."

"Serves him right." Boomer nudged his horse closer, leaning down to catch hold of Danny's arm. "Come on, boy. I've been storing up a heap of fury all these long weeks. You're going to pay for what you've put me through."

The moment he lay a hand on the boy Blue leapt up and with a feral snarl sank his teeth into Boomer's wrist. Howling in pain, the man managed to shake off the dog before firing a shot that had Blue dropping to the grass.

In some distant part of her mind Kate heard the boy's whimpering as he was hauled up behind his father. Through a haze of tears she saw

Boomer's leering grin as he shoved his rifle into the boot of his saddle and spat a stream of tobacco juice before wheeling his mount.

Desperation gave her a strength she never knew she possessed. Getting to her feet she threw herself against the man in the saddle, catching him off guard.

As he tumbled to the ground she was on him, pummeling him with her fists. In those first moments she had the advantage of surprise. But she was no match for his brute strength. He brought his hand back and slapped her so hard she saw stars. While she was still reeling he scrambled to his feet and tossed her like a rag doll against the trunk of a tree.

She lay, bruised and broken, struggling for breath as he pulled his rifle from the boot of his saddle and walked over to take aim. "Kate McCrea, I should have killed you the minute you told me who you were."

As Kate lay in the grass, she felt the cold steel of Danny's knife beneath her hand. Her fingers closed around the hilt. Using the trunk of the tree for support, she got slowly to her feet.

The effort cost her. Her words were little more than a whisper. "You mean the way you killed Fiona?"

"That one wasn't even worth the cost of a

bullet. Weak little pissant. All I needed were my fists.''

With a cry of pain and rage Danny leapt from the saddle. With one arm around Boomer's neck, he used the other to beat at him ineffectively.

Boomer shook him off like an irritating gnat. ''You're going to have to grow some to take me on, boy.''

As he turned toward Kate, Danny picked up a tree limb and swung it against Boomer's head with all his might. Using the distraction, Kate brought her hand back and tossed the knife. At the same moment she heard the roar of gunfire and turned to see Ethan, kneeling in the grass, holding the rifle to his shoulder.

Boomer dropped to the ground, eyes wide, jaw slack, while the grass around him slowly turned blood-red.

With a cry Kate raced to Ethan's side. The rifle had slipped from his nerveless fingers. His shirt, his pants, his boots, were all soaked with his blood.

She turned to Danny, who was standing, stiff and rigid, staring at the figure of his dead father. ''I need water from the kettle and clean linen right away.''

The boy turned away and ran to the cabin.

Kate closed her eyes, each strained breath

coming from Ethan's throat adding another layer to her guilt. She had brought death and destruction to his doorstep. She would have been more than willing to pay the price for her sins. But it was not to be. Instead, it was this good man who must now pay.

Bending close she whispered against his ear, "Please don't die, Ethan."

Kate felt fingers close weakly around her wrist. "Not...dead."

"Oh, my darling. Oh, Ethan." She buried her face in his neck, breathing him in. "Hold on. I'll clean your wounds and get you to your bed."

"What about you and Danny?" He squinted up at her, trying to see through the blood and sweat that burned his eyes. "Are you hurt?"

"No." She shook her head. "We're both fine."

He sighed with relief.

Minutes later Danny knelt beside him, tearing strips of linen while Kate bathed away the blood. Ethan seemed to drift in an out of consciousness.

"The bullet?" he suddenly asked.

"Went clean through your side. Missed your vitals." Kate bound him tightly and heard his little hiss of pain. "I know it hurts, but we'll soon be finished here.'' She touched a hand to his. "Do you think you can stand?''

"I'll try.'' With his arm around her waist he got slowly to his feet. Leaning heavily on her, he made it to the cabin where he fell into bed.

After covering him, Kate walked outside to find Danny kneeling beside the dog.

She hurried over. "Is he…?''

The boy shook his head. "I can feel him breathing.''

Kate leaned close and listened to the shallow breaths, then began working over the dog in the same way she'd worked on Ethan, probing the wound, cleaning the blood, relieved that the bullet seemed to have missed any vital organs. A short time later she and Danny carried Blue inside and lay him on the rug in front of the fire.

She wrapped a blanket around the boy, who was trembling so violently, even his hair seemed to be vibrating. "You stay here.''

As she started out, Danny glanced up with a look of absolute terror. She managed a reassuring smile, which faded the moment she stepped out the door.

As distasteful as it was, she needed to do this one last thing before she gave in to the weariness that was slowly draining her.

In the barn she hitched Ethan's horse to the

small cart. Though it required superhuman effort, she managed to roll the body of Ezra Boomer into a blanket, and lift it into the back of the cart. In the barn she unhitched the horse and led it to its stall.

When she returned to the cabin, she found Danny sleeping beside Blue. She banked the fire, then made her way to Ethan's bedroom.

Setting a kitchen chair beside his bed she wrapped herself in a blanket, determined to stay awake and alert, so that she could keep a bedside vigil all through the night, seeing to his needs.

Once again the guilt came creeping over her, filling her with shame.

She closed her eyes as tears streaked down her cheeks. "Please let him live," she whispered. "I promise you, if you let Ethan live, I'll not ask another favor."

CHAPTER NINE

ETHAN SAT UP and waited until the dizziness cleared before swinging his feet to the floor. The night had passed in a blur of pain. Whenever he woke, Kate was there, giving him sips of water, stroking his fevered brow, whispering words of encouragement.

Though even the smallest movement caused him pain, he managed to pull on his clothes and boots before walking from the bedroom.

Everything looked so normal. Coffee bubbled over the fire, filling the little cabin with its wonderful aroma. Danny and Blue slept on the rug in front of the fire. The old dog lifted his head and peered at Ethan before closing his eyes again.

Ethan paused, running a hand down the dog's back, before getting slowly to his feet. At the front door he stared at the spot where he'd last seen Ezra Boomer lying in the grass. Except for bloodstains, everything looked as it had before Boomer's unexpected arrival. The sun was just breaking out of a bank of clouds. Clothes were drying on tree branches. Birds were chirping.

Kate was just making her way from the coop with a basket of eggs on her arm. Seeing him she stopped for a moment, then looked concerned as she hurried toward him.

"You shouldn't be out of bed yet. Your wounds need time to heal."

He was staring at her in that piercing way that always made her heart beat a little too fast. "What did you do with the body?"

"I put it…" She swallowed. "It's in the cart in the barn."

"As soon as Danny wakes, we'll need to go to town."

Her heart trembled at the controlled tone. "Do you think you're up to such a journey?"

"It has to be done, Kate."

She heard the steel beneath the words and nodded, then squared her shoulders. "You'll need some food before we go."

A short time later she touched a hand to Danny's shoulder, where he lay beside the dog. "It's time you were up and dressed. We're going into town."

When the boy joined them at the table, the three ate in silence. Nobody seemed willing to talk about what had happened. It was as though each of them had locked it away in a little room in their minds.

While Kate washed the dishes and packed up enough food for their journey, Ethan made his way to the barn and hitched the horse to the cart, leaving the cow and calf with extra food and water.

When it was time to go, all three sat up front on the hard wooden bench, with Blue lying beside Danny. Ethan flicked the reins and the horse leaned into the harness.

Kate turned for a glimpse of the cabin and felt her eyes fill with tears.

Ethan looked down at her. "You all right?"

She nodded, and realized it was the first words he'd spoken in more than an hour. Not that she blamed him. He must be still stunned and reeling from all that had happened.

The journey was slow and difficult, leaving Ethan pale and sweating by late afternoon. Danny passed the time whittling on the piece of wood with such concentration, it seemed his very life depended on seeing it finished.

They made camp beside a stream. By the time Kate had supper ready, Ethan was asleep in his bedroll. Danny and Blue curled up beside him, leaving Kate alone with her bleak thoughts. She sat by the fire, sipping coffee and wondering at the strange twists and turns her young life had taken.

In the morning Ethan seemed a bit stronger as he ate a quick meal of cold meat and biscuits before hitching the horse to the cart.

The horse soon ate up the miles across the rolling hills and began the descent into the valley below. Each mile that brought them closer to the town of Heaven dragged Kate deeper into an abyss of despair. She had no one to blame but herself. This was all her own doing. She had freely chosen to come here to rescue her nephew from a hellish situation. But Ethan had been the innocent victim in all this. Not only had she lied to him from the very beginning, but she had brought death and dishonor to his very doorstep.

As they rolled into town Kate felt the press of Ethan's hip to hers, the brush of his shoulder against hers, and nearly wept.

Ethan reined in the horse in front of the jail and stepped down. Then he helped both Kate and Danny down before leading the way inside.

The sheriff's middle may have gone to fat, and the once-dark hair threaded with silver. Even the badge glinting on his shirtfront looked a bit tarnished. But his eyes were as dark and probing as a curious child's.

He looked up with interest when Ethan announced that they'd brought in a dead man.

"Dead, eh? What's his name?"

"Boomer."

"Ezra Boomer?" The lawman's head came up sharply.

"That's right. You know him?"

"In a way." The sheriff looked beyond Ethan to the woman and boy. "Didn't know you'd acquired a family, Ethan."

"This is Kate McCrea and her nephew, Danny."

The sheriff doffed his hat. "Ma'am. Son."

Ethan cleared his throat. "Danny is Boomer's son."

The sheriff peered at him in such a way, Kate moved closer to drape an arm around the boy's shoulders protectively.

The sheriff turned his attention to Ethan. "How does Boomer happen to be in the back of your wagon?"

Ethan said simply, "I shot him."

"That's not true." Kate saw the sheriff glance over in surprise and lifted her chin, as though prepared to fight. "I killed Ezra Boomer with a knife."

"You don't say?"

Danny stepped away from Kate, his voice

trembling. "My aunt is just trying to protect me. I killed my pa with a tree limb."

"Well now." The sheriff turned to study each of them in turn. "This is mighty interesting. I suppose if I examine the body, I'll find out who's telling the truth."

"You'll find my bullet wound, sheriff." Ethan shot a glare at Kate.

"You'll find my knife wound in his chest." She glared back.

Danny shot them both pleading looks before turning to the sheriff. "You'll find the lump on my pa's head where I hit him."

"Why'd you hit him, son?"

"He was going to shoot my aunt."

"Why was he going to do that?"

"Because she stole me from him."

"I see." The lawman looked over at Kate. "That so, ma'am?"

She nodded. "It's true that I took him away from his father. But only because my sister had written telling me she feared for her life and that of her son. By the time I got here my sister was already dead and buried." She swallowed the knot of pain that seemed to engulf her without warning. "I wasn't about to leave Danny at the mercy of that madman's beatings."

The sheriff turned to Ethan. "Now how'd a

straight-arrow rancher like you get involved in all this?''

Ethan shrugged. ''Kate and Danny took shelter at my place. When Boomer arrived, I couldn't let him hurt them. So I shot him.'' He gave them both stern looks as he added, ''I'm the only one who caused his death.''

''I figure I'll be the judge of that.'' The sheriff left them standing inside as he walked out the door and made his way to the wagon.

While he was gone, Ethan, Kate and Danny stood staring at the floor. No one said a word.

When the lawman returned he crossed to his desk and opened a drawer, then began writing on a sheet of paper.

When he was finished he looked up. ''I've listed the cause of death as unknown.''

Ethan took a step closer. ''But I told you...''

The sheriff cut him off by lifting a hand. ''I saw the bullet wound. And the knife wound. And the lump on his head. Any one of which, in my opinion, could have killed a man. The cause of death will read 'unknown.'''

He could see matching looks on confusion on their faces. He folded his hands on the desktop. ''Most folks around here knew about Ezra Boomer's temper. The few who'd seen his pretty wife said they could see the evidence of his beatings. We figured his son wouldn't fare any better. But the truth is, most of us were reluctant to interfere in what we considered a man's own business. I'm not saying I'm proud of that, but that's just the way it is.''

He picked up the document. "Now I think you folks ought to be about your business, and let me get back to mine." He looked beyond them to where a cloud of dust came rolling up the little patch of dirt the town called a main street. "Looks like the stage is here. I'll have to get this information ready to send along to the federal judge.''

Kate couldn't seem to take it all in. "You're…through with us?"

"That's right, ma'am. You're free to go."

Free. The word seemed to echo in her mind.

Numbly she put her arm around Danny's shoulders and walked out the door, noting that the back of Ethan's cart was now empty.

Ethan turned toward the big wooden building next door. The sign over the door read McGuire Mercantile.

"While I'm here, I need to pick up some supplies."

He led the way, with Kate and Danny following. Once inside, Ethan hauled sacks of sugar and flour to his wagon until it was piled high with supplies.

When Ethan's wagon was loaded, and he'd

settled his bill, he turned to find Danny sitting in the dust of the street, his face buried in Blue's neck. When he saw Ethan, he got to his feet. In his hands was the box he'd been whittling.

Without a word he held it out to Ethan.

Ethan studied the smooth lid, the carefully hollowed-out interior. "You did a fine job, Danny."

As he started to hand it back Danny shook his head. "It's for you."

"Me?" Ethan arched a brow.

"To hold your tobacco pouch. I figure if you keep it on the mantel, you'll never have to search for it again."

For the space of a heartbeat Ethan couldn't think of a thing to say. Then he tucked it inside his shirt and offered his hand to the boy. "I thank you, Danny. I'll treasure it."

He expected the boy to be flushed with pleasure. Instead, the look on Danny's face nearly broke his heart. "What's wrong, son?"

The boy shook his head, searching for the words. "I'll miss you... And Blue."

"Miss?" Ethan's eyes narrowed. "Where's your aunt?"

Danny looked away, unable to meet that dark look. "She's talking to the stage driver."

With a muttered oath Ethan swept past him

and stormed down the street, leaving Danny running as fast as he could to catch up, with Blue keeping pace. At the stage, the driver was unloading the last of the bundles and carpet-bags. Standing to one side was Kate.

Ethan paused, curling his hands into fists to keep from shaking her. "Danny said you were inquiring about the fare east."

She nodded, avoiding his eyes.

His tone was bleak. "Why, Kate? I thought..." He cleared his throat. "I thought we had a future together."

She fiddled with the buttons on her shabby gown. "You don't have to do this, Ethan."

"Do what?"

"Try to be kind." She looked up, then away. "You're such a good man, Ethan. And I'm..." She licked her lips. "I lied to you. And because of that, look at all the trouble I brought to your door."

"Yeah." His tone was gruff. "Look at all the trouble. A woman who melts my heart every time I look at her. A boy I'd be proud to call my own." He saw the way both Kate and Danny stared at him, with matching looks of amazement.

His tone softened. "I thought I was happy living on my ranch all alone. I never thought to ask for more. But then you came along, Kate, and made me food, and mended my clothes, and made my heart so happy." He turned to Danny. "And you, son. There's so much I was hoping to teach you. Not just about whittling, and ranching, but about life."

The boy turned to Kate with a look so filled with pleading, her heart nearly broke.

Her brogue thickened. "Are you saying you still want us, Ethan? Even after all this?"

"I've never wanted anything so badly. I'm thinking there's a preacher here in town. We could have him say the words, and then if you'd like, we could spend the night here in town at the rooming house. You could sleep in a soft feather bed, and eat someone else's cooking for a change."

She touched a hand to her heart, afraid it might leap clear out of her chest. "I'd be your wife?"

He nodded. "And Danny would be our son."

"Oh, Ethan." She wrapped her arms around his neck and hugged him fiercely, then opened her arms so that Danny could step between them and share the hug. "You make me so proud."

Sensing the excitement, old Blue wiggled his way inside the circle, his tail twitching.

"And you make me so happy, Kate." Ethan caught her hand in his, then draped his arm around Danny's shoulders. ''Come on. Let's go find that preacher.''

As they danced down the street, she gave a delighted laugh. ''If you don't mind, I'd just as soon not stay the night at the rooming house, though. I'd much rather go home.''

Home.

Ethan thought it the grandest word. And now that he had this angel in his life, and a fine lad for a son, it truly would be a home. In fact, it was the closest thing to heaven he would ever know.

Dear Reader,

I was not an ideal mail-order bride, at least from a male viewpoint. I resembled the bottom of the barrel, to tell the truth. My only hope was for kindness and understanding from the man who'd sent for me. When the tall, stern-appearing but handsome farmer approached me on the train platform I prayed as never before. Jebediah Marshall wore the look of one who would live up to his promises.

Once we said our vows, I decided, he would be pretty well committed to me. I only had to get him that far. But beyond that point I'd no doubt find myself in a peck of trouble. Especially when he discovered the truth about his bride.

Louisa Winifred Applegate Palmer

SECOND CHANCE BRIDE

Carolyn Davidson

To the newest brides in the Davidson clan,
Brandi and Emily,
who have each found a place in my heart

CHAPTER ONE

Bender's Hill, Colorado
1890

JEBEDIAH MARSHALL stood apart from the
crowd. Not in just his physical appearance,
which was enough to make him stand out in
any company, but in actuality this morning. He
couldn't bring himself to join the group; just
watched the hubbub on the train platform from
a distance. Not that he wouldn't soon be involved in the ruckus going on.

He needed a few moments to think, to cogi-
tate on what he had set into motion with his
letter. It was too late to change his mind. He
was only too aware of that. But marriage was
a big step to take, and he was about half an
hour from leaping headlong into that state.

The train could be seen and heard. Whistle
blowing, smoke puffing from the engine, it approached from the east, vying with the rising
sun to make an appearance in the town of

Bender's Mill, Colorado. And aboard that train were close to twenty women. Women who had come from various cities and towns in the east to make their homes in this harsh land.

And one of those women was Louisa Winifred Applegate Palmer. His bride.

He pulled the paper from his pocket, reading it in the glow of the rising sun. She was a widow woman, which was fine with him. He wouldn't be expected to pamper and coddle her, since she would already be well used to married life. "Efficient in the home," the letter said. Hard to say what that meant. So long as she could put a meal on the table and keep his house and clothes clean, he wouldn't quibble.

The advertisement had been simple: Women Available. It didn't get any more basic than that. A woman was available, and he needed a wife.

The folded paper slid into his pocket and he straightened from his stance against the side of the train station. The men on the platform huddled beside the tracks, peering at the slowing engine, and he sauntered in their direction, satisfied with lingering on the edge of the crowd. Seventeen were expected, according to the wire sent by the agent handling the transaction. The original number was twenty, but three of them had changed their minds at the last moment.

Jeb felt a twinge of apprehension but shook it off. Just her name, *Louisa Winifred Applegate Palmer* was enough to project an aura of dependability. His bride would be among the number soon to depart the train. He'd spent long moments trying to visualize her, having only the briefest of descriptions offered in the letter. Dark hair, blue eyes, healthy constitution and of an age to have been married.

Now, as the train came to a halt, spewing cinders from beneath its wheels, he watched the conductor make an exit from the passenger car, his step stool in hand. Behind him, a golden-haired creature peered past the man's considerable bulk and Jeb could not help but wish his bride had the pink-and-white coloring of the first woman to make an appearance. She offered her hand to the jowly conductor and moved down the platform, as if she adhered to a script.

And so it seemed she had, for the rest of the women followed her lead, lining up three feet from the side of the train, their small valises and portmanteaus in hand. From the baggage car, down the platform twenty feet or so, a veritable stream of luggage spewed onto the platform, two men tossing trunks and suitcases to the waiting station master. He stacked them haphazardly, already sweating profusely, his face glowing, grumbling loudly at the work inherent with so many passengers departing the train at one time.

Jeb counted, an almost unconscious activity, as the women assembled. An assortment of females, ranging from small to large, several of them downright plump, he noticed with a grin. They wore decent clothing, hats perched atop hair in various styles, curled, braided or in buns. Some were comely, easy on the eyes. Others were homely, but to the men who waited, that was a small matter.

They were *women*. Here for a purpose. And the men hovered in a semicircle in front of them, like so many turkey buzzards closing in on their prey.

Sixteen. He'd counted sixteen, and the wire from the marriage agent had promised one more than that. The ladies themselves checked their number, then turned as one to where the conductor handed down the last of their group. Dark hair, Jeb noted. Somewhat on the rotund side, but with a pleasing face to balance out that fact. She stepped onto the step—a hushed whisper met her appearance as a heavy shoe touched, its sole built three inches higher than its mate—then down to the platform. A small murmur swept the waiting crowd of men.

The woman was a cripple, and Jeb felt a moment's sympathy for the man who had spoken for this creature. Not for her the hard life to be expected on a farm. She would require a bit of pampering, he'd warrant. No wonder she was somewhat on the plump side. Probably didn't get much chance to work it off, with a handicap that would prevent her getting around easily.

The women glanced at each other, and as if it were prearranged, they lifted pieces of paperboard from inside their outer clothing, the carefully printed signs appearing like magic from cloaks and coats to be displayed in front of their bodies. *Sue Ellen McPherson* read the nearest one, she of the golden hair and pert features. The next was *Isobel Jackson,* and beyond her the letters blurred as men moved forward, reaching nicely for their brides, their eagerness almost overcoming their gentlemanly behavior.

Voices rose as couples formed, and Jeb circled the crowd, looking over several heads in search of the name he sought. Only three women remained unclaimed, separated by several feet, as their companions were towed away by the men who had paid their fare. A cluster of buggies and wagons awaited, and young boys who'd gathered early to view the happenings this morning were pressed into service to help with baggage.

It was a hubbub of movement and Jeb felt his heart beat heavily as he waited for the

crowd in front of him to part. Like the movement of the Red Sea at Moses' command, it
flowed to either side and he was faced with his
future.

Hands trembling, she stood before him. Even
from the distance of four yards he noted the
wobbling of her paperboard. The sign that read
Louisa Winifred Applegate Palmer. There was
no mistake. Not only was she the last to be
claimed, she was his bride. Dark hair, blue eyes,
eyes that possessed a calm detachment, no matter the trembling of long fingers against the
identifying sign she held.

And on her feet were black, sturdy shoes, one
looking normal to his eyes, the other proclaim-
ing her problem, its three-inch sole allowing her
to walk in a manner that might be considered
normal. Whatever that word meant. And as if
that were not enough, on closer inspection he
could not help but note she was plump, her
outer clothing obviously covering a figure that
promised to take its full share of the wagon
seat.

Her face was narrow, her nose straight, her
eyes wide-set, and her hands were slender. Yet,
she was certainly a fleshy woman. And unless
he missed his guess, the other men were all
more than thankful that they had not drawn the
short straw. He stepped forward and met blue

eyes that were shiny. Surely not with tears, he hoped. She was presentable enough, but he could not abide a crying woman.

And the fact remained that she was not equipped to run a house and do all the chores expected of a farm wife. Still, he'd made a bargain, and he'd stick to it.

"Ma'am?" he spoke the single syllable in his rough voice, and she nodded.

"You're Jeb Marshall?"

"Yes, ma'am. I see by your sign that you're the woman I sent for."

"Am I what you expected?" she asked quietly. "If I don't suit, I can return on the next train to the east."

"You'll do," he told her, turning to where the pile of luggage was rapidly diminishing as farmers carried their brides' belongings away. Only a small trunk remained, and he looked at her questioningly. "That one yours?"

She nodded and stood there, as if rooted to the spot. Maybe she didn't want him to see her walk, he decided. If so, he'd allow her that small favor.

"My wagon's over there, the big one with the black team. I'll bring your trunk."

He stalked to where the leather-bound trunk waited, lifting it easily to his shoulder. At least she was traveling light, he thought, turning to follow her to the wagon.

She was there already, perched on the seat like a hen might set on a clutch of eggs. How she'd made it across the platform and onto his wagon so rapidly was a conundrum. He shrugged. Apparently he'd shortchanged her, thinking she could not get around easily. One point in her favor.

Her trunk slid into the back of the wagon, pushed to one side to make room for the supplies he planned on picking up at the general store. And then he climbed into the seat, beside her. "We're to go directly to the church," he said, shooting another glance in her direction. She nodded, then clutched at the wagon seat, preparing for the lurch of movement, and he lifted the reins, urging his horses into motion.

The small churchyard was crowded, even at this early hour being filled with townsfolk who were sightseeing, joining forces to welcome the women into their community. The ladies of the town made no attempt to conceal their curiosity, scanning the assembled group of brides. Some of their number had come to Bender's Mill under the same circumstances and been absorbed into the life of the town without hesitation. Women were a scarce commodity in the state and enjoyed a certain amount of prestige among the menfolk.

Outside the church, Jeb and his bride sat atop the wagon as the crowd gathered, waiting for the preacher to arrive. And then the Reverend Niles made an appearance, walking around the side of the small, white building, the parsonage being only fifty yards distant from the church. A small cemetery separated the two buildings and the town had left vacant a suitably large area for further development, death being a fact of life.

The double doors opened with a flourish and the man of the cloth stood to one side, welcoming each couple as they crossed the threshold. Jeb turned to the woman beside him, looking fully into her face for his first assessment.

"You ready?" he asked bluntly, waiting for her nod of agreement before he jumped from the wagon seat to the ground.

She swung to one side on the seat and gripped it firmly. "Hold on a minute," he said gruffly. "I'll give you a hand." Her nod was quick, and she waited until he rounded the team, tying them to the hitching rail before he approached her. His hands lifted and she placed one foot carefully on the top of the wagon wheel. Her good foot, he noted.

His hands clutched at her waist through the

layers of fabric and told the tale. She was rotund. He'd chosen the right word to describe
her. With a smothered grunt of effort, he lifted
her, noting that her heavy shoe swung freely as
he lowered her to the ground. Releasing her, he
met her gaze and she tilted her chin, a bit ar-
rogantly, he thought.

"You don't have to do this," she said quietly. "There's still time to change your mind,
if you're having second thoughts."

"No, ma'am. I made a bargain, and I'll stick
to it," he told her. "We'll sort everything out
later on." He offered his arm and she grasped
it, not a token touch against his forearm, but a
genuine clutch as her fingers held him for support.

They walked through the gate and up the dirt
path to the church door. One step led to the
small porch, another into the vestibule, and Jeb
watched carefully as she placed her foot firmly
before allowing the second to join it. She
limped, although not with as much notice as
he'd feared. But she obviously did not move as
readily as the other brides, who had made their
way inside with a flourish. He walked by her
side, allowing her to set the pace, and as she
paused beside one of the front pews, she
glanced up at him. With a nod, he ushered her
in and slid next to her onto the seat.

The preacher was at the pulpit, smiling benevolently at the assemblage before him. "Will you all rise," he said brightly. "Take the right hand of the woman you are going to marry," he told them, watching through his spectacles as the men followed his command.

Jeb glanced at the woman beside him and she offered her hand, ungloved and slender, fingers long and well-tended. Probably hadn't done much hard work in her life from the looks of the unlined skin.

"Now repeat after me," the preacher told them, and in unison they claimed their brides, speaking seventeen names at once, the clamor of male voices surrounding Jeb.

"I, Jebediah, take thee, Louisa Winifred," he said quietly. The words were familiar, since he'd been in the congregation during several weddings in the community over the past year. And then she spoke, her voice clear, yet soft. Hushed, as if she felt a sense of dignity in the vows she took.

"I, Louisa Winifred, take thee, Jebediah as my husband."

I'M PROMISING TO MARRY this man, and I don't even know his middle name. Louisa said the words, then repeated the vows she had taken twelve years ago, in another lifetime. *I've just promised to obey him.* The vow had stuck in her throat, but she'd repeated the syllables, aware that they must be spoken aloud.

And then the preacher raised his hands, blessing the gathering as a group, repeating words that should have made this a joyous occasion. And indeed it was, she realized as the menfolk surrounding her, with few exceptions, gathered their brides close and kissed them with enthusiasm.

Her own groom looked down at her, his eyes touching on the narrow, gold band he'd slid onto her finger. "We can exchange it for the right size at the general store," he told her. "I wasn't sure what size to get."

She examined her wedding band. "It's fine," she told him. In actuality, it was a bit snug, but time would take care of that issue. And then his arm circled her shoulders and she looked up at dark eyes that met hers, as a frown furrowed his brow.

"I think we're expected to kiss," he said quietly. His other arm pulled her closer and settled at the middle of her back. She turned awkwardly to face him, her heavily shod foot catching on the pew in front of them. Off balance, she fell heavily against his solid form, and he was delivered a solid kick against his groin.

"I'm sorry," she whispered, catching a quick

breath as she wished fervently for the child she carried to remain quiet. It was not to be. Another nudge pressed against Jebediah's body, and his eyes narrowed as he looked down at her.

Then his head dipped and firm lips touched hers, a brief touch of warmth against her chilled flesh. Without thinking, her tongue touched the center of her upper lip, and his gaze focused on that small movement.

"Well, ma'am," he said quietly. "It seems we're married. And I'd say we have something to discuss."

CHAPTER TWO

THE ROAD WAS ROUGH, two ruts, wide enough
for but one vehicle. At either side, Louisa saw
evidence that another wagon had pulled over,
perhaps making way for oncoming wagons to
pass. The grassy meadows surrounding them
spoke of moisture in the ground as spring flowers bloomed amid the tall, green growth. In the
distance, mountains loomed, and foothills took
on a lower stance before them.

She'd wondered what this country looked
like, and a faint sense of excitement rose within
her, contending with the apprehension that
seemed to be part and parcel of her these days.
Obviously, the man was angry. His jaw was set,
his eyes shadowed beneath his hat brim, and the
wide, tanned hands held the reins firmly.

He'd spoken not a word upon leaving the
church, only nodding politely at the minister
and those who called out well-wishes in their
direction. The other couples lingered a bit, the
brides obviously wanting to become acquainted

with the womenfolk. Jebediah had not given her that choice, just grasped her elbow securely and ushered her with as much haste as he could manage to the wagon.

"I can get up myself," she'd told him, darting a look at his set face, but he'd not allowed it. His hands grasping her with an abundance of strength, he'd helped her climb to the seat and then untied his team before he joined her. She'd sent shy smiles at the women who turned to watch her leave, sensing the sympathy they felt for her plight.

She'd overheard several of them talking on the train when they thought she was asleep, and knew that their interest was sincere. Voices muffled and heads together, they'd wondered aloud what fate awaited her. None of them had shunned her, only lent a hand when they thought she needed it, and for that she was grateful.

The ability to move around was rarely hindered by her leg, unless she wore no shoes. Then her impediment was obvious, and only Harry's love and encouragement had given her the courage to appear in public on his arm.

Harry. The man she'd loved wholeheartedly, who had given her two children. Three, counting the one she carried now. He'd never known of this babe, his death seven months ago coming before her pregnancy became apparent. The son and daughter she'd borne him were buried beside him in the small town outside Boston, and she knew that a part of her heart would remain there forever.

"We're almost there," Jebediah said brusquely from beside her. "We'll turn off just to the right, over this rise." He tugged a bit on the reins, and the horses slowed their trot, drawing the wagon into the lane that was as wide as the road they'd traveled. Well-worn by his coming and going, it stretched ahead of them for over a hundred yards, ending behind a house that faced the road.

It was not a large dwelling by any means, but stood two stories tall. Freshly painted, by the looks of it, it wore shutters on the front windows. Four of them, two on either side of the door. A porch stretched across the front, fully forty feet in length, and Louisa caught sight of a swing hanging from the ceiling. And then the wagon rounded the corner and halted near the back of the house.

Two rosebushes grew beside the porch, one on each side of the steps, their leaves fragile as they unfurled. The earth surrounding them looked damp, as if someone had recently poured water on the thirsty soil. That someone could only be her new husband, Louisa thought, and somehow that knowledge brought her comfort.

She sat on the wagon seat, watching as he tied the team and walked silently around the hitching rail to where she waited. His gaze was accusing as his eyes met hers, his mouth a thin line. Yet he held up his hands and she swung her feet over the side of the wagon.

"I can step on the wheel if that will make it easier," she offered. "I know I'm heavy."

Ignoring her words, his hands gripped firmly, his thumbs digging into her midriff as he lifted her, again holding fast until she could gain her feet. "I'll get your trunk," he said, turning aside. "Go on in the house."

Louisa reached to grasp her valise, lifting it over the side of the wagon, then climbed the three steps to the porch. The back door opened readily when she turned the handle, and she walked into the kitchen. Behind her, the screened door shut with a bang, but she paid it no notice, her eyes widening in surprise as she looked around the cluttered room.

Dishes stacked in the sink were crusted with dried food, and several flies rose from the pile to buzz overhead as she approached to examine the mess. Scum covered the surface of a wash pan, and the odor of stale, standing water met her nostrils. She turned to the stove, where heat

still radiated from an early-morning fire, and
shook her head in dismay. Food spilled on the
black burners had been allowed to turn to ashes,
and the scent of burnt coffee turned her stomach.

She looked around for a towel amid the clutter, and found one on the kitchen table. The
empty coffeepot was hot, and the towel protected her hand from being burned. Laying the
lid aside, she held the pot beneath the pump and
cooled it with a gush of water. The dregs of
coffee baptized the dirty dishes, and grounds
settled amid the clutter of plates and cups.

The closest window opened at her urging,
and she pushed back dingy curtains to allow the
spring breeze entry. Another window next to
the door was more difficult, sliding back down
when she removed her supporting hands, and
she noticed a piece of lumber on the floor at
her feet. Lodging it between the sill and the
bottom of the window frame, she managed to
keep the window open, and inhaled deeply of
the fresh air.

"I haven't spent much time cleaning up in
here," Jeb said from the doorway. His narrowed eyes dared her to criticize his house-
keeping efforts, and she refrained, reaching for
her valise as he crossed the room and went into

a hallway. "I'll put your trunk upstairs," he said, his footsteps heavy on the bare steps.

Louisa followed him, her breathing hampered by climbing and the effort of placing her foot firmly on each step as she followed in his wake. Standing at the top of the flight of stairs, she surveyed her surroundings. Four doors opened from the central hallway, and only one of them stood ajar. She watched as Jeb pushed it fully open and stowed her trunk beneath a window, then turned to face her.

"You want to talk now, or after you fix us something to eat?" he asked. "I don't know what you ate on the train, but I haven't had breakfast."

She dropped her valise to the floor and worked at the buttons of her enveloping cloak. It slid from her shoulders and she placed it on the back of a nearby chair. "If you expect me to cook, you'll have to wait until I do some cleaning up first," she said. "I don't work in a dirty kitchen."

His mouth twitched, and he approached her, his gaze sweeping over her belly and then up to meet her eyes. "You're treading on thin ice, ma'am," he said, his voice soft, but filled with a menace she respected, given his frame of mind. "There's eggs in the pantry, and a slab of bacon hanging from a hook there. I've got part of a loaf of bread and a bit of butter.''

"Do you by chance have a clean skillet?" she asked.

"If you don't know how to wash a frying pan, we have a real problem.''

"Well, if it's in the same condition as your coffeepot, breakfast may be a while coming,'' she retorted.

"You've got until I take care of the milk and feed the stock. I expect food on the table when I come back in the house.'' He walked past her and she heard his boots against the stairs, across the hallway and through the kitchen. The screened door slammed behind him, and she sucked in her breath, aware of the scents of horse and hay that permeated this room. Somehow he managed to keep his clothing in a decent state, but from the pile of trousers and shirts in a basket near the door, he hadn't used a scrub board in some time.

LOUISA WAS IN THE KITCHEN, sleeves rolled up, and searching for firewood to stoke the stove when he appeared at the back door. One arm stacked high with split wood, he marched across the floor and deposited his load into the kindling box. "You'll need that,'' he said, his mouth firm, his forehead set in a scowl.

She waited until the door slammed again, then chose several lengths of wood and added them to the coals deep within the stove. A reservoir on the side held warm water and she rinsed the wash pan, then filled it, adding soft soap she found in a jar beneath the sink. Her own skillets, back home, had been seasoned and only needed to be wiped before each use, but the one she found in Jeb Marshall's sink needed a full-scale scrubbing before she would place food on its surface.

The sound of chickens wafted in the windows, and she surmised he was feeding them their morning rations, maybe gathering eggs. Coffee being the first order of the day, she backtracked, washing the pot, then filling it with water. A sack of coffee sat on the kitchen table, and she measured a handful into the pot and placed it on the stove.

In the pantry, a crock on the shelf yielded over a dozen eggs and she cracked six of them into a bowl, then reached for the slab of bacon. The knife she found needed sharpening, but it would do for now, she decided, wiping the slab of meat with another towel, one that seemed fairly clean. After cutting thick slices, she placed them in the skillet, and put it on the hottest part of the stove.

The fire was blazing now, and she turned the

damper to better contain the heat, listening to the bacon sizzle as she stacked dirty dishes in the pan and poured more warm water over them. The buffet yielded more plates and cups, and she wondered if he just got them all dirty before he did a wholesale job of cleaning up. Somehow that thought tickled her funny bone, and she turned from the sink with a smile on her lips.

"I'm glad you've found something amusing," he said from the kitchen doorway. He stalked to the sink and viewed the soaking dishes. "If you'll move these, I'll wash for breakfast," he told her, then stood aside as she approached.

"I would think you could lift that pan to the drainboard," she said quietly. "I'm ready to slice bread and put it in the oven to toast."

His silence was followed by the sound of the wash pan being thumped on the wooden board, and then water splashed from the pump; and she sent a cautious glance in his direction as she opened the oven door. He bent over the sink, suds turning dark as he scrubbed at his hands and forearms. The pump splashed again and he rinsed his hands, then ran his fingers through his hair.

"There's clean towels in the pantry, second

shelf," he said, his voice brusque. "I'm in need of one."

She hesitated but a moment, then entered the pantry again and located the stack of dingy towels. Careful not to touch him, she gave the towel to him, then found a fork and turned back to the stove. The bacon smelled good, and she was pleased. At least his meat was not rancid. Aware of him at the table behind her, she felt clumsy, her movements stilted, and she felt perspiration gather on her forehead as she stood before the hot stove.

The eggs were fresh, the yolks yellow and the whites clear, and her fork beat them to a frothy mixture. The bacon was lifted to a plate and she poured the grease into an empty cup. With one more whisk of her fork, she turned out the eggs into the skillet and placed them back on the stove.

And still he was silent.

The bread was toasted to a turn and she drew it from the oven, feeling nausea wash over her as she straightened, a cramp in her back catching her unaware. Butter sat beneath a glass dome on the table, and she examined a knife from the drawer, deeming it clean before she brought it to place beside his plate. "You might butter the toast while you're waiting," she suggested. Though the questions in her mind begged to be spoken aloud, now did not seem the time, not if his stiff posture was any measure of his mood.

In moments, they sat across from each other, and she watched as he picked up his fork. "Will you ask the blessing, or shall I?" she asked.

His glare was answer enough, but he added to it with words that left no doubt in her mind as to where he stood in relation to the Almighty. "I work the farm and tend the stock. I buy the coffee and chop the wood to feed the stove. I don't see that I need to thank anyone for the work of my own hands."

Well, so much for saying grace. She bent her head, murmuring beneath her breath, mostly asking for patience to deal with the man who watched her from across the table. The eggs were perfect, light and fluffy, and the bacon crumbled nicely as she chewed. He would not rob her of her appetite. There was a house to be tended, and if the rest of it resembled the kitchen, she had her work cut out for her.

"Do you have a mop and a supply of soap and vinegar?" she asked, picking up her coffee to sip at the dark brew.

"Vinegar?" he asked. "What for?"

"To clean windows."

"Look in the pantry. If I have any, it's in

there. The mop is hanging on the wall. Hasn't been used in a while."

She looked up at him, swallowing the words she yearned to speak. Whatever she'd expected, it wasn't the surly man she'd gotten. Anger she could live with. His scorn was deserved, after being made the butt of gossip. For there would be that, she was certain. By now, every man who'd married a woman from the train would know that Jeb Marshall had gotten himself a pregnant bride. And with a limp to boot.

But she'd hoped for some discussion, a chance to explain her circumstances. Now it seemed she was not to be allowed that much courtesy. And then he pushed his chair back from the table and placed his hands on his thighs.

"When is your child expected?"

"In a month," she answered quietly.

"And where is the father? You said you were a widow."

She raised her head and forced the words from her lips. "I am a widow. He died seven months ago."

"Don't you have family to take care of you?"

She shook her head. "No one I could ask." Certainly not the elegant mother-in-law who had hated her from the first, certain her beloved son had married beneath himself. Nor Harry's brother, who had tried to comfort her with hands that took liberties and a mouth that searched out hers in a vulgar parody of the mating act.

"Didn't you think I deserved to know that you were in the family way?" he asked.

She shrugged and took in a deep breath. "If you'd known ahead of time, you wouldn't have married me. I needed a place to stay. Once I'm on my feet, I can leave, if you like, and you can divorce me. You'll certainly have grounds that will stand up in any court in the land."

"So we're to make the best of it until…" His pause was long, and then he spoke again. "Perhaps not. I'll make a bargain with you. Stay here until I can bring in a harvest. You can plant a garden and put it up so there'll be food for the winter months. And then," he said firmly, his chin jutting forward, "I'll put you and your child on a train, heading in any direction you like."

Without waiting for her reaction, barely looking in her direction, he rose from the table and headed for the back door. "There are a couple of old hens about ready for the stew pot," he told her over his shoulder. "Kill one of them and fix it for dinner. I won't be hungry until midafternoon.'' From the porch, his voice called out more instructions.

''I left the eggs here on the porch. They need to be washed. And there are vegetables in the root cellar. Some aren't worth using, but there's enough potatoes to last another few months if you sort them out.'' And then he was gone, long legs carrying him across the expanse of bare ground toward the barn.

CHAPTER THREE

SHE'D NEVER CLEANED a chicken in her life, let alone kill it first. Surely there was a prescribed way to go about the task, and that route must certainly begin with snuffing out the poor creature's life as rapidly and painlessly as possible.

Louisa thought of the corner butcher shop, where a chopping block stood at the back of the lot. Chickens had been brought there by some unknown farmer and the crates left in the shade, until the butcher's wife came out the back door to select them, one at a time, from the crate. From that point on, they were slaughtered and plucked, their innards removed and the bird washed before it took its place in the glass-fronted cabinet, where housewives pointed at the chicken of their choice and had it weighed.

But, for the life of her, she couldn't remember ever actually watching as the chickens went through the process. Her brother had described in great detail how the creatures flapped and tried to fly; all this, after the butcher's wife had

managed to eliminate their heads. Perhaps with
a hatchet, she thought as she removed her traveling dress and donned a wrapper more suited
to housework. Although, if the truth be known,
she didn't think she owned an article of clothing designed for wear while killing and cleaning a chicken.

The two hens Jeb mentioned must be the pair
ruffling their feathers in the dust, she decided.
Larger than the others, they seemed to be in
charge of the chicken yard, with the exception
of the rooster, who was noticeable because of
his bright red comb and his size. Wherever he
walked in the fenced-off area hens scattered before him, and Louisa developed an instant dislike to the vain creature.

From the barn, she heard the sound of a
man's voice and, following her hunch, went toward the big structure. Larger than the house,
it boasted two big doors, both of them open,
and within its depths she caught sight of Jeb.
He held a horse's hoof in his hand, bracing it
with his knee as he pried at it with an instru-
ment of some sort.

"Excuse me?" Louisa stood at the door,
scanning the wall to her left in hopes of finding
a hatchet hanging there amid the assortment of
tools.

"You're in my light," Jeb said. "I can't see

what I'm doing." She stepped inside, allowing the sun to shine past her to where he worked, and a moment later, he finished his task and lowered the horse's foot to the floor. "He had a stone lodged," he said, with a glance in her direction.

She shoved her hands in her pockets and stepped toward him. "At the risk of bothering you, I wondered where I might find a hatchet?"

"What will you do with it when you find it?" His eyes made a slow survey of her body, and she flinched, wishing for just a moment that the presence of a child within her belly did not make her so undesirable as a wife. If it were his own, his gaze would soften, she thought, and his mouth might curve in a smile.

Instead he glared. "Well? What do you want a hatchet for?"

"To kill a chicken." The answer seemed obvious to her, but he only shook his head, and wiped his hands on his trousers.

"Why can't you use a butcher knife?" he asked, stalking toward her. "There are two of them in the kitchen."

"I'm not sure I can do that." She knew very well she couldn't figure out how to saw at a live chicken's neck with a knife, even if she wanted to. A hatchet would surely be quicker and more humane.

"How many chickens have you butchered?" he asked, moving past her. And then he turned with his hands on his hips and eyed her with distaste. "Do you even know how to cook?" he asked dubiously. "Or isn't that one of your many talents?"

"Yes," she said sharply, "I can cook. I can also clean house and do the washing and bake bread." She limped toward him, painfully aware of her awkward movements. "But I grew up in town, where the butcher's wife prepared the meat, and my mother simply bought it, already cleaned."

Her hands imitated his, her palms and fingers spread wide across her hipbones. "Now. If you'll find a hatchet for me, I'll chase down a chicken and chop its head off and do all the rest of it."

"You grew up in town." He repeated her words woodenly. "Did you ever work in a garden? Or put up food in canning jars? Can you churn butter?"

"I grew up in a town, but not in *ignorance*," she told him. "We had a garden, and I used a churn at my aunt's farm."

"I'll get the chicken and take off its head. You go in and boil water to pluck the feathers."

"Boil water?"

"In a kettle on the stove," he said slowly,

enunciating each word carefully. "You do know what a kettle is, don't you?"

Arrogant and overbearing did not begin to describe the man, and the urge to smack him with the flat of her hand was almost overpowering. Instead, she nodded and made her way to the house, earnestly hoping he was not watching her progress. Sitting upright in a seat on the train for hundreds of miles had not been good for her hip, and it ached like the worst toothache she'd ever had.

As she gained the porch, she glanced back and saw him approaching the hens in the chicken yard. With a mighty squawk, one of them spread its wings, flapping them as it ran. The other was held tightly in Jeb's hand, his fingers clutching the feet as the hen twisted, trying to gain her freedom. Watching the proceedings was not Louisa's first choice, and she hastened to open the door and enter the kitchen.

The largest kettle in the pantry was called into use, and she filled it with warm water from the reservoir. Stoking the fire took only a moment, but refilling the reservoir with a bucket from the pump in the sink meant three trips across the kitchen floor. Water dripped from the bucket as she tracked back and forth, and the floor began to take on the sheen of mud. The man had obviously not washed up behind himself in months, if the state of his floors was anything to go by. Once the chicken was plucked and its innards removed, she'd best plan on scrubbing the wide planks beneath her feet.

"Let me know when the water comes to a boil," Jeb said from the porch. "I'll carry it outside for you."

"Thank you," she answered, thankful for small favors, then watched as he stalked back toward the barn. The chicken hung from a sagging clothesline just beyond the outhouse, limp and bedraggled, its head nowhere to be seen.

IF SHE NEVER ATE another piece of chicken, it would be too soon. Louisa sat down at the table and silently said grace over her plate of vegetables. She'd made a pan of biscuits, since the supply of bread was short, and then set a fresh batch to rise on top of the warming oven. Once they were mashed, the potatoes didn't show signs of age, and the carrots she'd salvaged from the pile in the root cellar had cleaned up well. A pint jar of green beans cooked to a fare-thee-well with bits of bacon made up the rest of her meal.

Jeb ate his way through a platter of fried chicken, and she watched him scan each piece as he lifted it to his plate, his look puzzled. As if he'd never seen its like before, he took his fourth helping, turning it to peer at the underside. "What's this?" he asked.

"Chicken." She filled her fork and ate with relish. Perhaps next time would be easier, but cleaning her first chicken had not done much for her appetite, and cutting it into pieces was a new experience. The grocer back home had always done it for her.

Jeb's shrug was dismissive and he bit into the crusty brown meat with relish. "I take back my snide remark, ma'am," he said politely. "You're a good cook, if this is any example."

She moved the platter a bit farther from his plate. "If you don't eat it all, you'll have some left for your supper."

"I can make do with bread and a glass of milk before I go to bed," he told her. "We're eating late. This isn't my usual time for a midday meal."

Louisa pushed her chair back from the table and rose, feeling some bit of advantage as she looked down at him. "I was wondering. Is it necessary for me to share your bedroom? Seeing as how you've already made plans to ship me off once your crops are in?"

"You're my wife. You'll sleep in my bed." He wiped his mouth with the napkin she'd provided, having found a store of them in the buffet drawer. "There aren't any beds in the other rooms that will fit you."

"I don't require anything larger than a single bed," she said quietly. "I'm sure you'd be more comfortable sleeping alone."

"I don't have any spare beds," he said stubbornly. "You'll sleep in mine."

She looked down at the floor, searching for words that would express her dislike of that idea, and caught sight of dark clumps of dirt beneath his feet. "I washed this floor just before we ate. I'd appreciate it if you took your boots off at the door, or at least thumped them on the porch to get rid of the dirt before you come in the house."

He glanced down and nodded. "All right. I didn't notice." And then his eyes roamed the room and he nodded. "You've washed the windows." He looked toward the sink and his gaze touched her, one eyebrow lifting as he spoke. "And the dishes. Now I'll take back the other remark."

"Which one?" She stifled a smile of triumph.

"When I doubted your abilities. Now, if you are able to produce clean clothes from a wash boiler and scrub board in the morning, I'll fix the clothesline for you."

"I'd say you are the soul of generosity," she

told him, willing her blood not to come to the boiling point. "I'll do the washing out in the yard, but I'll need you to carry out the copper boiler for me."

"All right." He pushed back from the table, eyeing the rest of the chicken. "Maybe I'll have that with my bread and milk before bedtime," he said.

Louisa watched him leave, then snatched up the broom from the pantry and made short work of his trail of dirt. Opening the screened door, she swept the mess out on the porch, then in moments used the broom to briskly scatter the leaves that had blown beneath the swing and vanquish the dirt that lingered in the corners.

Weary and more than ready to rest, she worked on, unable to sit with her hands folded when the house cried out for attention. Someone, sometime, had lovingly placed pieces of bric-a-brac around in the parlor. Pictures in oval frames sat atop the mantel and on the library table before the front window. Middle-aged men and women, several of them with children in various poses, caught her eye. And in the center of a piecrust table, beside the sofa, a formally posed woman looked up at a man whose handsome face was bent to return her silent gaze.

Dressed in a pale gown, she held a small

nosegay of flowers, and a band of the same blossoms circled her head. Louisa bent closer, her cloth touching the glass, removing the layer of dust specks from the frame as she examined the pair who were so intent on each other. Oblivious to all but themselves, they'd obviously ignored the presence of the man who caught their image with his camera lens.

"What are you doing?" From behind her, Jeb's voice was strident, his movements swift as he approached and snatched the picture from her hand.

"Dusting," Louisa said quietly. "I didn't realize there were things I mustn't touch in the house. Perhaps you'd better make a list for me."

She turned awkwardly and walked from the room, hearing the opening and closing of a drawer behind her.

BEDTIME CAME with the rising of the moon, and Louisa looked around at the kitchen before she headed for the staircase. One room in decent shape, except for the walls, which she had only managed to dust with a rag on a pole. The parlor was as clean as a carpet sweeper and dust cloth could make it. The rug must be thrown over a line and beat, but not this week, she thought stoically. Probably not even this month.

Not unless the man she had married, just this morning, was willing to take on the task. And that didn't seem likely.

As she reached the bottom of the staircase, he came in from the back porch, and she heard the solid thud of the heavy door as he closed it for the night. She was halfway up the flight of stairs when the distinct sound of the lamp chimney settling into place reached her ears. Her hand on the railing, she pulled her weight up the final step.

Behind her, his feet made no sound on the hallway floor, and she realized he must have removed his boots. *That's one for my side.* The thought might be snide, but she gloried in it, recognizing that she had made a small inroad. Now to find her nightgown and get undressed and find her way into the bed before he appeared.

"I'll give you ten minutes," he said from the foot of the stairs. "Do you need warm water?"

"No, thank you. I've already washed." She moved slowly, carefully, aware of pain that radiated from her spine to her hip and down the length of her leg. Soaking in a hot tub might help, but that was out of the question tonight. Perhaps tomorrow, while he was working somewhere on the farm and she had a bit of privacy.

Holding her candle high, Louisa paused to rest for a moment at the top of the stairway, then bit at her lip. Only a few more minutes and she could slide between the sheets and close her eyes. Her foot dragged as she labored toward the bedroom door, and once inside, she leaned back against the solid piece of wood, tears forming in her eyes as she remembered other nights, in another place. Another life.

And then she shook her head at the foolishness of her thoughts. Not for her, ever again, the loving arms of a husband to hold her against the darkness, whose hand might massage the painful joint and bring relief to the pain that plagued her daily.

Harry was gone and, with him, the happiness she'd found. Some women never have what I had with him, she thought. I'll be satisfied with memories, and not wish for what will never be. Depositing the candle on the table beside the bed, she straightened and looked around the room.

Her trunk was where Jeb had dropped it early this morning, and with more effort than she'd realized it would take, she lifted it, to place it on the bed. Beneath the top layer of clothing and personal items lay a blue batiste gown. It had seemed quite modest the day she'd packed it there. Now she held it up to where the candle cast its glow and decided it was anything but.

Not that there was much to take a man's eye should he look at her, she realized, peering down at the heavy bulge beneath her wrapper. And with that, the child within her jerked and kicked as if protesting its mother's dour thoughts. Louisa smiled, resting her hand against the curve of her pregnancy. A small fist or knee poked at her palm and she smiled, love for her unborn child filling her almost to overflowing. This baby would help to fill the void in her heart. Not that another child could take the place of the two she'd lost, but her arms would be empty no longer.

The sound of pressure against a step, with an ensuing creak, caught her attention and she gathered up the gown and carried it to the far side of the room, where shadows gave a small vestige of privacy. A screen made a triangle of that corner of the room and she moved it, standing behind it as the door opened.

"Are you ready for bed?" Jeb asked, standing in the doorway, his head only an inch or two from the lintel overhead.

"Not yet," Louisa said, knowing she was effectively hidden in the shadows, yet feeling vulnerable as he scanned the corner where she stood. "I'm just putting on my gown."

"All right," he said, stepping back through

the doorway and into the hall. "Let me know when you're decent."

"I've been decent all my life," she muttered, pulling the gown over her head, then tackling the buttons and ties that bound her into her clothing. It was a struggle, working within the folds of the gown, but she managed. The wrapper, and the vest she wore beneath it, joined the petticoat on the floor at her feet. Then she wriggled from her drawers, aware that continued growth of her belly would necessitate the addition of another gusset to their width.

Her heavy shoe caught in the fabric as she lifted her foot and she bent to snatch at the drawers, unwilling to remove her shoes here and be forced to walk the width of the room without their support. The wrapper, vest and petticoat were ready to be washed, all of them soiled from the work she'd accomplished today, and she folded the drawers with them, forming a bundle to place with Jeb's clothing in the basket. With no reason to linger any longer, she crossed to the bed, sitting on the edge of the mattress to remove her shoes and stockings.

As always, she made short work of the task, allowing only a glance at the leg that was disfigured. Then lifting the quilt and sheet, she slid beneath them. With an impatient rap on the door, Jeb called her name.

"I'm in bed," she said quickly, the words spoken in unison with the sound of the door opening. Stocking-footed, he walked across the floor and she heard the whispers of clothing being shed, then felt his weight on the opposite side of the mattress.

"Do you wear your hair up all night?" he asked, and she felt the penetrating warmth of his gaze against her back.

"Not usually." The pins were uncomfortable against her head, but the intimacy of taking them out and allowing her long hair to flow freely was not to be considered.

"You'd might as well be comfortable," he said, blowing out the candle she'd left on his side of the bed. And then he sighed and yawned. "Good night, Louisa Winifred Applegate Palmer Marshall."

Her lips compressed as she heard his sardonic recitation of her long list of names. A movement of her head caused one of the bone hairpins to jab into her scalp, and she sat upright, muttering beneath her breath. In mere seconds, the pins were removed and placed on the table beside her, and she ran her fingers through the weight of waist-length hair before she tucked the pillow beneath her head and closed her eyes.

CHAPTER FOUR

THE BEAUTY OF HER HAIR almost made up for her lack of grace and pleasing personality, Jeb decided, his footsteps heavy on the stairs. She'd risen at the first sound of the rooster greeting the dawn, and he'd watched her as she'd slid from the bed. Dark waves covered her back, almost touching the bed as she bent to put on her shoes and stockings. And then she stood, balancing herself on the footboard before she walked across the room.

Her limp was less noticeable this morning, and he'd wondered again how she'd been injured, what calamity had caused her to be cursed with the affliction that hindered her movement. Though his eyes were closed, he'd been only too aware of her as she stood at the window, sorting through the trunk that appeared to hold all her earthly belongings. And then she'd walked across to where the screen would shield her from his sight. In moments, she was out the door and he was left to linger behind, rolling to his back, hands propped behind his head as he contemplated the woman he'd married.

Now, entering the kitchen, he noted her deft handling of the knife as she cut bacon and placed it in the skillet. The bread she'd baked yesterday afternoon sat on the buffet, and she wiped her knife before she used it to slice thick slabs for their breakfast. It was obvious she'd cooked for a man, he decided.

"I'll milk the cow while you finish up," he told her, walking behind her to the door. She'd opened it already, allowing the breeze to waft through the kitchen, and he stepped out onto the porch as he heard her murmured assent.

She wasn't what he'd expected, but then life had a habit of dealing from the bottom of the deck where he was concerned. Seeming to have no fear of his moods, she'd given as good as she got yesterday, and his mouth twitched as he recalled her quick retorts. He'd see just how smart she was today, when Abigail showed up.

ELBOW DEEP IN WARM WATER and soapsuds, Louisa looked up as a buggy turned around the corner of the house and came to a stop near the porch. She wiped her brow with her forearm and halted the movement of her fingers against the scrub board, as the woman holding the reins lifted a hand in greeting.

"I'm Abigail, Jeb's sister," she said warmly. "And you must be Louisa."

"I was last time I looked," she answered, unprepared for company and feeling more than disheveled. Her hair caught up in a braid, then left to dangle down her back, garbed in her oldest dress and damp from the splashing of wash water, she knew she looked a sight. And kneeling beside the square washtub certainly didn't give her an air of dignity as she faced the visitor.

"I've come to bring Elizabeth back," the woman said brightly, ignoring her taciturn reply. She climbed down from the buggy and reached up to lift a small child from the seat. "Go say hello, sweetie," she said, her hand on the girl's shoulder as she urged her in Louisa's direction.

"Hello, Elizabeth," Louisa said obligingly, loathe to look long into the innocent blue eyes. The smile was dimpled, the hair blond and curling over her shoulders, and the little girl approached gingerly, as if she sounded out her welcome. And then Louisa looked up at the woman who watched her from beside the buggy.

"What do you mean, you brought her *back*?"

"I mean, I brought her back home. I kept her so Jeb could pick you up and get you settled in without having to cope with a four-year-old your first day here."

"She lives here?" Her disbelief was apparent, and the woman named Abigail only nodded.

"Hello, Abigail." Jeb's welcoming words brought Louisa to her feet, leaning heavily on the tub as she rose. She shook her dress, smoothing down the skirt, and looked directly into Abigail's eyes, her chin held high, prepared for whatever words were hurled in her direction.

Abigail's eyes widened as she inspected Louisa's girth, and then she flushed as she looked helplessly at Jeb. "That didn't take you long," she said, almost choking on the words, her hand flying to cover her mouth.

Jeb cast Abigail a fulminating glare, then held out his arms to the child. For the first time, Louisa saw a genuine smile light his eyes as he crouched to welcome his daughter to his embrace. "Come here, sweetheart."

Elizabeth ran to him and was swung from her feet as she reached for his neck, clutching him as if this reunion had been long in coming. "I missed you, Papa,'' she said. ''Auntie Abigail read me a story, but she can't do the voices like you.''

''What can I say?'' Abigail spread her hands in a gesture of defeat. ''I'll never be a success as an actress.'' And then she met Louisa's eyes. ''I'm not much on tact, either.''

Now that was something she could relate to, Louisa decided, and for all the other woman's inept behavior, she could not help but like her.

Insofar as acting was concerned, it seemed that the man who held the child to his chest had done an admirable job, Louisa thought. He'd made much of the fact that his bride was not as promised, but had failed to mention the fact that he himself came equipped with a child. She allowed her gaze to speak for her, holding her silence as she watched and listened.

''...and then we made cookies, Papa. And Auntie Abigail—''

His index finger on the child's lips effectively halted her effusive tale and Jeb shook his head. ''Later, sweet. For now, you need to speak with Louisa.'' He lowered her to the ground and led her three steps to where his bride waited. ''Louisa is going to live with us, Elizabeth. We got married yesterday.''

''What's that mean?'' The child darted a look at Louisa, then backed up to press against

266   SECOND CHANCE BRIDE

her father's legs. "Are you really gonna live here?" she asked, excitement rising in her voice. "Can you bake cookies like my auntie Abigail?"

It was not in her to shun the child or to be rude to such a guileless moppet, and Louisa dredged up a smile, nodding agreeably. "Yes, I'm going to live here," she allowed, with a quick look at Jeb. "And I can bake cookies, and I know how to make clothes for a baby doll. Do you have one?"

Elizabeth shook her head. "I got a grown-up-looking dolly, but she's not a baby."

"Well, maybe we can make her some grown-up clothes," Louisa told her. "But right now I have to wash some grown-up clothes, so your papa will have a clean shirt to wear tomorrow."

"Come and get Elizabeth's washing, Jeb," Abigail told her brother, tugging a wicker basket from beneath the buggy seat. She shot a glance at Louisa and grinned. "It looks to me like you've got enough there to keep you busy all morning. I'm glad I thought to do Elizabeth's things up with ours."

Jeb reached for the basket and let it thump on the ground before he lifted his arms to assist Abigail from the buggy. "You planning on staying for a while?" he asked.

"I think we need to discuss some things for

a few minutes," Abigail told her brother, grasping his arm. "Talk to Louisa a bit, why don't you, Elizabeth? Then we'll take a look at the new kittens. All right?" Without awaiting a reply, she steered Jeb toward the barn, and Elizabeth turned her attention to Louisa.

"We got babies in the barn," she said cheerfully. "And when they get their eyes open I can hold them. Only they got claws and they might scratch if I'm not careful."

"Kittens will do that," Louisa said, watching as Abigail bent her head toward Jeb, speaking quietly as they walked inside the barn.

"Will you go and see them with me every day?" the child asked. "It's more fun if you come along, because big people can pick them up, and then I can put my finger on their fur and pet them a little bit." Elizabeth squatted beside the washtub and brushed a stray lock of hair from her eyes.

"Will you wash my dirty clothes next time?" she asked after a moment, and Louisa's hands stilled their movement on the scrub board as the child's expression sobered. "Are you sure you're gonna still be here tomorrow? For every day, from now on?" she asked.

"I'll be here," Louisa told her firmly, her heart expanding as the moppet crept into that place which ached to hold just such a elfin being. Feeling a tug, Louisa looked down at the golden-haired child, and noticed one dimpled hand clutching firmly at the side of her wash dress, as if a modicum of security were to be found there.

And then blue eyes looked up and simple trust glowed from their depths. "Did you know I used to have a mama?"

"I suppose you did," Louisa said quietly. "Do you know I used to have a little girl?" She hesitated and then her hand lifted to touch the sunlit hair. "I used to have a little boy, too."

"Did they die, like my mama?"

The words, so easily spoken, touched her as if a sword had been driven into her heart, and Louisa could only nod. Her fingers sifted through the curls and caught on a tangle, and she bent her head to separate the strands. A fullness in her throat warned her of tears to come and she swallowed, attempting to stave them off as Elizabeth stepped closer to her, her fingers buried now in the drab fabric of Louisa's skirt.

"It makes me cry, too, sometimes, when I think about my mama." And then she whispered softly, as if it were a confession, "I don't really remember her, you know, but I just feel funny inside when my papa looks sad, and it makes me want to cry a little bit."

"Well, we're not going to cry today," Louisa said briskly, blinking rapidly. "We've got too much to do."

"Can I help you?" Hopeful eyes lifted and a smile played around the pink lips.

"You can hand me the clothespins when I get ready to hang the clothes." She looked up to where Jeb and Abigail stood just outside the barn, and lifted her voice for their benefit. "Your papa told me he'd fix the clothesline, but he hasn't done it yet."

JEB HEARD THE WORDS that repeated his promise and nodded. "I'll have the line strung tight and washed by the time you're ready for it." He held out a hand to Elizabeth. "Come say goodbye to your aunt Abigail."

"Aren't you going to stay for a while?" She ran to her aunt and hugged her, her arms not long enough to enclose her hips in an embrace. Abigail bent to place a warm kiss on Elizabeth's forehead and then looked up at Louisa.

"No, I have to go home. Your uncle Tim will be looking for his dinner pretty soon, and I need to get it ready for him. I'll come another day, and maybe Louisa and I can have a nice, long visit."

"That would be...interesting," Louisa said,

drawing out the word as if she were already anticipating the event.

She bent to her task, wringing a shirt between strong fingers, gripping to the fabric firmly, as if it were the neck of the man she watched.

"I THINK I'd better take a look upstairs," she announced at the dinner table. "I might not have been taken unaware had I known there was a little girl's bedroom up there. And on top of that, I could have washed her bedding when I did yours." She lifted a slice of bread and bit into it neatly. "Does she still use a crib to sleep in?" she asked, flashing a look at the man across the table.

"No, of course not," he answered. "What I should have told you was that there isn't an extra bed available in the house for your use. Elizabeth sleeps in it." He dished up a second helping of stew from the bowl, not meeting her gaze. "You know you're free to look in any room in the house. Although you'll find two of the bedrooms upstairs empty. I haven't needed them."

She latched onto his claim. *You're free to look in any room in the house,* he'd said, and the words begged a disclaimer. "No, I didn't know that. The doors upstairs are closed, and

I'm sure I felt a distinct lack of welcome when I was in the parlor.''

"That was something else, altogether,'' he said gruffly. ''I hadn't mentioned everything you needed to know, and you caught me unaware.''

"Well, then perhaps we need to discuss things a bit more thoroughly,'' she told him, suddenly recognizing the silence from Elizabeth. Her eyes had widened as she took in each and every word spoken, and she had ceased eating, seeming to shrivel against the back of her chair.

Louisa shot a quick smile at the little girl. ''But for now,'' she said quickly, ''Elizabeth and I have some chores to do, and then we're going to visit the kittens in the barn.'' Rising, she beckoned his daughter, and bent her attention to the girl as she led her from the kitchen.

"What chores do we gotta do?'' Elizabeth asked, her good spirits restored as she skipped by Louisa's side across the yard.

"Well, the clothes are dry, so we have to take them off the line. Then we'll put the pins away and fold the sheets so they won't get wrinkled before we make the bed.'' With quick movements, Louisa gathered the assortment of garments in her left arm, handing the clothespins to Elizabeth as she slowly moved the length of the line. With her arms loaded, and almost unable to look over the top of her dry laundry, she headed toward the house.

"Wait for me," she said. "I'll be right back." Elizabeth nodded agreeably, and squatted where she was, idly playing with the clothespins in the small wicker basket.

"I'll just leave these here for now," Louisa told Jeb, dumping her load into the waiting clothes basket. Quickly, she held up the sheets for his bed and folded them in quarters before placing them over the back of a chair.

He watched her silently, and she walked out onto the porch, grasping the upright post as she carefully descended the steps.

THE HOUSE WAS DARK and silent when he entered the kitchen door. Elizabeth had been asleep for hours, as probably was Louisa. Surely the woman must be weary, after the day of work she'd managed to handle. He'd held Elizabeth on his lap in the parlor, told her the requested story, then kissed her cheek and watched as she climbed the stairs. Pacing herself to Louisa's gait, she clung to the woman's fingers, and chattered happily as they made their way to the second floor.

He'd headed from the house to walk through the pasture, hoping he would dodge the leavings of his cow and horses. He couldn't face her right now, and felt a cowardly impulse to find a place in the barn to spend the night. After making a big to-do about her keeping secrets, he'd had to face the fact that his own motives were not lily-white. And had been shamed by her easy acceptance of his child.

As if she'd spent years tending children, she'd known what to do with Elizabeth, her movements almost involuntary. From issuing small orders as they set the table together, to the final wiping of hands and face and brushing of the child's golden hair as she readied her for bed, Louisa had filled the gap he'd labeled in his mind as *mother*.

He knew she was bristling with questions, much as he had found them beating at the back of his mind upon her arrival only yesterday. And that was another thing he could not fathom. Could it be less than forty-eight hours since he'd spoken those words of commitment inside the small church in Bender's Mill? It seemed a lifetime had passed since he'd felt the definite nudge of a small hand or foot against his groin. And known that the woman he'd just spoke vows with, and held in an embrace, carried another man's child in her body.

He'd watched as the lamp went out in the kitchen, then seen the flickering glow of candlelight in the upstairs bedroom. Standing beneath a tree, he'd caught a glimpse of her form, well-rounded with the child she carried, wearing a voluminous gown as she passed in front of the window. The candle glow vanished, and still he'd waited.

Now, in the silence, he thought he heard her breathing as he entered the bedroom. Shedding his clothing near the door, he approached the bed, and spoke softly.

"How angry are you?"

She laughed, the sound smothered as though she feared to wake his daughter with her mirth, and rolled to her back, a shadowed form against the pale sheet. "I'd say we're about even, Mr. Marshall, each of us with our own surprises."

He sat on the edge of the bed and looked over his shoulder at her. "Maybe so. But I still think you're one up on me."

"Because I limp? Certainly not because I'm going to have a child. You're years ahead of me on that one." She shifted in the bed, her movements clumsy as she rolled to her side. "And while we're talking about years, I think I'm well beyond you."

"Beyond me?" He'd wondered, noting the fine lines at the corners of her eyes, and a small streak of white that touched her left temple. "How old are you, Louisa?"

"Thirty-two. Thirty-two, going on sixty, some days."

"Because of your loss?"

She was silent, and he waited, although patience was not a quality he could boast of. But now it seemed to be required of him.

"More because of my leg, I think," she said finally. "Although sorrow tends to age a person, I've found." She waited until he lifted the sheet and made himself comfortable beside her. "I think you know what I'm talking about, don't you?"

He laughed, a brittle sound that held no amusement in its depths. "I've lived with grief for over three years," he said. "Since Elizabeth's mother died."

"Then it's time to put it aside," she said firmly, and he turned his head, seeking her gaze in the shadows of the room.

"Have you?" His words doubted it, and then he remembered her grim determination to cope with the situation he'd thrown at her. "Yes, I think you have. Perhaps better than I."

"It was either handle it or jump into Boston harbor," she said flatly. "And I chose to live."

CHAPTER FIVE

HIS DAUGHTER certainly didn't believe in beating around the bush, Jeb decided. Her voice in the kitchen was loud and clear, and he hesitated on the porch, watching through the screened door as he waited for Louisa's reaction to the child's query.

"Are you gonna be my new mama for always?" Her blue eyes were wide as Elizabeth climbed up onto a chair and pulled her skirts down to cover her legs. She looked up expectantly at Louisa. "My papa said this morning I could call you mama if I wanted to."

As indeed he had, he recalled, grinning widely. Elizabeth had been adamant that such a thing should be, and he'd nodded and agreed that she should approach Louisa with her idea.

Now Louisa stilled the movement of her spoon, gazing down at the scrambled eggs as if she searched for some brilliant answer to the child's query. "Did your papa think that was a good idea?" She glanced at Elizabeth and her hand hesitated its movement, as if the child's answer was of great importance.

Elizabeth considered that notion for a moment, and then grinned widely. "Well, I asked him first if I could, and he didn't say anything till I asked him again. But then he said did I think I needed a new mama, and I said if it was gonna be Louisa, then it was all right." She folded her hands and looked up expectantly.

"I think it would be nice to have a little girl call me mama," Louisa said quietly, her movements stilling, her back stiff, and Jeb thought he caught a whisper of tears in her voice.

Elizabeth continued her coaxing in earnest. "I told my papa that I'd be extra good and not be any trouble to you. And I told him it would make you feel better and maybe you wouldn't cry anymore about how your babies died and my mama died, if you had somebody to call you mama."

"You told your papa..." Louisa's spoon went into motion, working rapidly as the scent of scorched eggs wafted upward.

"It seems my daughter knows more than I do about any number of things," Jeb said from the kitchen doorway, taking pity on his wife and her dilemma. Opening the screened door, he came in the kitchen and Elizabeth slid from her chair to clutch at him, gleefully announcing her good news.

"Did you hear, Papa? Did you hear my new mama telling me?" He reached down and lifted her into his arms, and she hugged him, whispering her victorious plans in his ear.

Louisa turned, skillet in hand, and carefully spooned out the parts that were still edible. "The eggs got away from me," she said, refusing to meet Jeb's eye. "You two go on and eat, and I'll cook some more."

Jeb, his arms full of an exuberant child, came across the kitchen to where she was scraping the burnt residue from the pan into the bucket of scraps for the pigs. "I think there's enough for the three of us, Louisa. We'll have plenty to eat." The urge to include her in his embrace was strong, but he feared it would result in her embarrassment, and that would never do.

She nodded, and settled the skillet on the drainboard. "I'll clean this up later," she said, wiping her hands on her apron as she headed back to the stove. A plate of sausage waited in the warming oven, toasted bread already buttered beside it. A quick trip to the pantry provided a jar of jam, and breakfast was ready.

Elizabeth waited in her chair and Jeb washed his hands at the sink, aware of Louisa's apprehension. She was not willing to speak of her past with him, yet Elizabeth had been her confidante and it stung him to be excluded.

As he watched, she bent her head over her plate and whispered a short prayer beneath her breath, lifting her head to see Elizabeth's eyes intent on her.

"Who were you talkin' to?" the child asked bluntly.

Louisa hesitated for only a moment, then casting a glance at Jeb she answered simply, "I was thanking God for my food."

Elizabeth's smile was quick. "Aunt Abigail goes to church to visit with God sometimes. And when I was at her house, we all held hands and Uncle Tim said stuff out loud about being thankful for his food." She tore off a piece of toast and looked at it, then darted a glance at Louisa. "Am I supposed to do that before I eat my toast?"

"Maybe your father—"

"I think we could let Louisa say her prayer out loud from now on, and it would probably cover everyone's food, Elizabeth. Does that sound like a good idea?" Jeb's jaw was set as he looked at Louisa, and she agreed with a quick nod.

"Let's do it over, then," the child said firmly. "And when I get big, maybe I can do the talking to God."

"Maybe tonight, before you go to bed, we can discuss this a little," Louisa told her. "And if you want me to, I'll say grace for our breakfast." Her look in Jeb's direction was inquiring, but he only nodded briefly.

Elizabeth held out her hands to her father and Louisa, then closed her eyes tightly, thus missing the awkward moment when Jeb's wide palm engulfed Louisa's narrow fingers. Her fingers trembled in his grip, her flesh was chill against his warm palm, and she spoke quickly, as if she could scrape up nothing more than a simple line of thanksgiving, then a halting "Amen."

Elizabeth repeated the final word in a solemn tone. "Aunt Abigail says that, too, after Uncle Tim says the other stuff," she announced, picking up her fork and digging into the eggs on her plate.

Louisa ate the eggs Jeb scraped onto her plate, chewed dutifully at the sausage, and spread jam over her slice of bread. Her head was bent over her plate, yet he'd be willing to bet his bottom dollar she was aware of the attention he shed on her every movement. His ponderings must be spoken aloud, he decided. There was much to be discussed, and he had waited long enough to have his curiosity put to rest.

The first item on his agenda was to have Elizabeth out of hearing, and so he turned to her with an encouraging smile. "I think you need to go up and take the sheets from your bed, Elizabeth. Bring them downstairs, along with any other dirty clothing we missed, and I'll get the washtub ready for Louisa to use."

"All right," the child said agreeably. "I can help her hang them on the line, too." She skipped from the kitchen and clattered up the stairs, her father silent as he listened to the sound of her shoes on bare wood. And then he turned his attention to Louisa.

"I eavesdropped shamelessly, and I owe you an apology for that. On the other hand, I'm not sorry I heard what Elizabeth said. If her turning you into a mother again is too painful for you, I'll talk to her and set things straight." He spread a generous helping of jam on his bread and took a bite, watching her as he chewed.

"No, I don't mind if Elizabeth wants to pretend I'm her mother. I just fear that she will be hurt when you send me away after harvest. And I would never do anything, knowingly, to hurt a child."

"I believe that, Louisa. I watched you with her yesterday. She's taken to you in a big hurry. Maybe she really does need a mother. I thought I'd done well by her, but a woman's touch is another thing altogether when it comes to a girl.''

Louise lifted a hand, shaking her head. ''I can't find any fault in you as a father. She wouldn't be the child she is if you hadn't taken good care of her and loved her.''

''Well, for now, let's not worry about what will happen after the harvest,'' he said harshly, wishing she hadn't brought up the deadline he'd set. Louisa watched as he rose from the table and headed for the backyard. Shame swept over him as he looked out into the yard and remembered her as she'd knelt before the washtub just yesterday.

''Call me in when the water for washing is hot, and I'll carry it out for you,'' he said, turning back to offer an offhand apology. ''You needn't kneel on the ground to scrub clothes. I'm sorry I didn't think of carrying out the bench from the back room for you to put the washtub on yesterday. I'll do it from now on.''

She nodded, smiling, her eyes lighting at his words, and he added regret to the shame he felt. Struggling up and down from the ground was a difficulty he could have prevented, had he thought ahead. No matter. It would no longer be an issue.

Perhaps he needed to provide some sort of delight that would bring that smile to her lips again. He'd put forth very little effort to please her, and for the most part, she was without complaint. She was sassy and outspoken, but not a complainer.

"Make a list for the general store," he told her. "We'll go to town tomorrow and get whatever you think we need."

THE TRIP TO TOWN yielded seed for the garden, and between caring for the house and planting vegetables in the soil Jeb made ready for her use, Louisa managed to only plan ahead one day at a time. She'd gardened before, but not to this extent, and some days only Elizabeth's joyous enthusiasm kept her going. And yet, she found satisfaction in the tasks inherent in being a wife and mother, even the chores of cleaning and cooking.

Watching the first tiny, green tendrils of peas, beans and carrots was a delight, one Elizabeth greeted with applause and an announcement to her father that he must come and look at the garden. He approved of it at great length, and then spoke quietly to Louisa.

"I'll take care of the hoeing and weeding until you're back on your feet." His gaze touched her belly and his words were soft. "It won't be long now, will it?"

"No. A few weeks, perhaps." And it couldn't be too soon to suit her.

THE DAYS BEGAN to run together, with one small obstacle after another being faced and dealt with. Louisa was beginning to feel languid, her back aching most days, sending her to bed as soon as Elizabeth's nightly ritual was complete. She didn't have the energy to argue with Jeb, it seemed, and he in turn spent most of his time in the fields, having hired on a pair of young men from town for the summer months.

They spoke little, Louisa intent on the coming birth, giving all her energy into Elizabeth's care, and Jeb putting in long hours, cutting hay and bringing it into the barn. He rose early, yet most mornings Louisa was up first, dressing with haste and leaving the bedroom while he lingered in bed. When he arrived in the kitchen, it was the usual thing to find the coffee brewing and breakfast begun.

Until one morning a little more than a month after her arrival.

No scent of coffee met his nostrils as he entered the kitchen, and stranger yet, Louisa's familiar form was nowhere to be seen. His heart jolted as he stood in the doorway and looked expectantly toward the pantry. "Louisa?" He called her softly, and then, when there was no reply, spoke her name a bit louder.

The stove sent off no warmth as he walked past, and he touched the coffeepot, already certain that it was still cold from the day before. Louisa was nowhere in sight.

Birds called from the orchard and the cat sat on the porch, silently begging a handout. Nursing six kittens was hungry work, and Louisa had taken to giving her scraps from the table. They could have been better used in the pig trough, but if it pleased the woman to feed the cat, Jeb was willing to let her have her way.

He stepped onto the back porch and looked around the yard. From the barn the cow sent forth an appeal, her bag no doubt heavy with milk, and Jeb stopped to pull on his boots before he headed in that direction. "Louisa!" His call was louder now and concern edged his voice. And then he heard her.

"Jeb?" She stood in the doorway of the outhouse, her robe barely meeting over the enormous rounding of her pregnancy. Her fingers were clasped beneath her belly, and she leaned her head against the door.

"What's wrong?" And even as he spoke the question, his heart sank. "Are you having pains?" He ran toward her and, without thinking, he reached for her, holding her against his chest, recalling another woman at another time. Louisa should feel strange in his arms, he thought. But she didn't. Instead, she leaned her head to nestle beneath his chin and relaxed her weight against his greater strength.

"I don't feel well," she whispered. "I threw up and my stomach feels funny."

"Let's get you in the house," he told her, his arm sliding around her back, his other palm cradling her hands as he led her back to the porch. "Come on. I'll help you up the steps."

She faltered, her game leg dragging, and once more, he recognized the courage she exhibited every day as she followed the routine she'd set for herself. "Is your leg paining you?" It was the first time he'd asked, and shame washed over him as he rued his thoughtlessness.

"Only all the time," she said with a small chuckle, lifting it to the first step and heaving herself upward as it wobbled beneath her weight.

"I meant to put a railing here for you, but…"

"You've got a whole farm to run, Jeb. You can't be worrying about catering to me." He lifted her then, easing her up the other step and across the porch. On the other side of the screened door, Elizabeth's small face was squashed against the metal mesh, and she watched, wide-eyed, as the adults in her life neared.

Louisa reached for the handle and pulled the door open, then stepped across the threshold as Elizabeth moved from her path. "Are you all right?" Blue eyes filled with tears as the child reached to touch Louisa's arm. "Are you sick?"

"Just a little," Louisa told her. "I'll sit down for a bit and then I'll feel better. I had a backache all night, and an upset stomach, to boot."

"You should have wakened me," Jeb said, easing her into a chair. He squatted in front of her, brushing tendrils of hair from her cheek. "Your forehead is clammy," he told her. "I'm thinking you need to spend the day in bed, Lou."

She looked up quickly, her attention gained as he spoke her name, and she repeated it as if she had not heard him aright. "Lou?"

A flush ridged his cheekbones, and he felt its heat. He reached for her, and his hand trembled against her skin as he curved it beneath her jaw. It was a simple gesture, but one he hadn't intended. They were married, but she was not yet his *wife*. And though he lay beside her nightly, knew her scent and heard her soft mumbles in the darkness as she slept, they were separate.

Two people sharing a home and a life, yet walking apart, one from the other.

"Am I taking liberties?" he asked, a crooked smile masking his heavily beating heart. Somehow, he felt foolish asking the question, as if he were a green lad gone courting. And perhaps he was, he thought, though this did not seem a good time for such a thing to happen. Yet, in her distress, Louisa brought forth a male part of him that begged for release, and he felt protective of her, drawn to her as a woman in need.

"Liberties?" The word seemed to amuse her, for a trembling smile appeared for a moment and then was gone as she bent her forehead to the tabletop, and her voice was muffled against its surface. "I doubt you'll be much interested in a woman about to give birth," she muttered.

He'd argue that point later, he decided, rising to stand over her. "Let me carry you upstairs to bed," he said, and was gifted by an incredulous look as she lifted her head to peer up at him.

"You couldn't lift me without a block and tackle," she muttered. "I weigh a ton."

"Don't be too sure about that," he said quietly. "I'm probably stronger than you think."

"My papa is real strong," Elizabeth reiterated, nodding her head in emphasis.

"I believe you, sweetie," Louisa told her,

"but it would be just my luck to take a tumble down the stairs."

She looked up at him, her eyes narrowing as she scanned his upper body. "Believe me, I've noticed your strength. You were the biggest man on that train platform. With shoulders the width of an ax handle."

She'd noticed. And that thought pleased Jeb immensely. Though why it should was foolishness. He was a grown man, not a fuzzy-cheeked lad. These days he felt far beyond the age of seeking a woman's favors. Unless...perhaps when things changed.

For Louisa was different. She didn't offer pretty words. She was bold sometimes, and he admired her for her ability to speak her mind, even as he bristled at her audacity. Yet there was a gentleness, a kindness about her that had Elizabeth following her around like a foal behind a mare in the pasture.

With his child she was ever pleasant, ever loving.

As for himself... He grinned, feeling foolish, but it could not be helped. *For, she'd noticed him.* Before he'd known she was to be his bride, she'd seen him and noted his size, his broad shoulders. Well, wasn't that a bit of news, he thought, feeling his chest expand as he lifted her to her feet. She looked up at him, and panic churned within his belly. There was something about her, whether it be the dazed look in her eyes, or the waxen appearance of her skin, he didn't know. But there was a new element in his concern.

"Are you sure this isn't just a touch of summer influenza?" he asked, suddenly unwilling to face the fact of her coming labor.

She slanted him a long look and shook her head, grimacing at his words. "Don't be foolish. This is definitely not influenza. I've got a bellyache. It may last awhile, but trust me, by tomorrow I'll be right as rain."

Stubbornness rose within him, and he shook his head. "A bellyache? Is that what you call it? I think you need to be in bed, Lou."

She seemed to be in the mood for compromise, pursing her lips and then offering another suggestion. "I'll go up later on. Maybe for now I'll just lie down on the sofa in the parlor for a while."

He turned to look at his daughter. "Go upstairs, Elizabeth, and bring down the pretty flowered quilt out of the closet in the hallway. You'll need to sit on the stairs and go bump-bump, the way you did when you were just a little girl. Do you remember how you used to do that?"

Elizabeth nodded. "Should I pull my sheet

up and cover everything with my quilt like we always do, Mama? And pick up my dirty clothes?'' As if she needed some sort of assurance that all was well, the child stood before Louisa, reaching to touch her knee with a small hand.

''Yes, that'll be fine,'' Louisa said, smiling encouragement at the child. ''And now I'm going in to sit on the sofa for a while.'' She bent closer and whispered in an undertone, ''It'll make your papa happy.'' Her head lifted and she met Jeb's gaze. ''And be easier for me than going upstairs. Although, later on...'' Her pause spoke of concern that she would not be able to climb.

For the first time she'd admitted to having a problem with the everyday tasks she handled. He'd watched her when she was unaware of his attention. Climbing the stairs had been difficult for her. He'd seen her careful placing of her shorter leg several times, and surmised that pain accompanied the movement. Now she'd confessed to that small bit of weakness, and he viewed it as a landmark.

''Whatever keeps you from hurting, Lou,'' he said as Elizabeth backed toward the doorway, her smile wobbling a bit.

Louisa's eyebrow quirked at his soothing words, and it was a dead giveaway. He'd learned much about her, he decided as he smothered a chuckle. From previous experience he knew it was a sure sign she was about to deliver a smart remark, that sarcastic tongue of hers probing at his ego. Today, he would not have it, and he wrapped both arms around her as she stood before him, and bent his head to touch his lips to hers.

Her indrawn breath made him smile, and he brushed kisses across her lips. "Now I know how to keep you quiet, ma'am," he said quietly, leaning back to look into her eyes. They were bright blue, and shiny with unshed tears. "Are you angry with me again?" he asked.

She shook her head. "No, just...surprised, I think. I haven't been touched by a man for a long time." Her tongue touched her lip in a tentative gesture. "Although I'd say *that* could be construed as *taking liberties,* Mr. Marshall."

He looked down at her, and held her more firmly against himself, nodding as he felt the movement of her child against his groin. "A long time since you've been touched? I'd say so. Almost nine months, in fact." The child moved again, a slow rolling pressure against him. "He did that once before, remember?"

Her cheeks bloomed with color and she nodded. "I remember. You were angry."

"Yeah, I was. But not for long."

"Really? I recall several days of you berating me every chance you got. Making fun of me and keeping secrets."

"Ah, we're back to that, are we?" He turned her, leading her from the kitchen, across the wide hallway to the parlor. "I thought we'd gotten beyond that the past few weeks. In fact, I think you said we were even on that score. Although, you've told Elizabeth more about your past than what you've allowed me to know."

"Well, this isn't the day to give you all the details," she said, easing down onto the sofa.

"Lean forward," he said curtly as he reached to prop a small, embroidered pillow behind her back.

"Thank you." It was a whisper of sound, her breath taken with the first tightening of her abdomen.

"You're not going to lie down?"

"I'll just sit here for a while if you'll pull the footstool over."

"Do I need to get the doctor?"

She looked up quickly, and saw the drawn, taut look of his mouth, the darkening of his eyes as he bent over her. "No, I don't think so. Not yet, anyway. What you need to do is make your daughter some breakfast, and eat something yourself. I can use a cup of coffee when you get a chance to make some.'' She settled back against the pillow and sighed. "By that time I should know for certain what's going on.''

"Just so you know, Louisa, I'm not much of a hand at delivering babies. And you sure don't want to do this by yourself.'' He straightened and his hands cocked against his hips. "Although I understand you have done it before. Twice, in fact, if I heard right.''

"This is a fine time to bring that up,'' she said, her palms massaging the tense muscles beneath the load she carried.

"I've got you cornered, for a few minutes anyway,'' he said, listening for Elizabeth's return. "I need to tell you this one thing. If you need me…you know, while you're having the baby, I'll be close by.''

"Were you with your wife while she had Elizabeth?''

"Her name was Hannah,'' he said quietly. "And, yes, I was with her.''

"This is different. This baby is mine alone. Elizabeth was your child.''

"Yes,'' he said, "she was. But that matters little now. Whatever comes or goes, I owe you my support. You're my wife.''

CHAPTER SIX

THE PROCESS OF DELIVERING a child was familiar, but the surroundings were different this time, not to mention the man who stood beside her bed as she labored. Louisa gripped the hand he offered and bit back a groan. It was not seemly to have him here, and yet, she could not bear to have him leave.

He was silent, as he'd been for the past hour, just offering his support, yet seemingly willing to do as she asked. And for that she was grateful. He'd gone at her bidding to find a doctor, and returned alone, the doctor being out on a call. At first she'd been frightened, but at the first touch of those long fingers, and the firm grip of his palm wrapping around hers, she'd relaxed against the sofa and offered no argument as Jeb took over the whole procedure.

He'd left her only to stoke up the fire in the stove and fill the big teakettle with water, then taken up his post at her side. When she decreed it necessary, he'd helped her, almost carrying her up the stairs. For a few awkward moments, she'd protested, then given in to his quiet persuasion as he'd stripped her from her clothing and drawn the white gown over her head.

Careful not to lower his eyes, he'd only looked into hers, as if aware of her modesty and unwilling to cause further distress when she was already coping with such an enormous amount of it. With sure and capable hands, he'd lent his help to the proceedings, then he'd covered her with the sheet and settled back to wait.

Surely, she thought, the doctor would arrive soon, and things would go as they should. Surely the man would be here in time to deliver her child. Surely—

Louisa shifted against the mattress, caught by a swiftly escalating spasm that wrapped her in hot tentacles of pain. She bit her lip, looking up at the man beside her, and he bent to her. His hands were gentle, placing the cool cloth he held on her forehead as he sat down beside her on the bed.

SURELY, SHE'D BE all right, he thought. Surely, the doctor would come soon and get him out of the midst of this muddle. Jeb rose and walked to the window as Louisa's pain receded and her eyes closed. The lane was empty, and the road to town was not visible from the bedroom window. He'd ridden quickly on his gelding to fetch the doctor, Elizabeth perched on the saddle in front of him. A quick stop at Abigail's home had found the child wailing her distress at being left with her aunt.

"I want to see my mama," she'd cried piteously, reaching her arms to Jeb as he mounted his horse. Abigail had bent to gather Elizabeth into her arms, a few quiet words from Jeb having made her aware of the situation.

"You'll see your mama tomorrow," he'd told Elizabeth staunchly. "Maybe even this evening. It all depends. And best of all, sweetie, we may have a surprise for you."

Elizabeth looked hopeful. "I like surprises," she'd sniffed through her tears, waving her goodbyes.

"The doctor ain't in." Tall, thin, and wrapped in a white apron, Mrs. Henderson had met him at the door of Doc Henderson's office, waving toward the center of town as she spoke. "Got a call to go clear the other side of town. I'll send him out when he comes back."

And then she'd lowered her voice. "I heard you got hung with a woman in the family way. Oughta be a law about such things," she'd said, sniffing with obvious righteous indignation. "Puts you in a bind, don't it?"

"Baby or not, Louisa is my wife," he'd told

her quietly. "I married her, and I'll take care of her."

"Well, she wouldn't be so lucky, were it some of the other fellas who sent for their women. Sight unseen…I declare, I can't imagine such a thing."

She was still muttering words of disapproval when Jeb mounted his horse and set off for the farm. He dug his heels into the gelding's sides and the patient animal went from a walk to a quick trot. Then, at Jeb's urging, the horse broke into a lope that would guarantee a fast ride back home.

Watching from across the room, he thought of the doctor's wife and her disdain for Louisa. Back a month or so in the past, he might have had the same thoughts himself, he admitted silently. Now, after weeks of sleeping beside the woman, learning to know her, and sharing his home with her, he looked at her differently.

She intrigued him with her quiet ways, her tender care of his daughter, and the quick intelligence that surfaced so readily. During the nightly supper hour they spoke of many things, usually beginning with the day's events, during which she gave a recital of Elizabeth's doings, including the child in the discussion. From there she sometimes asked questions about the farm and his plans for the crops, and he found her to be well educated and filled with knowledge he would not have given most women credit for possessing.

If only she didn't have such a sharp tongue, he thought, his lips pursing as he remembered some of their more heated discussions. And yet, it was that refusal to be downtrodden, the pride that kept her head high and her back straight, that appealed to him the most.

She would not kowtow to him, and for that he respected her. As wives go, he decided, he hadn't done too badly. He'd warrant that the pink-and-white specimen named Sue Ellen McPherson wouldn't be able to find her way around a kitchen like Louisa could. The younger ones, the ones who'd been snatched up by their new husbands like a handful of five-dollar gold pieces, probably couldn't even bake a decent batch of bread.

And not a one of them would have taken to Elizabeth the way Louisa had. He was almost certain of that. Louisa knew what it was to have a child and love it, and her mother's heart had opened to Elizabeth without urging.

He rubbed his neck and looked back at the bed where the silent woman labored. "Were your other childbirths long?" he asked quietly, and watched as her eyes opened.

She seemed to consider the query for a moment, then shook her head. "Not long, I suppose. All night long and half a day, with my first. A little shorter, when my son was born."

"How long has it been going on this time?" he asked, turning from the window to cross the room. For a moment he stood at the footboard of the bed, then moved to settle beside her on the mattress again.

"Forever," she muttered, closing her eyes again as a pain took her from him.

He smiled, aware of her wry grin. Even in the midst of pain, her answers were edged and touched with a sense of humor he wondered at. Certainly, she didn't have much to be sassy about right now. Yet, as the pain relented its hold, her eyes opened and a glimmer of irony shimmered in their depths.

"You ready to call it quits yet?" she asked, her breath trembling between each word. "I can probably do this alone if it's too much for you."

He lifted her hand and examined it minutely. "I'll just bet you can," he murmured. "But there's no need. I'm sure the doctor will be here soon." His fingers rubbed with long, precise strokes the length of hers. "You have strong hands, Lou. You've worked hard in your life."

"Hard work is a fact of life," she said, "but, in fact, I was a pampered wife. I had to argue with Harry before he'd let me do the gardening or any heavy work in the house.''

Well, that was another bit he'd tuck away and think about later, Jeb thought. Amazing that any woman would find housework to her liking, given a choice. Yet, it seemed that Louisa had. *Pampering.* He certainly hadn't done any of that in recent weeks, he decided, and felt a pang of guilt that he'd expected so much of her.

Her hand clenched in his grip, and as he watched, perspiration broke out on her forehead. The damp cloth lay against the pillow, and he picked it up to refresh it in the basin. By the time he placed it on her brow, her eyes had closed and tears squeezed from beneath her lids to roll across her temples and dampen the pillowcase beneath her head.

''Is it getting worse?'' He possessed an urge to touch her belly, that swollen, distended knot that rose from her slender body like a mountain. As her pain mounted, it formed a taut, rounded bulge that surely must stretch her skin painfully. And then, in a gesture he seemed unable to control, his palm curved against the hard, ungiving form of her child.

She inhaled sharply, then sighed, settling limply against the mattress. For the first time since the beginning of their marriage, she was totally relaxed in his presence. Only a layer of sheet, and the fabric of her nightgown separated the palm of his hand from the taut flesh of her belly. It was a moment fraught with intimacy and he closed his eyes, lest he disturb her with his gaze.

Beneath his hand the muscles gathered again, and he recognized the onset of another pain. He heard her tight gasp as it rose to a peak, and then her soft moan as the crescendo continued and she was wrapped in the midst of it. A hiccup escaped her lips as the muscles relaxed beneath his touch and he bent to touch his mouth to her forehead.

"Would you like some water?" he asked, willing to do whatever he could to relieve her solitary plight.

She nodded and her lips moved, the whisper almost inaudible. "Tea. A box in my trunk."

"Yes. All right. I'll get it." Rising quickly, he went to the window, kneeling before her trunk, and lifted the lid. The contents were hers, each item a part of the woman he'd married. From the soft, lace-trimmed gown on top to the stack of flannel squares just beneath its delicate weight, each was part and parcel of Louisa.

A cardboard box in one corner looked to be a likely spot to hold tea, and he opened the lid. Various tubes and jars were neatly arranged within, and a wooden box was marked with black ink, in what he recognized as Louisa's penmanship. Red Baneberry For Childbirth read the label, and beneath those words was a dire warning that made him shudder. Use Sparingly. Danger Of Poison.

And how much of this tea could be considered a safe dosage? he wondered, lifting the box from its corner. The flannel squares were newly made, stitched with care, and he chose several from the stack to be set aside for use before he closed the trunk lid. The tea was probably for pain, and would only be of use once he added the boiled water to brew it. But first, he must be certain he'd found what she asked for.

"Louisa?" He knelt beside the bed, noting the tension that gripped her as her hands clasped firmly to her belly. A line of perspiration filmed her forehead and her head rolled against the pillow once, then again, as she inhaled sharply.

He placed his hand above hers, where muscles clenched in a rhythm as old as time itself, and felt the tension ooze from her body as he whispered her name again. "I'm here, Louisa." His hand moved in a slow, firm, circling movement, and she groaned, biting at her lip, even as her breathing evened into a sigh.

"I'll brew the tea for you now," he said quietly. "But I need to be sure I have the right thing." He read aloud the words on the wooden box, and she nodded, then whispered an assent. "I'll put the kettle on, and be right back," he told her, waiting until she moved her head, acknowledging his words.

His feet sped down the stairs, missing every other one, and he skidded into the kitchen just as the back door opened. "Well, I'd say you're in a hurry," the doctor said, doffing his hat as he entered. "Haven't seen you for quite a spell, Jeb. Sorry I wasn't home when you came by." He placed his bag on the table and slid from his coat, stepping to the sink to wash his hands.

He glanced back over his shoulder at Jeb, and his words were sober. "I'll warrant you weren't expecting something like this when you sent for a bride, were you?"

"I guess that's a safe assumption," Jeb told him. "But we've worked things out between us. I'm not going to go back on my bargain."

Doc Henderson pushed down on the pump handle, then held his hands beneath the flowing water to rinse them. His voice was brisk as he turned to Jeb. "Is it safe to assume that the woman hasn't delivered yet?"

"No, but I don't think it'll be long. She's having pains pretty close together." Jeb held up the box of tea he carried. "She told me to brew some of this."

"Let's take a look," Doc Henderson said, peering at the label through his spectacles. "Red baneberry. Yup, that oughta do some good. Just a half teaspoonful for a cup, mind you. It's potent stuff." He turned back to scrubbing his hands and forearms. "Is she upstairs?"

"First room on the right," Jeb told him, sliding the kettle to the hottest spot on the stove. "I'll be there in a minute."

"Bring my bag and a couple of clean towels with you, son," the doctor told him, heading for the hallway, hands uplifted. "And the hot water, too," he called back, his footsteps audible as he climbed the stairs.

Louisa sipped at the tea, leaning against Jeb's arm, her hand covering his on the cup. "Thank you," she whispered, allowing her head to rest against his chest. He held her a moment, unwilling to release her from his touch, but a quickly indrawn breath told him she was once more in the throes of a pain that held her in its grip. His hands were gentle as he placed her back on the pillow, and he looked up to meet the doctor's gaze.

"How long?" Jeb asked, hoping the answer would be to his liking.

"Not much longer," Doc Henderson said. "She needs to start pushing." He looked cautiously at Jeb. "You sure you want to stay for this?"

"I'll stay. I told her I would." No matter that his memories were bleak, as he recalled Hannah's travail with Elizabeth's delivery. He'd promised Louisa, and the import of that weighed heavily on him. She was brave, above all women he'd known, and deserving of his loyalty.

"It's all right," she whispered, and her eyes opened, seeking his face. "You don't have to."

He grasped her hand and felt her fingers curve strongly around his. "You need to push, Lou. I'll help."

In between pains, he held the cup for her to drink, and during the strong contractions that brought smothered moans from her lips, he held her hands, allowing her to pull on him, imbuing her with his strength. Doc Henderson spoke quietly to her, offering encouragement, and examining her with care as she labored.

A glimpse of Louisa's thigh met Jeb's vision as the doctor uncovered her and then draped clean towels over her, and he looked aside, unwilling to invade her privacy when she could not escape his gaze. But the vision of a scarred, twisted limb burned in his mind and left its indelible imprint. She'd been hurt, and badly, and his heart ached for the proud woman who walked with pain.

"Jeb?" She called his name and he gripped her hands anew as a high, eerie cry slipped from her throat. She clutched at him, biting at her lip as the spasm slammed her against the mattress. And then the doctor laughed aloud, lifting high the plump form of a squalling infant.

"It's a boy, ma'am," he said loudly. And with one hand he wrapped a flannel square around the squirming body.

"Here, take ahold," he told Jeb. "I need to tie the cord and cut it."

Jeb reached out for the bundle, holding it on his cupped palms, gripping firmly the tiny arms and legs, lest he drop the baby on the bed. Blood and mucus covered the head, and slate-blue eyes blinked against the moisture that covered them. And then the child's cries ceased as he looked up at Jeb.

A pang of yearning enveloped Jeb's heart as he examined the infant who seemed to return his gaze. And, to his amazement, in the aftermath of pain and heartache, the babe became no longer only Louisa's child, but his own.

With a resounding clearing of his throat, he watched as the cord was cut, and then offered the tiny bundle to Louisa's care. "Will you hold him?" he asked, already knowing her reply before it was uttered.

"Oh, yes," she said, breathless from her labors, but eager to touch the babe she'd spent all of her energy to deliver. Softly, she kissed the damp, dark hair. Tenderly, she held the wrapped bundle against her breast. And quietly, she spoke his name. "David," she whispered. "I'll call him David."

"He's a beautiful baby," Jeb said, reaching to touch the stained skin where the blood had begun to dry. "Let me wash his face, Lou," he offered, reaching for the cloth he'd used earlier to wipe her brow.

She watched as he wiped the birth fluids from the baby, her eyes intent on his every move, and when he'd finished, she looked up at him. "I can't thank you enough," she told him quietly. "I don't know how I could have done it without you."

He could find no words to explain his feelings, no simple phrases to assure her that these hours had begun to provide a measure of healing to his weary soul. And so he could only offer a gift he hoped might express his acceptance of the child she held.

"I'll go up in the attic after a while," he told her. "The cradle I made for Elizabeth is there, beneath the eaves. If you like, we can use it for David."

CHAPTER SEVEN

"HE'S BEAUTIFUL," Abigail said, her eyes shining with awe as she held the baby in the crook of her arm. "I've never seen a newborn so alert."

"And how many have you seen?" Jeb asked dryly, standing by with an air of protection enveloping him. He seemed poised to reach for David should Abigail's grip falter, and Louisa could barely stifle her laughter.

Abigail shot him a look that promised revenge. "Probably more than you, brother dear. *I* manage to get out and around and visit folks on a regular basis." She looked down at the infant in her arms and her eyes softened as a tear slid down her cheek. "But you might as well know that I'll be housebound for a while, myself, Jeb. In about six months, if I have it figured right."

"You're going to have a baby?" Louisa asked, her heartbeat quickening as she understood the emotion expressed by that single, salty drop. "How wonderful for you."

Abigail looked up and blinked, and her arms cradled the babe even more closely. "Seeing David makes it seem real. Does that make sense to you?"

"Oh, yes," Louisa told her. "I remember when—" Her words faltered and she bit at her lip, unwilling to recite the thoughts and feelings of days gone by. "If you like," she offered haltingly, "I'd be glad to share David with you over the next couple of months. Perhaps it would make it easier when your time comes to have handled a newborn a bit."

"Would you?" Abigail's eyes lit with pleasure. "I'm afraid I'll be a pest. You'll just have to send me home when you're tired of having me around." She crossed the room to put the sleeping baby in the cradle Jeb had washed and made ready.

A voice seeking her mama's whereabouts floated up from the kitchen, announcing the arrival of Elizabeth, and Louisa looked quickly at Jeb. "Does she know about the baby?"

"I told her we might have a surprise for her," he said.

"I didn't say anything," Abigail said quickly, "and when she wanted to run to see the kittens before she came in the house, I thought it would give you a chance to be ready for all her questions when she comes up those stairs.''

"Mama?" Elizabeth darted through the doorway and stopped in the middle of the room. "How come you're in bed?" she asked, her gaze moving from one to another of the adults watching her.

"I didn't feel well yesterday. Remember?" Louisa asked her. "And do you know what happened?"

Elizabeth's head shook slowly from side to side, her eyes growing larger by the second. And then she ran headlong toward the bed. "Mama, are you sick?" Fear brought quick tears to the blue eyes, and Louisa reached for her.

"Oh, sweetheart, I'm just fine. I just had to get your surprise ready for you. Would you like to see him?"

"Him?" If Elizabeth's eyes had been enormous before, now they defied description, Louisa thought as the child leaned back in her arms and looked around the room. "Do you mean my papa?" she asked quickly before dissolving into laughter. "He's no surprise, Mama. He's always been here."

Louisa shook her head. "No, the surprise is in the cradle on the other side of my bed. Do you remember the cradle?'' And at Elizabeth's puzzled look, Louisa whispered soft words in her ear. ''You used to sleep in it when you were a baby.''

''It's too small for me now,'' the girl said, sliding from the bed and rounding the footboard quickly. ''It's only big enough for a baby.'' And then she peered within the depths of the handmade bed, her mouth forming an ''Oh'' as she reached forth her hand, one cautious finger extended, to touch the sleeping babe.

''It's a real baby,'' she breathed. ''When I first looked, I thought it might be a baby doll for me, 'cause I told you I only had a grown-up dolly.'' Her face took on an earnest aspect as she turned back to look solemnly at Louisa. ''I'd rather have a real baby than a pretend one.''

''We'll have to share him,'' Louisa said quickly. ''Real babies are harder to tend to than dolls. But you can help me take care of him.''

''Do we have to make clothes for him?'' Elizabeth's fingers touched the white flannel square Louisa had wrapped around the infant. ''Does he got shirts and stuff to wear?''

''We have a few things already made, that I brought with me,'' Louisa told her, ''but we'll make some more pretty soon.''

"I can help," Abigail offered. "I'm handy with a needle and thread."

"I thought maybe Elizabeth and I could take a ride to town and pick up a few things for him," Jeb said quietly. "We need supplies from the general store, anyway."

"Can we go pretty soon, Papa?" his daughter asked eagerly. "I want to tell everybody about our new surprise."

"You need to stop by the church and make arrangements for his christening, too," Abigail told him. "Louisa should be feeling up to it in a couple of weeks, I'd think."

"We'll talk about that later," Louisa said quickly, shooting a look at Jeb. For all she knew, he might not be the least bit interested in claiming this child in a ceremony that would include the name *Marshall* on the certificate.

He was silent for a moment, his brows lowered. "Maybe you need to sort out a few things in your mind," he said, "before we talk about giving him a name." He turned to Elizabeth, ushering her from the room. "Come along," he told the child. "We'll be needing to do some chores and then get dinner on the stove. Louisa will be staying in bed for a few days, and there's a lot for the two of us to take care of."

Abigail looked exceedingly uncomfortable as her brother walked out the door. She sat on the edge of the chair by the bed and stared at her hands for a moment, then lifted her head to meet Louisa's gaze. "He seems to be upset about something, doesn't he?"

"Maybe he's just tired," Louisa offered. If Jeb was having second thoughts about being a part of her son's life, he'd might as well say so now. And if she knew anything about it, his frown signified doubt of some sort.

"If you want to get the rest of the baby things out of my trunk, I'd appreciate it, Abigail. Just dig under my clothes and you'll find a few gowns and some diapers. I'll send some money and a list along with Jeb to buy whatever else I need later on."

"I doubt Jeb will allow you to pay for anything for the baby," Abigail said stoutly. "He seems to be taking hold of things here. This may be the best thing that ever happened to him. Since Hannah died, he's been about as gloomy as any man could be, just moping around this house and letting things go generally to pot.

"In fact, I told Tim I was surprised you stuck around when you got here and saw the mess he was in. Jeb just hauled Elizabeth around with him most days on the wagon or on his horse, and let her watch while he worked the farm. Didn't take time to do much else but get meals together. I was coming in for a day, every week, and cleaning what little bit I could, but I couldn't keep up with it.''

"He should have had someone here for Elizabeth full time," Louisa said, thinking of the child being dragged around behind her father all day long.

Abigail slanted her a long look and grinned. "Why do you think he sent for you?"

Louisa couldn't help the smile that curved her lips. "And look what he got."

"I told you before, you're the best thing that could have happened to him. He's alive these days. His eyes have been sparkling the past weeks, like he's got a new lease on life." Abigail crossed to the trunk and knelt before it, delving amid its contents as she searched for the flannel bits Louisa had brought with her.

"You're good for him," Abigail said, rising with both hands full. Inspecting the tiny garments, she sat on the edge of the bed. "You sew beautifully, Louisa. My stitches aren't nearly so fine as yours."

"Well, I suspect I'll have my hands full, making things for him to grow into," Louisa said. "I don't have any hand-me-downs to fall back on this time."

Abigail's hands stilled, and she cast a cautious look at her sister-in-law. "Elizabeth told me you had a son and daughter, and they died. Can you talk about it?''

She hadn't, not with strangers, not till now. But if it were to ever become less of a bleeding wound in her heart, this might be the best time to begin, Louisa thought. ''My husband's name was Harry. My daughter, Patricia, was four years old. Little Harry only two.'' There, she'd gotten the facts out of the way. Now for the tough part.

''They were coming home from the market one afternoon, walking across the street, when a runaway team rounded the corner and ran them down.'' Louisa caught her breath, aware of tears that neared the surface as she spoke. And so, she rapidly completed her recitation, having committed it to memory the day a policeman had stood at her door and delivered the facts with tears of his own streaming down ruddy cheeks.

''Harry could have gotten to safety,'' she said, her voice breaking, ''but he picked the children up, and when the team swerved in the middle of the street, he was trampled. And then the wagon ran over them.''

''Oh, my dear!'' Abigail dumped the contents of her lap on the quilt and reached out for Louisa, sweeping her into her embrace, weeping unashamedly as she clutched her against her breast. "How could you live through such a horrible thing?"

Louisa found herself comforting Jeb's sister, much to her amazement. "It's all right, Abigail. I've gotten used to being without them, most days. And coming to Colorado was the best thing I could have done. It's made me think about something other than the loss of my family." She patted ineffectively at her sister-in-law's back, spilling her thoughts to another woman for the first time in eight months.

"I should have been honest when I wrote the letter to your brother. I suppose I knew he wouldn't want a pregnant wife, but I was stuck, like a square peg in a round hole, with nowhere to go." She smoothed back Abigail's hair as the younger woman sat upright and wiped at her eyes.

"If I'd had someone like you back home, I might have been able to handle things better. But, then," she said with a sigh, "I'd have missed out on you and Elizabeth...and even Jeb. Most of all, Jeb, I guess."

Abigail looked at her with understanding dawning in the depths of dark eyes. "Are you in love with my brother?" she asked quietly.

Louisa was silent as she considered the idea. "I think I love him, yes. Not like I did my husband. But then, he was my childhood sweetheart, and he treated me like I was made from sugar candy.'' She thought back and smiled. ''Sometimes I hated it, that he always protected me, looked after me. But when I got on that train and I was on my own, I sure missed him. And when I got off and saw the look on Jeb's face, I knew I was in for trouble, once he found out I was in the family way.''

''I think he's happy with you,'' Abigail said firmly, her dark hair bouncing as she rose from the bed and stalked around the room, as if she could not tolerate sitting still. Her face glowed with excitement as she spun to face Louisa. ''I'll just bet he loves you to pieces. Why wouldn't he? His house is clean, and he's eating like a king, and his daughter is happy as a lark.''

''I'm not sure that's all it takes to make a man happy,'' Louisa said dryly. ''Or to keep him that way.''

Abigail's cheeks flushed as her final spin left her breathless. ''Oh, that!'' she said with a wave of her hand. ''From what I've heard from other women you'll be able to…well, you know, in just a couple of weeks or so.''

''How old is your brother?'' Louisa asked abruptly.

''Twenty-eight. But, what difference does that make?''

"Four years difference. I'm not only older than he is, I'm a woman who has had three pregnancies and has the marks to show for it. My hair is beginning to turn white around the edges, and I have a limp that makes me terribly unattractive. All of that is guaranteed to make Jeb turn tail and run, first chance he gets." She ran out of breath as she listed her defects, and one brow lifted as she waited for Abigail's reaction.

"I don't think he cares about any of those things," Abigail said, her words firm, even as she dodged Louisa's gaze.

"You don't think he cares about what?" From the doorway, Jeb's voice posed the question, and his sister muttered beneath her breath.

"This is woman talk," she said. "Go do something in the barn, why don't you?"

"When my name comes up in the *woman talk*, as you put it, then I figure I have a right to be interested, sis." He leaned against the door jamb and Louisa turned her face to the window, lying back on the pillow.

"Neither of you planning on talking to me?" he asked, and his voice held a tone much like that she'd heard on the day of her arrival in Bender's Mill. He turned after a moment and stalked away, his boots clumping noisily on the stairs as he descended with haste.

"I think I made him angry," Abigail said after a moment. "Maybe I'd better go and try to mend my fences." She stood by the side of the bed and looked down into the cradle. "No matter what happens, this baby is going to wear Jeb's name, you know. He was your husband when the baby arrived. Legally, he's the father, unless he should choose to protest that in court."

"I think he just figured that out a little while ago," Louisa said, looking out the window, where white clouds swept regally across the blue sky. "And I don't think he's very happy about it." Her fingers tightened on the sheet, holding it firmly at her waist. "Don't mention a christening again, will you? Let him do it on his own if he wants to. I don't want to push him into anything."

JEB BROUGHT A TRAY up the stairs with soup from Abigail's kitchen in a bowl, and bread from a loaf she'd supplied for their supper. He'd toasted two slices, buttered it lavishly and brought a jar of jam from the pantry. "Would you like anything else?" he asked, reserve alive in his voice.

"No, this is fine," Louisa answered, smiling up at him. "I appreciate what you're doing for me, Jeb. I'll be back in the kitchen in a couple of days.''

"Hannah was in bed for ten days when Elizabeth was born, and even that wasn't long enough," he told her stubbornly. "You have the same right to linger here as long as you need. I don't want you up and around until you're all healed up."

"Well, that might be longer than you've bargained for," she said sharply. "Usually takes a month or so until things are back to normal for a woman. I don't intend to lollygag around that long."

"We'll see," he said politely, and then backed toward the doorway. "I'll come back up and get the tray later on." He hesitated in the doorway. "And I'll sleep downstairs on the sofa for a while. Till you're feeling better anyway."

Louisa shot upright in bed, almost upsetting the tray she held across her lap. "You'll do no such thing. Someone told me, about five weeks ago if I remember right, that, being your wife, I must sleep in your bed." She gritted her teeth and settled the tray beside her on the mattress, then threw back the sheet and slid to the side of the bed.

"I've done as I was told, sleeping right here every single night, probably taking up more than my share of space. Are you telling me now that your edict no longer holds true? Because if so, then I'll be the one to move to the sofa." She got to her feet, swaying as she reached for the bedpost to steady herself.

"Louisa!" He crossed the room in three long strides and grasped her by the shoulders. Anger reflected from dark eyes as he looked down at her, his and hers combined, and she sensed his latent strength in the grip of long fingers against her skin.

"Get back in that bed," he growled, his teeth clenched, his jaw a taut line.

"No one tells me what to do," she said, tilting her chin, the better to look in his face. "I'm a woman grown. You need to respect your elders."

"My elders? Isn't that stretching it a bit, ma'am? I'd say the truth is you need to respect your husband," he returned roughly. "I won't have you hemorrhaging all over the floor, just because you're trying to do more than you ought."

"What ever gave you idea I'm going to hemorrhage?" she asked bluntly. "I'm fine. I know what to expect, and if I think I'm in trouble I'll let you know."

"Women do." His chin jutted forward. "Hannah did. And she was never the same after that. She died..." He turned his head aside, but his shoulders slumped with the sound of those words that shuddered from his chest. And then he turned his head back and faced her with stormy eyes and a determined look that bode ill for any more defiance from her.

"She died just a year later, Louisa. Because she hemorrhaged two weeks after Elizabeth was born, and then didn't take care of herself." His fingers tightened, sliding the length of her arms to clasp hers with a strength that threatened to crush the small bones he held in his grip.

"I won't let that happen to you."

Beside her, the baby squirmed in the cradle and a whisper of sound foretold more to come. "He's waking up. I'll need to nurse him," she said, forcing calm into each syllable. "Let me sit down, Jeb."

His dark eyes blinked, and then his gaze touched her hands, lifting them. "I didn't mean to hurt you," he said quietly. "I fear I've bruised you, Louisa." Carefully he assisted her to the rocking chair he'd placed before the window, and then returned to the cradle, lifting the baby and scooping up two diapers as he carried the squirming infant to his mother's arms.

"I'll take the tray down and reheat the soup when you're done with the baby. Just call out when you're ready to eat."

"Yes, all right," she said, already intent on the unwrapping and diapering of the babe. She glanced up, soiled diaper in her hand. "I'll need a bucket of water up here to soak these. It'll save you carrying them downstairs each time."

"All right." He backed away. "Call me. You hear?"

CHAPTER EIGHT

THERE WAS NOTHING in this world like caring for a new baby to take your mind off your troubles, Louisa decided. Rocking and nursing little David, keeping him clean and dry, and rising during the night to tend him all combined to keep her mind totally focused on the tasks inherent in being a new mother. Elizabeth was her second concern, and allowing her to help in the infant's care was simple, the girl being enthralled by the idea of having a baby in the house.

Careful not to designate David as Elizabeth's brother, Louisa simply told her they would share the baby, and with that, the child was satisfied. On the other hand, it seemed there was little she could do to satisfy Jeb. He was morose for the most part, but she'd surprised him several times as he stood by the cradle or the basket where she kept David during the day. He'd bent over to touch the downy hair more than once, and Louisa had been careful to keep her distance, as if she failed to note Jeb's interest in her child.

Doc Henderson dropped by during the fourth week, checked out Louisa's progress and pronounced her "healthy as a horse," a condition she wasn't sure she approved of. He'd looked the baby over and smiled into the unfocused eyes. "A beautiful child, Mrs. Marshall. He resembles you through the eyes and nose. Kinda looks like Jeb, too, and that's not all bad, I'd say."

She'd privately thought the same thing herself, so she only nodded in agreement.

"What did Doc say about the baby?" Jeb asked at the dinner table. "Is everything all right? And how about you?" Fork in hand, he waited for her answer, as if it might be of great import, and she was quick to reply.

"We're both fine. I'm healthy and he's beautiful."

"That might be true for both of you, I'd say," Jeb told her, spearing a piece of meat from his plate. His look from beneath half-lowered lids dared her to debate the issue, and she declined, choosing to help Elizabeth with her plate instead.

"When are you going to tell me what's wrong?" he asked quietly. "I've felt for weeks that I'm on the outside looking in, Louisa. I think I've been patient enough."

"If either of us has something to talk about, I'd say it was you," she retorted politely, fearful of including Elizabeth in their exchange. "I'm only doing what I was told when I arrived here. And as I see it, by the time I get the garden harvested and into jars, I'll be more than able to begin the next stage of my life."

"And that is?" His words were taunting, as if he dared her to speak aloud the vision that chased through her dreams nightly. Of standing on a train platform, watching the approaching engine and wondering where her destination would be.

"I believe you said you'd put me and my child on a train, heading in any direction I liked."

"What child?" Elizabeth asked, peering up at Louisa's face. "Me or David?"

"Neither," Jeb said shortly. "No one's going anywhere, Elizabeth. Louisa was just talking out of turn."

"Was I?" Her brow rose and her jaw thrust forward as Louisa met his anger head-on. "It seems to me I was merely quoting, chapter and verse, from your very words."

"Well, you can stop the foolishness right now," he told her firmly. "You're not going anywhere, as you very well know. You're my wife and you belong here with Elizabeth and me. I don't want to hear any more of this from you."

"My mama once said that what you want and what you get might be two very different things," Louisa said quietly. "I'll not remain with no sense of security."

"Security? I've given you a home and a name for your child. What more do you want from me?"

Elizabeth's mouth drew down and a wail erupted from pink lips as she cast fearful looks at both of the adults in her life. "I don't like it when you talk loud," she sobbed. "You make me all scared inside."

"Oh, sweetheart," Louisa said, rising to scoop the child from her chair.

"Let me take her. She's too heavy for you to lift," Jeb said, rounding the table with arms outstretched.

"I've got her," Louisa said stubbornly, bending her head to hide the misery she knew must be obvious in her eyes.

His arms encompassed them both, as if he found it a better thing to do than just stand by, watching. Louisa allowed it, glorying in the warmth of male flesh surrounding her shoulders. She inhaled, enjoying the scent of a freshly shaved jaw next to her face.

For the first time since the day of David's birth, Jeb was *with* her. Not in just a physical sense, but in such a way that his concern was a viable entity, enveloping and comforting her, even as she held Elizabeth between them.

"I don't like you to be mad," Elizabeth whimpered. "Please be nice to my mama," she said, reaching to touch Jeb's cheek with small fingers.

"I'm trying," he said quietly. "I just don't seem to be doing a good job of it." He shot a look at Louisa. "Maybe I don't know what your mama wants from me."

"I want to be more important to you than your memories," she blurted, and then flushed when she realized the futility of such a thing.

"And am I playing second fiddle to Harry?" he asked, as if goaded into such a response.

At a loss for words, unable to speak in Elizabeth's presence, she could only press her lips together and turn aside. He allowed it and she bent to lower Elizabeth to the floor. "I think we need to finish our dinner," she told the girl. "We have a line full of diapers to fold before David wakes up for his feeding."

Easily swayed by the prospect of helping at the clothesline, Elizabeth agreeably climbed onto her chair, and Louisa sent a warning glance in Jeb's direction.

"We'll finish this later," he told her quietly, holding her chair as she sat down.

It was a small thing, this bit of courtesy he exhibited, one she would not have expected from a farmer in the flatlands of eastern Colorado, but she accepted it with a nod and picked up her fork. Jeb was aware of the small amenities she'd thought to be sole possessions of those raised in the city, and she once more was thankful for his upbringing. In some ways, he was a puzzle to her. In most ways, he confounded her.

And yet she knew that deep within her grew and flourished an abiding love for the man that was not dependent on his manners for its survival. She had only to look at him to recognize the feelings that filled her heart for his generosity of spirit and the care he'd given her during David's birth. For that reason alone, she would harbor deep feelings toward him, no matter if she remained here or left him behind.

The bottom of her trunk held sufficient funds for her to begin anew if she must, the results of the sale of her home and the proceeds of Harry's insurance policy. And she knew with certainty that Jeb had never gone deeper into her luggage than to find her small box of herbs and salves, had never seen beneath the bits and pieces of her belongings. Unless she offered the information, he would never know that she was financially capable of caring for herself, should the need arise.

But the issues between them were not resolved later that day, or even in the hours of darkness when they lay beside each other in the bedroom on the second floor.

Whether Jeb thought it prudent to let things simmer for a while, or simply had too much on his mind to pry further into her intentions, she didn't know. But the matter was put on the back burner and their private times in the bedroom during the next weeks were few. And those few only involved caring for the baby or speaking of their daily life together.

THE DAYS OF SUMMER passed quickly, with the garden coming in at a rapid pace. Abigail came several times to help Louisa put up vegetables in glass jars, both quarts and pints, of peas and beans, pickled beets and small, whole carrots, that lined the pantry shelves in colorful array.

Greens appeared on the dinner table daily, until Elizabeth groaned at the sight of them. Rows of potatoes, onions and carrots were left in the ground to develop fully, and the tomatoes flourished, providing them with more than Louisa had jars enough to hold.

"Take some home with you," she begged Abigail one afternoon as she prepared to leave after a full day of work in a hot kitchen. Boiling water filled the room with steam as the last of the tomatoes waited to be scalded and stripped of their skins. But Louisa had decreed that Abigail's duty for one day was done.

"I've already canned up two bushels," Abigail protested. "You need to have Jeb get you more jars from the general store."

"Jeb can get her anything she needs," he answered from the porch.

"You're in early," Louisa said quickly. "Is anything wrong?"

"No," he told her briefly. "I came up to the house to talk to you."

"Well, don't let me interfere," Abigail said brightly. "I was just leaving." She looked across the kitchen at the baby, asleep in his basket. "Give the children a hug for me, Lou. Elizabeth must have fallen asleep on the sofa. She was looking at a book when I glanced in there last."

"I'll give you a hand up in the buggy," Jeb told her. "It won't take a minute to hitch up your mare."

"I knew you'd come in handy if I kept you

around long enough,'' Abigail told him, reaching up to pat his cheek.

"You always did have a smart mouth on you.'' Jeb held the screened door open for his sister and then looked back at Louisa with a sharp admonition. "Don't go away.''

She looked incredulously at the stove where steam rose in a white cloud above her largest kettle. "Not for a while, anyway,'' she said. "Not with another peck of tomatoes to slip skins from before I can start supper.''

But it seemed their talk would wait, for when Jeb returned to the kitchen, Louisa had involved Elizabeth in the proceedings and his daughter was at the table, an apron protecting her dress as she knelt in front of a pan of tomatoes.

"I'm helping,'' she announced, her eyes still puffy from the nap she'd taken. "I heard Mama talkin' to you and Auntie Abigail and it woke me up.'' She grinned up at him and nodded at the pan before her. Tomatoes cooled in the water and she lifted one for his inspection.

"All I hafta do is dig in my nails a little, tiny bit and the skin just peels right off, just like magic. See?'' She demonstrated her skill, her small hands filled with the plump fruit as she diligently slid the skin off and placed the tomato in a bowl beside her.

"Louisa is lucky to have such a good

helper," he told Elizabeth. "Maybe she'll let me help, too, and then we can set the table for dinner." His look at Louisa was met by surprise, and a quick nod of agreement.

He'd wait till bedtime, he decided. The afternoon in the pasture, mending fences and stringing new wire, had given him time to think beyond the task at hand. His youthful farm hands were busy beside him, but his mind was not on their talk of girls in town and the coming dance on Saturday night. And then one of them spoke of walking out on Sunday afternoon with the young lady of his choice, and Jeb had a glimmer of an idea he hoped would bear fruit.

"DO YOU THINK we might go to church on Sunday morning?" he asked. Lying on his back, hands beneath his head, he glanced to the side, noting Louisa's quick intake of breath as her head turned in his direction.

"You don't generally go to church, do you?" she asked, lying beside him, ignoring the candle flickering on the table beside her.

"Haven't since Hannah died," he admitted. "But I've been thinking, it would be good to take Elizabeth. You know, get her in the habit like her mother would have wanted. And then, too," he said, with a glance at Louisa, "I thought you might like to talk to the minister about a christening for the baby.''

She was silent, unwilling to ask the question that preyed on her mind. And yet, it must be spoken aloud if they were to continue together. And it seemed that Jeb had decreed it to be so. ''Will it involve your name on his christening certificate?'' she asked.

The silence pounded in her ears and she rolled to face him. His face was set in stern lines and she feared the words he would speak, words that might cut her to the quick, should he deny the child that right.

''I planned from the first to claim your son,'' he said. ''If you wanted his father's name on his birth record, you should have said so at the beginning. I won't stand up in church with you and allow him to be christened as another man's child. There's a certain amount of pride involved in this, Louisa.''

''You want to claim him?'' she asked. ''You won't mind the gossip when folks realize you're planning on keeping me, and the baby, too?''

His frown grew deeper. ''What are you talking about?''

''I spoke to the woman at the general store that day you dropped me off to choose groceries while you went to the mill. She hinted that folks thought you'd probably send me on my way, once the baby was born. I think she wondered when I was leaving.''

"Why didn't you tell me?"

She sighed. "I didn't know for sure how you felt about anything at that point." A smile curved her mouth, and she gathered her courage as she touched his cheek with one finger, shifting for the comfort of her leg. "Still don't, I guess. But I'm willing to bet you wouldn't be accepting him this way, unless you planned on keeping me around."

"I thought I made that pretty clear one day awhile back. I told you you weren't going anywhere, and, in the process, managed to get my daughter all upset, as I recall." His hand slid beneath the sheet to touch her hip and she felt a wave of heat from that minute spot wash upward to enclose her in its warmth.

"Are you feeling more secure now?" he asked quietly, as if he recalled her words, spoken in the heat of anger.

I'll not remain with you with no sense of security. They rang false in her mind as she thought of the days since that time. "Yes, I suspect you could say that."

"I'd rather have you say it," he countered, his hand sliding upward to cup her ribs.

"I feel like I belong here," she admitted.

"I'd like it better if you had strong feelings for me, but I can't expect to take Hannah's place in your heart."

"Why not? I expect to push Harry into the past, just as soon as you let me."

Her fingers spread wide along his cheek, and she relished the rough bristles he wore at the end of the day. Would they leave rosy marks on her skin, she wondered, should he brush his cheek across tender flesh?

"He's already in the past," she told him. "I loved Harry. Still do, I guess. But he's gone." She felt tears fill her eyes as she recognized the words as a goodbye to the man she'd shared her life with for over six years. "He was good to me, Jeb. But he didn't treat me as an equal, the way you do."

"As an equal? Is that how I treat you?" His hand slid to her back and he pulled her across the sheet, sliding his other arm beneath her neck. His arms met, circling her in an embrace that sent shivers of anticipation down the length of her spine.

"You give as good as you get, Lou. I'll grant you that. And I've not always been kind to you, not at first anyway. But I've always realized how intelligent you are, how quick your mind works. I told you before, you're the strongest, bravest woman I've ever known, and I've admired you from the first.''

''Have you, now?'' she asked, the words he spoke a delight to her heart.

He bent his head and his lips touched her forehead.

''I did that before. And I've kissed your lips, too. Do you remember?''

She nodded, feeling the warmth of his mouth against her skin. ''I felt you kiss my forehead several times when I was in labor.''

''That was for comfort,'' he said, ''because I wanted so badly to do something to help, and I couldn't. This...'' His lips brushed again. ''This is because I want to offer something more.''

CHAPTER NINE

"SOMETHING MORE?" That *something* was hopefully what she'd wished for, these last few moments. These last few weeks, if she were to be honest with herself. Especially since she'd recognized that the healing from childbirth was complete, and her woman's heart was ready for the sealing of her love for Jeb Marshall.

"I want to be your husband, Lou. Not just on a piece of paper, or in the granting of my name to you." He leaned back and grinned at her. "Although I have to admit, I kinda like the sound of Louisa Winifred Applegate Palmer Marshall. It suits you, ma'am." And then his look grew tender and she felt an impulsive urge to pull him toward her, to grip the nape of his neck and lean into his embrace more fully.

"Are you healed enough?" he asked, and in the question she heard the implicit request for the giving of her body into his keeping.

"Healed?" The question was one she felt compelled to answer, on more levels than one.

"Yes, I'd say so, Jebediah Marshall. You've healed the pain in my heart and given me something to live for. As to what you're asking, yes, my body is back to normal. Well," she countered uneasily, "as normal as a woman's can ever be after bearing three children."

A sense of apprehension washed over her and she admitted it aloud. "I have stretch marks and my bosoms are more abundant than usual."

He smiled, quirking an eyebrow. "I've noticed that, the bosom thing, I mean.

"And don't forget the white streak in your hair." His hand moved to her face, then brushed at the strands he thought only enhanced her beauty. "And you have a limp that you think makes you terribly unattractive. Have I left anything out?"

She jolted in his embrace. "Did you hear *everything* Abigail and I said that day?"

"No," he said. "I only came up the stairs just before you asked Abigail how old I was. And I heard you tell her that you had four years on me." His grin was quick. "Or something of that sort."

"We talked about Harry and my babies," she admitted. "I almost wish you'd heard that part, too. It would save me telling you now."

"We can share it another time," he offered.

"It's in the past and only important to me because it hurts you to speak of it."

"Well, I feel I must," she said quietly. So she did, softly and simply, pulling the words and phrases from her memory, he thought, as a child would recite her alphabet. And then she sighed. "Isn't it strange that something so important should seem almost like a dream now? And it's only been a year since..." She paused, her eyes half closed as if she counted the days.

"It *has* been a year," she said. "A year last week. I can't believe I forgot the date. I thought I'd never be able to think about the second day of September without falling entirely apart." She looked at him and his heart ached for the tears that glistened in the candle glow. "You've given me a whole new life, Jeb. Without trying to take away my memories, you've given me new ones. I'll never forget my babies, but Patricia will always be four years old, and little Harry barely two."

"Four? Elizabeth's age?" And he had expected Louisa to accept his daughter, not knowing how difficult such a thing must have been.

"Yes, almost exactly. It was like holding Patricia in my arms at first, and then I realized that Elizabeth is a person in her own right, and though she gave me comfort, it wasn't long before I loved her for herself."

"And me?" he asked. "Can you find it in you to love me for myself? Not the man who was harsh and cruel to you. Not the husband who regretted, just for a while, that he had accepted you as his bride. But the man who loves you now."

"*Do* you love me?" she asked, wonderment in her eyes as she searched his face.

He nodded, fearful of the lump that had lodged in his throat. It would not do to declare his love aloud the first time in less than a firm, ringing tone. Yet it seemed she would demand it of him, her mouth firming, her eyes narrowing at his hesitation.

"I love you, Louisa." There. He'd said it, loud and clear, only a small tremor marring the sound of her name.

Leaning toward him, she pressed willing lips against his. Moist and eager, her mouth received him, and he knew the flavor of her lips and tongue as they blended with his own. A soft moan resounded from within her throat as his mouth traveled to the spot where her pulse beat heavily beneath the fragile skin. She lifted her hands to the back of his head, pressing his face against hers, shivering as his warm breath touched the hollow of her throat.

Desire washed over him; and though he struggled to keep it under control, it burst into a spark of flame that brought his body to readiness as he slid his hand down her back, urging her against the hard, rigid proof of his need.

"Well, I guess you feel something for me," she said breathlessly, a glitter of amusement lighting her expressive eyes as he looked up to meet her gaze. "I fear my old lady's heart is beginning to thump away at a rapid pace. I hope you won't be too much for me to cope with."

He laughed aloud, rolling her to her back as his mouth found new territory to explore, his hands impatient as he set aside the fastenings of her gown. "David got here before me," he murmured, inhaling the scent of milk and her infant son that suffused her flesh with an earthy aroma. "It will be a long time, I fear, before he lets me have full possession of these treasures."

"Not too long," she said quietly. "At least I hope not." She held his head against the lush curves that filled his hands. "I yearn for your mouth, Jeb. I want it to touch me in a million places."

"A million?" His mouth twitched at one corner, and he thought suddenly what fun it would be to share this bed with Louisa for the rest of his life.

"Well," she said, backtracking a bit. "Maybe a thousand."

"A thousand I can handle all right," he murmured, pressing hot, openmouthed kisses over her swollen breasts. "I don't want to alarm you, ma'am, but I'm planning on this being a long night."

"I'm not a virgin," she said simply. "I only want to please you, Jeb. And if I'm to do that, I need to blow out the candle."

His head lifted from her, and he felt apprehension touch him at her words. "Why?" he asked. "Haven't you ever made love with the lamp on or a candle glowing?"

She shook her head. "I couldn't. I knew it would bother Harry to see my leg. Much as he loved me, it hurt him to see the scars of my operations when they tried to make it perfect. And failed so miserably."

"Were you born with the problem?" he asked. He didn't need to know, but perhaps she needed to tell him.

"My hip was not formed properly. By the time I should have been walking, my mother noticed that one leg was shorter than the other and I couldn't put my weight on it. They tried. By the time I was ten, I'd had three surgeons cut on me, then my parents gave up on the idea, and just shoved me aside in order to concentrate fully on my brothers."

"They shoved you aside?" He heard the menace in his voice and could not suppress it.

That such a thing should happen was beyond belief.

"Well, not literally, I suppose. But I think they were ashamed of me. And when Harry asked to marry me, it was a big relief to them."

"Well, Harry missed his chance to know the whole woman," Jeb told her firmly. "I won't do the same. You'll allow me to see every inch of you. If you can't bring yourself to do it tonight, then we'll put it off a day or so. But know this, Louisa. I will be your husband in every possible way."

She bit at her lip and he felt a moment's pity for the hesitation she felt.

"I have something to confess," he said quietly. "I saw your leg. The day you had the baby, I caught a glimpse of it when Doc Henderson covered you with towels before David was born."

At her look of dismay, he shook his head. "I didn't do it a'purpose, sweetheart. I'd tried hard not to look when I got you into your gown, and I didn't mean to invade your privacy..."

"Invade my privacy?" She smothered a laugh. "That's a good one, Jeb. I had a baby right in front of you, for heaven's sake. And that's about as indelicate as a situation can get." She levered a hand against his chest and pushed at him, her other hand tugging at the sheet that covered them both.

"If it's important to you, then have at it," she told him, gritting her jaw as he watched her push the sheet down the length of her body. The gown was tugged up a bit, and he knelt beside her, pulling it even higher, their eyes caught in a seemingly endless exchange of emotion.

"Lift up and let me take this off," he told her, helping her to sit upright, then sliding the garment over her head. It drifted to the floor and he lowered her again to her pillow. "Now," he said. "Show me."

Her good leg rose to push at the sheet and it slid the length of a scarred, twisted thigh, his fingers aiding its progress. It was ugly. No other word could describe the waste of clean, un-blemished skin she'd suffered. It was shorter than her other upper limb, and she kept it bent just a bit at the knee, as if that small crook made a difference in the way it was attached at that point.

His hand curved beneath the limb and he bent to touch the scars with his mouth.

"Oh, don't," she whimpered, protesting his gesture, and he lifted his head.

"I can't make it better for you, Lou, but I can let you know that it doesn't appall me. It doesn't sicken me or make me want to turn aside. It's a part of you, and if I love you, then I have to love every inch that makes up the woman you are.''

"I wasn't including that in the thousand places I wanted you to kiss," she protested, but he thought her words faltered. And then she proved him right. "Maybe I was," she admitted. "Maybe I knew you would be accepting of me, with all my flaws, but I needed to know for sure."

He lowered the leg to the mattress, his hands sweeping its length, his fingers lingering where it connected to her hip, where the crease was edged with dark curls. "And do you know…for sure?"

She nodded, and he heard the sharp intake of breath as his fingertips brushed against her woman's secrets. "I'm ready to be your wife," she said, shifting to allow him access, should he choose.

"Not yet, you're not," he told her, lying down beside her, pulling her against him. "But you will be before long." His eyes watched her carefully as he moved her to his liking. "Tell me if anything I do hurts you."

She nodded, her cheeks flushing with a desire she made no effort to hide from him. Reaching for him, her hands were greedy, touching him eagerly. She'd been long without the pleasure of a man's body. And he wondered how it had been possible to sleep in the same bed for all the past weeks and months and not recognize the passion that dwelt within the woman he'd married.

Their palms pressed and soothed. Fingertips circled and teased. Mouths lingered and tasted, and teeth brushed against damp skin as they came together. His desire seemed endless, stretching beyond the limits he imposed. Need raged within him, but love kept it under a tight rein, though his fingers trembled in their search. And then he ventured past the barrier of feminine flesh, exploring the creases and folds of her womanhood, finding her slick and smooth to his touch.

The tender channel was open to him, yet clenched readily around his finger as he probed its length, and he gritted his teeth, anticipating the same treatment being afforded the male part that surged against her hip. Louisa moved beneath his touch, her cries muted against his shoulder as he brought her to a peak of desire that made her fitful and impatient, and then he heard her groan, as her hands grasped at him.

"Please, Jeb. Please." Her head fell back against the pillow, her hips rising to meet the promise he offered, and he could wait no longer. Kneeling between her thighs, he lifted them, the twisted limb handled with care as he lay it against his own. Her eyes opened and her hands moved to where they would join.

"Do it for me," he said, his tone guttural, his teeth clenched as he took short, uneven breaths. And she did, her fingers sure and certain of their task as she blended their bodies as one.

He sank within her, holding her in place for his thrusts, his only aim to complete the act she had brought about. Beneath him, she sobbed, clutching at his broad, muscular shoulders, and he arched low, their bodies swaying as one, his chest brushing the swell of her breasts as they moved in the age-old dance of mating. He touched her fragile flesh with care, impatient to hear the cries of completion he knew were hovering just beyond her next breath, and then groaned in triumph as she cried out her pleasure.

She whispered broken phrases he bent to hear and the sound of his name, blended with vows of love, threw him into a climax he could not control. "I love you, Jeb. I love you." The sounds vibrated in his mind as he gave her the essence of his manhood. They echoed in the air surrounding them as she met his passion with an equal force and then warmed his heart as she sobbed her love aloud against his throat.

"Lou..." He could speak only her name. And then he whispered the word he'd called her aloud only once before. Yet, in his mind she'd become the epitome of the syllables he spoke. "Sweetheart..."

He lifted from her, and she opened her eyes, a look of replete, abounding satisfaction softening the lines of her face, blurring the sharp, piercing gaze she was wont to cast in his direction. "I like it when you call me that. Although I'm not really very sweet, most of the time."

"No, maybe not," he agreed, bracing himself for the jab her fist aimed at his shoulder. He bent to touch his lips to hers. "But I love you anyway." He leaned over her, his forearms against the mattress. "I had *sweet* the first time around, Lou. It was a wonderful marriage, but I never knew before what it was to have a woman with a quick wit and a backbone like yours around the house."

She cocked her head. "Is that good or bad?"

His lips twitched in response. "Well, she never sassed me the way you do." He sobered and hesitated, then spoke quietly. "And she never laughed in this bed, the way you do. I'm not telling tales on her. Hannah was a wonderful woman, and I loved her. But you...you've managed to creep into every hollow place in my heart and fill it to overflowing."

He felt embarrassed speaking the words, fearful she would think him a total ninny, but she only clasped his face between her palms and kissed him, her lips touching his cheeks, his nose, and the edges of his mouth, murmuring soft promises he stored in his heart.

CHAPTER TEN

WITH A DREAD she could not speak aloud, Louisa entered the general store, almost tripping over the threshold as her heavy sole caught on the small obstruction. She lurched and caught herself, barely disturbing the baby she held in her arms. Jeb was only a step or two behind her, and he grasped her elbow quickly.

"Are you all right?" he asked quietly and she could only nod, knowing she was the focus of a dozen or so of the townsfolk in the store, bent on Saturday shopping. Behind the counter, the storekeeper's wife smiled a wary welcome.

"Come to do your shopping?" she asked. "Looks like that little one's growin' like a bad weed these days."

And if she were digging for a bit of gossip, Louisa figured she might as well give her something to chew on. "I need a few things for the house," she admitted, making her way slowly toward the counter, consulting a list she had tucked into her pocket. "But mostly some flannel to make up for the baby. He's about out-grown his smallest gowns. Doc Henderson said he's doing well."

She fingered a bolt of striped flannel that lay on the counter. "Do you have anything with flowers for our Elizabeth, some nightgowns?"

"*Our* Elizabeth?" His voice choked with laughter as Jeb repeated the possessive words in her ear, a low whisper lest he be heard by the gawking woman on the other side of the counter.

"Elizabeth? Hannah's girl?" The woman blurted out the words and then had the grace to look chagrined as Jeb cleared his throat.

"She's my daughter, too," he said quietly. "And now, she's Louisa's, as well." He slid his arm around Louisa's waist and, together, they faced the long counter. "Have I introduced you to my wife, Mrs. Pelfrey? This is Louisa."

"Well, of course, of course." Flustered, Mrs. Pelfrey turned to pull a bolt of blue-flowered flannel from the shelf. "I suppose I just didn't know your given name before," she said quickly, fastening a smile in place.

Another lady moved within hearing and offered a hand to Louisa. "I'm Claire Summers," she offered. "I haven't seen you in town before, Mrs. Marshall." She turned to call over her shoulder at another customer. "Hazel, come meet Jeb Marshall's wife."

In moments, Louisa had met four women and was in their midst as they admired the baby and laughed at his smiles. It was universal, she supposed, this attraction a new baby had for women, and she could not fault David's appeal to the ladies who gathered around him. As if he performed for their benefit, he cooed and batted his eyes, peering from one to another, as though admiring his audience.

"Will you be coming to church in the morning?" Claire Summers asked nicely. "We're having a church social afterward, sort of a harvest season dinner. Everyone brings a dish to pass. And we could use a hand setting up tables, Mr. Marshall," she said to Jeb, looking over Louisa's shoulder to where he leaned against the counter.

Louisa turned quickly, lest he be offended at the assumption, but he only grinned, his arms folded neatly across his wide chest, a possessive smile on his lips as he grinned at his wife. "I wouldn't mind helping," he said politely, "if Louisa can spare me."

"I'll certainly give it my best shot," she said, darting him a smug look. "And I'll bring a chicken casserole along, one Jeb enjoys," she told the ladies surrounding her. They had eyes only for Jeb, it seemed, for silence followed her proposal, only broken when Claire blinked and belatedly accepted the offer of Louisa's specialty.

Jeb walked away, crossing the store to where two men inspected hardware on the far counter, and Claire leaned closer to Louisa. "My, he's a fine-looking man, isn't he? I wondered why he felt he had to send off for a wife, when there's a couple of women here in town who'd give a cow and a calf to latch onto him."

And then she flushed as she recognized that the woman she addressed was the wife in question. "Oh, my," she whispered. "I didn't mean that the way it sounded."

"He is handsome," Louisa said quickly. "I'm most fortunate to have married him."

The door opened, a bell jingling to announce another arrival, and Elizabeth crossed the floor to Louisa's side. "Mama, I found a friend I almost forgot I had," she announced, tugging at Louisa's skirt. "Would you like to see her?"

"Certainly," Louisa told her, looking down at the dark-haired child beside Elizabeth. They were like two total opposites, she thought, Elizabeth so fair, the other child tanned, with brown eyes that glittered with mischief.

"We can play jacks on the porch," the older girl suggested, "if you say it's all right for Elizabeth to sit with me. I'll take good care of her," she promised.

Claire laughed aloud. "This is my daughter, Belinda," she said. "Six years old and a mother hen already." She brushed back a dark curl and the child smiled, revealing a missing tooth. "She'll look after Elizabeth, if it's all right with you."

"Yes, fine," Louisa told her, overwhelmed by the outpouring of friendship she'd received in less than ten minutes. And she'd so feared this moment. The two little girls vanished, giggling as they went out the door, and Louisa barely sent a second glance in Elizabeth's wake.

Claire bent closer. "Don't ever feel you don't belong here," she said quietly. "Some of the women aren't real friendly right off, but there's enough of *us* here so you'll never be alone."

"Us?" Louisa returned, puzzled by the single word that seemed to have a meaning beyond her comprehension.

"Brides, my dear. Most of the ladies in town, save the older ones who came here years ago, arrived as brides, sent for by the lonesome men who came here alone."

"You, too?" Louisa asked. Then she looked around at the women who listened. Two of them nodded, the third just shrugged her shoulders.

"I picked my Donald out, back in Philadelphia, and then had the pleasure of helping build a house while I was carrying our first baby. I think the rest of you had it easy. Most of the men came alone and then sent for a woman later."

And wasn't this a novel experience, Louisa decided. She'd might as well plunge in, she thought. "We're going to talk to the minister at church tomorrow about christening the baby next week. Do you think anyone would be interested in coming to a party?"

Hoots arose from the ladies. "Interested? In a party? I should say so," one of them said. Louisa was at a loss to remember her name, but decided it didn't matter. She suspected she'd have lots of time to get everyone straight in her head. No sense in working too hard at it today.

"WELL, WHAT DO YOU THINK?" Jeb held the reins loosely in his hand and waved at two men on the sidewalk as they neared the end of the row of stores that made up the main street of town. "Did they give you a decent welcome?"

"You think you're so smart," Louisa told him, unbuttoning her dress beneath the shelter of the baby's blanket. David was busily sucking at his fingers and a howl was about to erupt from those rosebud lips any moment now, if she was any judge of things.

"I didn't say that," Jeb told her. "I just wondered—ow!" he muttered as she reached up to tug at his forelock, and then laughed at her as she scrambled to cover her partially exposed breast. "That's what you get for being mean to me," he said righteously.

"You were so smug," Louisa said, guiding David's seeking lips toward her breast. "Introducing the baby as yours, when everyone in town knows the truth. Even the minister had to take a second look at you, and he sputtered when he—" She smothered a giggle as she recalled the look of amazement on the man's face as Jeb had offered David for inspection, there in the parlor of the parsonage.

"Well, he is mine," Jeb said firmly, "and no one had better ever deny me the right to call him that. I was there when he was born, and I'm married to his mother. What more proof do I need?"

"None, I suspect," she said with a sigh. "I just can't seem to get it through my head that you've claimed us both so readily. Me with my—"

"I know, I know," he said quickly, interrupting her. "You with your limp and your white streak, and being on the verge of old age like you are.''

She cast him a long look and firmed her lips, lest she laugh again. ''You know what I mean. Everyone was wondering when we drove into town if you were there to put me on the train to nowhere. And instead, you marched me into the general store and bought out half the stock of yard goods poor Mrs. Pelfrey got in last week.''

''And then I introduced you as my wife and let you find out that you're not such an oddball after all.''

''What's an 'oddball,' Papa?'' asked a small voice from behind the wagon seat.

''It's what makes one person different from another sometimes, sweet.''

''Like I'm big and David's little?'' Elizabeth asked seriously, one hand resting on Jeb's shoulder.

''No, it means being different, like I'm taller than a lot of people and my shoulders are as wide as an ax handle.''

While Elizabeth digested that bit of information, Louisa spoke quietly, turning to face the child. ''It means having to wear an ugly shoe with a heavy sole, and limping when you walk, the way I do.''

''I don't think that matters,'' Elizabeth said

judiciously, leaned her chin on the very edge of Louisa's shoulder until their foreheads almost touched. "Nobody notices if you walk different, Mama, cause they're all too busy looking at how pretty you are."

"Hear! Hear!" Jeb said beneath his breath.

"And I don't care if you're so tall you almost touch the top of the door, Papa," the child continued. "I love you anyway, even if you aren't as pretty as my mama. Or even as my first mama was."

"She was beautiful, sweet," Jeb agreed readily. "And you look a bit like her, but being pretty isn't the best part of either of your mothers."

"It's not?"

He shook his head. "No, the best part is that both of them were beautiful inside, where it doesn't show. But if you really get to know people, you can see how wonderfully they're made, both inside and out."

"All right," Elizabeth said after a moment. And then she scanned Louisa's features with care. Her tiny index finger traced the line of cheek and chin and ended precisely on her lips. "But no matter what you say, my mama was the prettiest lady in the whole store. So there."

SUNDAY MORNING found the entire family sitting in the third pew from the front of the church, and an announcement was made from the pulpit that the christening of tiny David Marshall would take place the following Lord's day, followed by a celebration at the home of Jeb and Louisa Marshall.

"That chicken casserole looks fit to eat," Claire Summers said, taking the unwrapped dish from Louisa's hands as the congregation gathered in the churchyard. The towels were good insulation, and the bowl was still more than warm as Claire placed it on the long table. Lined with similar offerings from the ladies of the town, it almost bowed in the middle from the weight of hearty food.

"Did you notice Sue Ellen McPherson?" Jeb whispered into Louisa's ear. "She's over there looking mighty unhappy with her bridegroom."

The pretty young woman indeed wore a glowering countenance and Louisa felt a pang of sorrow for whatever circumstance brought about such a down-turned mouth on a beautiful young woman. "Let me go talk to her," she said quietly, and at Jeb's nod, she walked across the uneven ground to where Sue Ellen watched from beneath a tree.

Her gait felt clumsier than usual as she made her way past several groups of people, a few of whom nodded and smiled in her direction. And then she stood before the young woman who had been the pet of all the others on the train from the east.

"How are you doing?" she asked kindly, and as she spoke the words, Sue Ellen's eyes filled with tears, her gaze darting to the baby in Louisa's arms.

"I don't know," the younger woman answered. "I'm going to have a baby, Louisa, and I'm so scared. And Tommy just laughed at me and said that women have babies every day, and I'm acting like a sissy."

"Well, Tommy needs to have his mouth washed out with soap, if you ask me," Louisa said promptly. "What a thing to say to a woman, especially one without any kin to turn to."

"My mama's dead anyway," the girl said, "and my pa married somebody else right away. That's why I accepted Tommy's letter of proposal." Her mouth looked sullen as she glared at the young man in question, who stood in a small group a few feet away. He looked up and his smile was uncertain as he favored Louisa with a nod.

"Maybe Tommy just needs someone to talk to. I'll ask Jeb to give him a few words of advice," Louisa said. "And why don't the two of you come out and visit us one day? In fact," she said quickly, "why not come to the party next Sunday after the baby is christened?"

Sue Ellen brightened. "I'd like that, ma'am. And I'll bet Tommy will agree. He's nice most of the time, but he doesn't like it that I'm not a very good cook."

"Well," Louisa said soothingly, "maybe I can help you with that, too. And we can talk about your having a baby."

Jeb waved a plate in her direction and Louisa made her apologies, then met him halfway across the churchyard. "I should have known if I turned you loose, you'd be off gallivanting, leaving me all alone," he said morosely, pulling a face for her benefit.

She just laughed at him and took his arm with her free hand as he led her to the table where folks gathered to spoon up various offerings onto their plates.

"Here, give me the baby, and you can fix both of our plates," he told her, lifting David from her arms and looking around to search out a likely place to sit. "I'll get a quilt from the buggy and spread it under that tree," he told her, and she watched as he strolled away, offering a glimpse at his precious bundle to those who stopped his progress.

It was good, she decided, the way their lives had blended into one. More than good, actually, what with Elizabeth running to catch hold of her skirt, demanding a chicken leg on the plate she held. Surrounded by the people she'd feared would shun her, Louisa looked down at the child who had so wholeheartedly accepted her.

"You can have two legs, if you'll say please," she told Elizabeth.

"Yes, ma'am. Please, may I have a chicken leg." Properly chastened, she held out the plain white china plate and watched as Louisa spooned potato salad and green beans onto its surface. Two small, crusty, brown chicken legs completed the meal, and Louisa pointed the way to where Jeb was sitting with David beneath a tree, the center of attention from all those passing by.

In moments, she joined them there and offered him his plate. "I wasn't sure what all you liked, so I gave you a little of everything," she said, breathless as she lowered herself carefully to the ground beside him.

"I think you know exactly what I like," he whispered next to her ear, planting a kiss on the tender skin just beneath. "But I think I'll have to wait until later for that, won't I?"

Louisa looked up into the face of Hazel...Hazel something-or-other. The name fled from her mind as she caught the meaning of

Jeb's remark, and she could only smile and nod as Hazel commented on the gown David wore.

"Thank you, Hazel," she managed to say. "I'll be glad to show you how to do that sort of buttonhole. It's really quite easy."

With an invitation to join the sewing circle at her home the next month, Hazel walked on, and Louisa gave Jeb a disgruntled look. "Don't get me all confused, Mr. Marshall. I was trying to sound reasonably intelligent, and you made me feel like a doddering idiot. I couldn't even remember the woman's last name."

"As long as you remember mine, I'll be satisfied," he said, forking up a mouthful of potato salad. "Can you make this stuff?" he asked, his eyes lighting as the flavorful food was swallowed.

"I can do anything," she said smartly. "And if you're very nice to me, I'll make you some for your supper tomorrow." She leaned against the tree and prepared herself for the next round of visitors. Mrs. Pelfrey came into view and cast an admiring look at the baby's new gown.

"Is that a piece of the yard goods I sold you yesterday?" she asked, bending low to inspect the finely bound buttons.

"Yes, it is," Louisa said. "And is this your husband?"

Mrs. Pelfrey placed her hand on the gentleman's arm who accompanied her. "This is the mister," she announced. "And this," she told her husband, "is Jeb Marshall's bride."

"And my new son," Jeb added. "Isn't he a dandy little fella?"

CHAPTER ELEVEN

THE HOUSE, filled with merriment and the scent of food all afternoon long, was now silent. Louisa leaned heavily on Jeb's arm, watching as the last buggy rolled down the lane, and lifted a hand to wave at Abigail and Tim. "I'll see you in a couple of days," Abigail promised, as Tim's long arm hauled her close to his side.

"Everybody's gone," Elizabeth said sadly, sitting on the bottom step, her chin propped atop her fists. "I like it when we have company, but I don't like it when they all go home."

"Didn't you hear your auntie Abigail?" Louisa asked her, bending to touch the golden hair. "She's coming to visit one day this week. Move over, sweetie. Let me climb the steps." Her palm clutched at the railing Jeb had put in place only the day before, and she pulled herself up the steps with care.

"You're tired, aren't you?" he asked, his arm circling her waist.

"Um...yes, I am," she admitted. "But it's a

nice tired.'' And then she grinned up at him. ''Does that make sense to you?''

''Nice? I don't wonder that you're not exhausted,'' he told her. ''You've cooked everything you could lay your hands on, and baked pies till I didn't know where you were going to put them.''

''You helped,'' she reminded him, ''and Elizabeth, too,'' she added quickly, lest the child feel slighted. ''And you put up the railing by the steps for me. Not to mention doing all the running up and down stairs when I did the washing and ironing.''

''We haven't had company for a long time,'' he said. ''I wanted everything to be just right for this occasion. The last time this house was full of people it was the darkest day in my life.''

''When Hannah...'' She hesitated, unwilling to speak the words aloud in Elizabeth's hearing. After Hannah's funeral, the town had turned out and filled Jeb's pantry with canned goods and supplies to last several months. He'd told her about it late last evening, and she'd held him close as he spoke the words.

''This celebration today managed to wipe out the sadness, Lou,'' he said. ''I can remember Hannah, and love her memory, but this baby has filled our home with joy, and there's not a trace of sorrow left.''

He held the door open for Louisa and Elizabeth to enter the kitchen and then reached to light the lamp over the table. ''It's getting dark out in a hurry,'' he said. ''We'll need the lamp to put everything in place.''

''The ladies did most of it,'' Louisa said, ''and the rest can wait till morning.'' She looked down at Elizabeth, just as the child's mouth opened in a yawn. ''I think it's time for this one to be getting ready for bed.''

The baby cooed and gurgled in the corner, where he'd held court for the whole afternoon. Propped in the basket, he stared at the bright light and waved a tiny fist in its direction. ''He's getting so big,'' Louisa said. ''He laughed out loud for Mrs. Pelfrey today. Tickled her half to death.''

''Was she nice to you?'' Jeb's voice took on a sharp tone as he spoke and Louisa reassured him quickly.

''They all were. Every last one of them. And Sue Ellen told me that her Tommy has been behaving better since you spoke to him last week at the harvest dinner.''

''I just told him women were kinda peculiar when they were in the family way, and he needed to be extra nice to her,'' Jeb drawled.

He winced as Louisa swatted at his arm. "See, I knew you'd take it the wrong way," he said, turning to her fully, pulling her into his arms. He bent his head and kissed her, a quick, hard caress that held promise.

"Now, you tend to the baby, and feed him or whatever you have to do to keep him quiet for the night. I'll take Elizabeth up and get her ready for bed and tuck her in. And then I'll be back down to help you get David upstairs."

"Sounds to me like you've got everything under control," she told him. "Far be it from me to argue with a headstrong man."

"That's a good one," he said, lifting Elizabeth into his arms. "Tell your mama good-night," he instructed her, holding her as she leaned down to kiss and hug Louisa. "And now wave to your brother, and I'll carry you up the stairs to bed."

"He's really my brother now, isn't he?" she asked Jeb. "When the preacher man at church said all those things about him and we were standing there watching, he said that David's name is the same as mine. We're both called Marshall, aren't we?"

"Yes, he's really your brother," Jeb said. "And one of these days, you might even have another brother or two, and maybe a sister, if your mama behaves herself and does what I tell her."

"What are you gonna tell her, Papa?" Elizabeth asked, eyes wide as she was carried from the kitchen.

"I'm going to tell her she has to love me forever and ever," he said, his foot on the first step. "And then I'm going to tell her that since we're probably gonna fill up the other two bedrooms upstairs, I'll have to build us a big bedroom down on the first floor, just as soon as we can afford it."

"Whatever for?" Louisa called out, following them to the staircase, looking up as Jeb climbed slowly, deliberately allowing her to hear his sing-song promises to Elizabeth.

"So you don't have to climb the stairs every day," he said, turning his head to look down at her. "We'll make it as big as the parlor, with full-length windows that will look out to the east, so we can see the sunrise every morning."

"Well, I know what I'll be spending my nest egg on, then," Louisa said, turning back to the kitchen. The silence behind her was ominous, she decided, but she smiled as she picked up David for his last feeding of the day.

"WHAT NEST EGG?" Jeb asked quietly as he watched her brush her hair. On his back, both pillows under his head, he yearned to take the brush from her hand and complete the task himself. Yet, he knew where such a move would end up, once he had his hands on her. And the matter of her *nest egg* was one he was determined to explore.

"The one I brought with me," she said. "I've been trying to figure out how to tell you about the money I kept from the sale of our home in Boston, and the proceeds of Harry's insurance."

"Where is it?" he asked. "I didn't know you'd gone to the bank."

"It's not in town. It's in my trunk," she said, turning to face him. "I kept it a secret at first, in case I had to leave. If you hadn't wanted me here, I couldn't have accepted money from you, after I'd lied to you and kept you from getting one of the other brides."

"You've known for weeks that you're staying here," he reminded her. "I have no intention of ever letting you go, Lou. You know that."

"Yes." Her smile was brilliant as she tossed the brush aside and crawled over the covers to sprawl across his chest. "I've just been trying to think of something you'd let me do with it. I knew there was no sense in offering to buy more stock or a new plow or any of the other things you're saving for. You wouldn't have let me.''

''What makes you think I'll let you pay for a new bedroom?''

''Because it's for both of us, but mostly for me, and I want to give you something to let you know how much I love you, Jeb.'' Her kisses were warm and damp against his face, and he struggled mightily to hold on to his male pride as she spoke, her words punctuated by those sweet brushes of lips and tongue against his skin.

''I'm not poor, Lou,'' he told her quietly. ''We can do it right away if you want to. I can always borrow a bit at the bank to help buy the lumber.''

''Let me do this?'' she asked, her eyes warm as she met his gaze. ''If you'd rather put the money in the bank for security, we can do that instead, I suppose. I just thought it would be fun to have a special place of our own.''

''Because Hannah slept in this room before you?'' he asked.

She shook her head. ''No, I don't fear Hannah's memory. Any more than you worry about the love I shared with Harry.''

''You're the one who needed security a while back, if I remember right,'' he reminded her.

''Well, I don't anymore,'' she said. ''I have

everything I need right here." And, as if to emphasize her meaning, she curled closer to him and he felt the weight of her breasts against his chest, the length of her legs twining with his. "You're my security, Jeb. I love you."

"Is the baby all settled for the night?" he asked, his mouth nuzzling against her throat.

"David Palmer Marshall won't stir till morning," she assured him, her hands smoothing the taut muscles of his shoulders and upper arms. "Thank you for allowing Harry to have a part of David's christening."

"Harry would have been his father if things hadn't happened the way they did. He'd be the one holding you in his arms." His eyes were solemn as he looked up at her. "I wouldn't have wished Harry any ill, but I'm sure glad it's me, instead, Lou. I needed you so much."

"Claire told me there were a couple of women in town who'd have jumped at the chance to be your wife. Did you know that?" she asked idly, her fingers tugging at the mat of hair on his chest.

"Yeah, I knew," he answered quietly. "But something told me..." He paused, and she was sensitive enough to his mood to wait out his hesitation. "Something told me to answer the ad. It was almost as if Hannah whispered in my ear.'' His eyebrow lifted and a smile tugged at his lips. ''You'll think I'm making this up.''

''No.'' She shook her head. ''I think this, our being together, was meant to be. I've always believed there's a plan for each of our lives, and somehow I feel that we were intended to find each other. I needed what you've given me, Jeb.''

''Well, I surely need what you're about to give me,'' he murmured, his hands finding her bottom. ''Elizabeth's out like a light,'' he told her, his arms shifting her upward, his teeth gently touching the tender flesh of her breast. ''There's only you and me left to finish up this celebration, sweetheart.''

''You aren't going to argue with me?'' she asked, peering down at him. ''About the money, I mean.''

''Arguing with you isn't the smartest thing for me to do tonight, Lou. You think faster than I do, and you've got a sharp tongue in your mouth. I never can manage to get the best of you when I've got other things on my mind.''

''What have you got on your mind?'' she asked, catching her breath sharply as he captured the crest of her breast in his mouth.

''Loving you.'' She felt the curl of his lips against her skin as he spoke the words.

''You won't get any argument out of me on

that score.'' Her submission was complete as she rolled to her side, drawing him with her, her arms enclosing him. ''You told Elizabeth I had to love you forever and ever, Jeb. I have no desire to give you an argument on that one, either.''

''For a woman who's prepared to be agreeable, you sure talk a lot,'' he whispered, his mouth hovering above hers, his breath warm and inviting.

''I won't say another word.'' The tone was solemn, but a chuckle bubbled in her throat. Jeb stifled it with his kiss, and she was captured by the magic of his hands and mouth and body...

...held breathlessly in thrall by the man whose love promised her a future that stretched forever and ever.

C'mon back home to Crystal Creek with
a BRAND-NEW anthology from

bestselling authors
Vicki Lewis Thompson
Cathy Gillen Thacker
Bethany Campbell

Return to Crystal Creek

**Nothing much
has changed in
Crystal Creek...
till now!**

The mysterious Nick Belyle has shown up in town,
and what he's up to is anyone's guess. But one
thing is certain. Something big is going down in
Crystal Creek, and folks aren't going to rest till
they find out what the future holds.

*Look for this exciting anthology,
on-sale in July 2002.*

HARLEQUIN®
Makes any time special ®

Visit us at www.eHarlequin.com

PHRTCC